FULL DISCLOSURE

BRUCE BRONSTEIN

Also by Bruce Bronstein

NONDISCLOSABLE

This novel is a work of fiction. While the novel is based on actual tax cases, I have taken certain dramatic liberties to embellish on specific events and characters. The characters in this novel are entirely fictitious and any resemblance to actual persons, living or dead, is entirely coincidental.

Published by Bruce Bronstein Books

Printed by CreateSpace

CHAPTER 1

"Please state and spell your name for the court," said the IRS trial attorney, which the witness did without any fanfare.

"Please state your occupation and employer, Mr. Lipschitz," asked Lindsay Cooke, the trial lawyer representing the IRS in the United States Tax Court.

"Revenue Agent for the Internal Revenue Service," answered Louie Lipschitz.

"How many years you have been employed as a revenue agent by the IRS," asked Lindsay.

"Twenty years."

"And during your twenty years as a revenue agent, has your job required that you testify in Tax Court?" asked Lindsay.

"Yes, on many occasions."

"Agent Lipschitz, did you conduct an examination of the petitioner's tax returns for the tax years in issue?" asked Lindsay.

"Yes."

"And did the petitioner submit documents to your office during the audit?" asked Lindsay.

"Yes."

"And did you examine these documents?" asked Lindsay.

"Yes."

"Can you tell the court how many documents were submitted to your office?" asked Lindsay.

"Approximately three thousand documents," answered the witness.

"Did you personally review each and every document?" asked Lindsay.

"Yes."

"What did you learn from reviewing these documents?" asked Lindsay.

"That the petitioner altered existing documents and created false documents in order to mislead me during the examination. I found that every document he submitted was fraudulent," answered Louie.

"Agent Lipschitz, please explain how you came to the determination that all of the approximately three thousand documents are fraudulent?" asked Lindsay.

"The petitioner prepared a schedule of various expenses that he claimed to have incurred on a daily basis. This schedule consisted of automobile expenses for mileage where he claimed to have traveled to different job sites, expenses for meals and the entertainment of clients, and so forth. The schedule that the petitioner prepared shows every day of the tax year. Actually, it lists more than every day of the tax year," said Louie.

"How is this possible?" asked Lindsay, who already knew.

BRUCE BRONSTEIN

"The petitioner inserted extra days that do not exist in any calendar year. He gave September an extra day. He also gave April an extra day. And, he gave February two extra days. Additionally, the petitioner claimed business expenses on weekends, federal holidays and days when the National Weather Service reported blizzard driving conditions," said Louie.

"In addition to this schedule, the petitioner submitted copies of various documents such as hotel, restaurant and airfare receipts. I then matched these receipts against the petitioner's schedule that he had prepared based on his travel calendar. However, it didn't match," said the witness.

"Please explain how it does not match," said Lindsay.

"According to the petitioner's calendar, he used his car every single day of the year, and then some, and claimed automobile expenses for each day. In contrast, there were documents that suggested the petitioner traveled out of town by airline because there were airfare receipts. Actually, there were multiple airfare receipts for the same day, which I will get to in a moment," said Louie.

"I obtained copies of the airlines' records which show the petitioner always flew Coach," said Louie, as he gave Lindsay a moment to pull these documents as well as other related documents from one of her files which she identified as government exhibits.

"I then obtained copies of the Employee Expense Reports which the petitioner submitted to his employer. These Employee Expense Reports confirm that the petitioner claimed reimbursement for airfare based on having flown First Class. As a consequence, the petitioner overcharged his employer for airfare," said Louie.

Throughout Louie's testimony, the petitioner sat in his chair without saying a word, unless mumbling counts. The petitioner, who was eighty five years old and ready for either an assisted living facility or institution for the criminally insane, was clearly overmatched in this proceeding when his opponents happened to be a very skillful trial attorney and a tenacious revenue agent who was very good at his job.

"Agent Lipschitz, did the petitioner also claim deductions for other expenses that he allegedly incurred for the same days?" asked Lindsay.

"Yes. These deductions appear on the tax returns on Schedule A as unreimbursed employee business expenses and on Schedule C as other expenses," replied Louie.

"Were the same expenses deducted more than once?" asked Lindsay.

"Yes."

"And were these expenses actually incurred by the petitioner?" asked Lindsay.

"No," stated the witness.

"Please explain how you concluded that these expenses could not have been incurred by the petitioner."

"It's actually quite simple. If you look at the entries recorded by the petitioner on his schedule which lists every day of the year, he claimed automobile mileage on his personal car while he flew out of town on company business and was away from home for more than one day. The petitioner also claimed business meals and entertainment expenses, yet he was served a complimentary lunch on the airplane. Also, the petitioner claimed multiple deductions for getting his car washed on those days he was out of town. Clearly, the petitioner could not have been in two different places at the same time," Louie said.

"Did you ask the petitioner to provide you with copies of his Employee Expense Reports during the audit?" asked Lindsay.

"Yes."

"And did he?"

"No."

"Why not?" asked Lindsay.

"According to the petitioner, he did not maintain copies of his Employee Expense Reports, but did have copies of every other document you could possibly imagine," answered Louie.

"What happened then?" asked Lindsay.

"The petitioner gave me a copy of a letter on company stationery that bore his supervisor's name. According to this letter, his supervisor was unable to find the petitioner's Employee Expense Reports," stated the revenue agent.

"Is this the letter you're referring to?" asked Lindsay, as she held up the letter so Louie could see the document.

"Yes, that's the letter."

"Your Honor, I would like to introduce this document into evidence at this time," said Lindsay.

"You may do so now," replied the judge. After the letter was introduced into evidence, Lindsay continued with her questioning of her witness.

"Agent Lipschitz, what can you tell me about this letter?" asked Lindsay.

"For starters, the signature is a forgery. I spoke with the petitioner's supervisor and he told me that he did not write this letter and that this is not his signature. He also provided me with official copies of the petitioner's Employee Expense Reports which you now have in your possession," stated Louie.

"Did you inform the petitioner's supervisor that the petitioner actually flew Coach and not First Class?"

"Yes." I presented him with copies of the airline tickets so he could compare these documents to the copies of the First Class airfare receipts that were attached to the petitioner's Employee Expense Reports," answered Louie.

"Please explain the tax consequences as to what the petitioner did," said Lindsay.

"Because the petitioner received more in reimbursement than he actually incurred, the excess funds constitute taxable income to him in the year of receipt. I included the excess amounts in my audit adjustments, to which the petitioner continues to disagree," stated Louie.

At this point in the trial, everyone turned to look at the Petitioner who didn't bother to acknowledge the stares because he was sound asleep. The judge nodded to a Sheriff's deputy who was standing in the back of the courtroom to wake up the petitioner.

Once the petitioner was awake, the judge advised him that it might be prudent for him to remain awake if he wanted to participate in this legal proceeding. The petitioner informed the judge that he would do his best to stay awake but that he was finding it difficult to do so because Ms. Cooke was boring him to death with her stupid questions.

"Ms. Cooke, you may continue with your witness," said the judge, who was hardly bored.

"Did the petitioner's supervisor inform you as to what he intended to do?" asked Lindsay.

"Yes. He said he was going to immediately terminate the petitioner's employment and demand full restitution of the money the petitioner was not entitled to receive. If full restitution was not repaid, he had said that the company would notify the Maryland State Attorney General's Office and file a criminal complaint against the petitioner," said Louie.

"And was the money repaid?"

"Eventually it was paid back."

"Agent Lipschitz, what are its tax consequences?"

"For federal income tax reporting purposes, the petitioner is required to include the excess funds in taxable income with respect to those years in issue, which are before the court. The restitution payment may be deductible, subject to limitations in the year of repayment," answered Louie.

"Turning to the petitioner's Form Schedule A, was there anything that jumped out as unusual when you first examined his tax returns?" asked Lindsay.

"Yes. I noticed substantial deductions were claimed for charitable contributions in every tax year. These amounts are significantly greater than what one might expect given the amount of income on the return in each year. I was able to determine that the cash donations the petitioner claimed to have made to his church were never made."

"Can you please tell the court how you discovered this?" asked Lindsay.

"The Petitioner provided me with Affidavits that he prepared. These Affidavits are supposed to be on stationery of the church. However, I noticed that the Affidavits show the church's name as having been misspelled and there was a typo with respect to the church's zip code. In addition, the name of the church official is bogus because no such person was employed or worked as a volunteer for the church," explained Louie.

"And the noncash donations?" asked Lindsay.

"The petitioner is single, yet he claimed thousands of dollars with respect to the donation of clothing, of which at least eighty percent consisted of women's clothing. I found this to be strange because the petitioner's wife passed away more than twenty years ago," stated the revenue agent.

"Female clothes?" questioned Lindsay.

"Yes. Items such as dresses, bras, panties, slips, stockings, some girdles and so forth."

"We get the picture. Did the petitioner explain this to you when the noncash donations were being questioned?" asked Lindsay.

"The petitioner said that after his wife passed away, he kept her clothing in his one bedroom apartment until he finally made the decision to part with her clothes."

"And you questioned the veracity of his statement because?" asked Lindsay.

"That would be because he lied about everything else. He altered documents, he forged his supervisor's signature on fake documents that he created, he cheated his employer and he fabricated false deductions in order to avoid paying income taxes. It seemed odd that he would keep female clothing in a cramped one bedroom apartment for more than twenty years. That is why the deduction for clothing was disallowed in its entirety," explained Louie.

As everyone turned to look at the petitioner once again, he just sat there shaking his head, gathered his folders, stood and said, "I've heard enough of this nonsense. The IRS is making all of this up to make me look bad. That agent is lying. And if you can't see through his lies, you're a really stupid judge. In fact, I don't even think you're a real judge. You're probably an IRS agent who's just playing a judge to fool me. Or, maybe you're one of those unemployed actors that go around playing impostors for lunch money." With that said, the eighty five year old Conrad Hogan started to walk out of the courtroom.

Before the petitioner made it to the door, he heard the judge say, "Based on the testimony in this case and the evidence presented, as well as your conduct in my courtroom, it is clear that you've wasted the court's time by filing a petition. Accordingly, I am imposing monetary sanctions for your having filed a frivolous petition in this matter."

Turning back to the judge, Lindsay asked, "Your Honor, would you like me to continue?"

"Why bother, counselor? I'm merely an impostor on loan to the IRS. No, I think we can dispense with the rest of the testimony and cut right to the chase. I'm prepared to render a bench decision right now. I hereby determine that the petitioner is liable for the entire deficiency amount, as set forth in the Notice for all tax years. In addition, all penalties, as asserted for all tax years in issue, are sustained. Furthermore, the court will impose a five thousand dollar penalty against the petitioner for filing a frivolous petition," ruled the judge.

***

The following day, Louie made a visit to Stanley Scherr's law office to examine his books and records in connection with the audit of Stanley's personal tax returns. Stanley has chosen not to be in the office because he does not want to have a conversation with the revenue agent concerning a certain matter.

The subject that is a sensitive topic for Stanley involves his representation of a client in a refund claim which was litigated in the United States District Court. The trial received a great deal of publicity because it was alleged that Stanley's client attempted to circumvent the taxation of exercised stock options by transferring the stock options to a foreign corporation that she formed, but later gifted to her husband who was not a US citizen. The IRS characterized this as tax avoidance and the Department of Justice defended the IRS's position in court.

The media heralded this as a major upset when the jury ruled in Stanley's favor. However, the victory was short lived when Louie learned that the foreman of the jury paid eighty thousand dollars in cash for a luxury car one day after the verdict was announced. Shortly thereafter, Louie discovered that the jury foreman accepted a one hundred thousand dollar bribe from Stanley's client, who promptly went into hiding to avoid arrest for bribery.

Stanley informed his secretary that his books and records could be examined in one of the small meeting rooms on the first floor by the revenue agent. As Louie reviewed Stanley's General Ledger, he had the secretary provide him with all client files so that he can match the payment in each client's account to the General Ledger.

After noting discrepancies with respect to how retainers were recorded, Louie inquired into Stanley's billing practices and found that she was eager to be of assistance.

While Erin Schlaffer has only been employed as Stanley's secretary for a very brief time, Louie got the sense that she is much sharper than he would have expected someone to be who is working for an idiot. Although Louie hasn't quite figured Erin out, he suspects that she is more than a secretary working for a fool.

CHAPTER 2

Stanley Scherr is not a happy camper. In fact, Stanley has been depressed ever since he learned that he has been suspended from practice before the IRS for a period of twelve months. At the same time, the media has reported that Stanley has been charged by the Maryland Attorney General's Office with criminal conspiracy in allowing a non-lawyer to falsely impersonate an attorney in his law office.

Stanley's law practice has gone down the toilet, as the majority of his clients have fired him for having lost their cases against the IRS. Ironically, the one case that did result in a temporary win has been ordered by the United States District Court to be re-tried.

Now that Louie Lipschitz is auditing Stanley's federal income tax returns, the notorious lawyer anticipating the absolute worst. Yet, the worst is still pending because the feds are conducting a criminal investigation into whether Stanley assisted his clients in facilitating tax evasion and conspiracy to defraud the United States Government.

Stanley decided that he should go into the office today and see if there is any work he can do. If Stanley can't find any work, he's prepared to play his favorite game of tossing paper basketballs on the floor for three or four hours.

Greeting him with a warm smile and hot cup of coffee is Erin, the young, attractive and hard-working secretary who has replaced Estelle Schwartz, the not so young, not so attractive and not so hard-working secretary.

Unaware that Erin is an undercover FBI agent who has been assigned to the Government's Task Force that is investigating Stanley for conspiracy to facilitate tax evasion, Stanley told Erin to locate his client who has gone into hiding and find out if she wants him to prepare her case for re-trial. Upon receiving this instruction, Erin wondered if Stanley knows that she is an undercover FBI agent.

"Stan, if Mrs. Lopez has disappeared, how am I supposed to find her? What if she has already fled the country?" asked Erin.

"Just find her and ask her if she wants me to argue her case again. If so, I'll need to be paid in advance," Stanley said. Recalling that she didn't have a problem paying off the jury foreman before the trial started, Stanley thought that this wouldn't be a problem for her now.

Bribery is considered a felony offense. If found guilty, Mrs. Lopez could be imprisoned, granted probation, given a fine, or combinations of all three sanctions. The punishment will eventually depend on the magnitude of the bribe. To Mrs. Lopez, prison is not an option.

Stanley is unaware that Mrs. Lopez, who is out on bail, is in the process of making a hasty departure to an undisclosed foreign country where she and her husband will establish residency. For Stanley, this means that he will not get an opportunity to argue her refund claim again.

However, Stanley's most immediate problem is Timothy Bell's absence. Since the boy wonder was charged with conspiracy, willfully failing to file tax returns, obstruction of tax administration, tax evasion, practicing law without a license, and who knows what else, Timmy has been unavailable for legal consultations. Actually, Timmy is available if Stanley wants to drive to a federal correctional facility while Timmy awaits his federal and state criminal trials. Without Timmy providing legal advice, Stanley is lost at sea with no rescue in sight.

While Stanley is barred from doing tax controversy work that involves representation before the IRS, he can still do advisory work such as tax research and planning, if only he knew how. Without Timmy to advise him, Stanley is unable to do this for his few remaining clients. To further complicate matters, Stanley is looking at the possibility of going to prison.

After doing nothing of consequence for the past hour, Stanley buzzed Erin to let her know about the next office meeting which is about to start in thirty seconds. Erin would prefer having a root canal rather than sit through another office meeting with her idiot boss. While Stanley has generally been civil to her, Erin would prefer not being in the same room with him.

When Stanley called the meeting to order, he told Erin that with his law practice doing virtually no business, he may have to terminate her job. Erin, who was ready to return to the FBI, is relieved that she now has an excuse to return to her real job.

Erin's only regret is that she has been unable to find more corroborating evidence of his complicity to having facilitated tax evasion schemes for his clients.

***

The boy wonder is now sitting in a holding cell while awaiting a formal reading of the charges against him.

An Arraignment Hearing is the first stage of the criminal trial process when a defendant is formally informed of the charges brought against him and is expected to respond by entering a plea. The Federal Rules of Criminal Procedure stipulate that at the hearing, the defendant is read the formal criminal complaint in open court. If Timothy Bell pleads not guilty, a trial date may be set at the hearing.

Timmy is about to meet with an attorney in the Office of the Public Defender. In all likelihood, Timmy probably knows far more about criminal law than his designated legal representative.

When the guards brought Timmy to one of the meeting rooms, he got a glimpse of his lawyer, who actually looks younger than he does. Timmy's first thought was whether the Public Defender hires its lawyers right out of high school.

"Mr. Bell, I'm Derick Mason. How are you holding up so far?" inquired the young Assistant Public Defender.

Derick stood about five feet nine inches and weighed no more than one hundred and forty pounds. If Derick were a different gender, he would be called petite. With a pale complexion and slight build, Derick looked like he spent his entire childhood and young adult life in a library.

"Please call me Timmy, and I'm fine."

"Timmy, I have to go over a few things with you. Once a person is arrested, a prosecutor must decide whether or not to file charges. The prosecutor may base this decision on several different factors. To proceed with a trial, the evidence must indicate that there is at least probable cause to believe that a crime has been committed and that you, as the suspect, are guilty of facilitating the crime. One way for prosecutors to initiate criminal charges is by filing what is called an Information document. An Information document is a charging document that lists the offenses that you are believed to have committed," explained the Assistant Public Defender.

"And the prosecutor is doing this instead of filing an Indictment against me?" asked Timmy.

"Yes. That is what I've been told," responded Derick. "You will be asked to enter a plea at your Arraignment Hearing. It's important that you enter a not guilty plea at the hearing," said Derick.

Entering a not guilty plea allows the defendant time to consider the respective strengths and weaknesses of his case and to determine the possibility of a favorable outcome in court. In addition, it allows the defendant time to prepare a defense and, in some instances, allows the defendant the right to appeal an adverse decision. This is important because defendants who plead guilty waive their right to a trial, to prepare a defense, and the right of appeal.

"I'm anxious to be released. Any chance the Magistrate will consider bail?" asked Timmy.

"I seriously doubt it. The DOJ prosecutors will argue that you're a flight risk given the seriousness of the criminal charges and the amount of money at issue. Of course, the financial resources that are available to you will also be a factor for denying you bail. While I'll make the request for bail, I don't see the Magistrate granting any request, regardless of the amount set," replied Derick.

"If denied, is it appealable?"

"We can appeal an adverse bail decision. However, the scope of the review is limited. The only question for an appellate court is whether the trial court abused its discretion," answered Derick.

"How old are you?" asked Timmy.

"Twenty seven. Why do you ask?" asked Derick

"Just curious."

"I get that from a lot of people. It seems that I don't look my age," said Derick.

Upon hearing this, Timmy thought to himself that he used to say the same thing.

"I've been with the PD's Office for the past two years. I've had my share of interesting cases and I've assisted the PD on several of his cases as second chair. If your case gets to be too much, I'll see if the PD is available to help out with your representation," said Derick.

"Good. But, if you can get me some legal materials on bail hearings and criminal procedures, I think it would be helpful. I want to assist in my defense and to do so, I'll need to do some legal research," Timmy said to his lawyer.

"Okay, but you're not a lawyer, are you?" inquired Derick.

"I just played a lawyer that got caught by the FBI. I'm not all that concerned with the state charge of practicing law without a license. It's the federal case against me which consists of multiple criminal tax offenses that worries me," said Timmy.

"Are you thinking about entering into a Plea Agreement?"

"If the terms and conditions are favorable," answered Timmy.

"I can talk to the PD and see how he wants to handle this. But my guess is that the Justice Department will insist that you serve substantial time in prison," responded Derick.

"I can't do a substantial stretch behind bars. It's not as if I murdered someone," complained Timmy.

"I understand. DOJ will insist on a significant prison sentence if you enter into a Plea Agreement. It's something you'll need to think about," suggested Derick.

As Derick got up to leave, he turned to Timmy and asked, "I'm curious as to why you haven't retained a prominent law firm that specializes in criminal defense work to represent you."

"So am I," replied Timmy.

Actually, Timmy was fully cognizant of the potential problem that could cause him if he were to hire a prominent law firm. Hiring expensive lawyers would require a substantial retainer, and to do so, Timmy would have to wire transfer money from an overseas bank account that he does not want the government to know about. For the time being, Timmy will have to utilize the talents of the Public Defender's Office.

CHAPTER 3

Louie has been called into the office of his Group Manager in order to discuss the status of Stanley Scherr's audit.

"Hey, boss. What's happening?" asked the stellar revenue agent.

"Louie, I don't have time to bullshit with you, so let's cut to the chase. Where do you stand with the Scherr audit?" asked Roger Smith.

"Rog, I'm almost finished. I have some housekeeping items to wrap up, including a referral memo to CID."

CID is the Criminal Investigation Division. Cases that merit criminal investigation are transferred to CID, which is responsible for referring the case to the Department of Justice for approval if the IRS believes criminal prosecution is warranted.

"A referral to CID? Why wasn't I informed before now?" wondered Roger.

"Relax. I just reached this determination only late yesterday."

"Okay. What evidence do you have that warrants a criminal referral?"

"The nitwit set up an escrow account that he used exclusively for the purpose of depositing all client retainers. The retainers are generally fifteen thousand dollars and represent advance payments for services to be rendered. However, these amounts are not reported in taxable income," stated Louie.

"You mean the retainer amounts are not reported in taxable income in the year received," wondered Roger.

"No, what I said was the retainer amounts are not reported in taxable income, period," said Louie.

"Then what is he reporting as his income?" asked Roger.

"Scherr is reporting only the amounts that he receives in excess of the retainer. For example, if the retainer was for fifteen thousand dollars and the client paid him a total of twenty two thousand dollars for legal work, only seven thousand dollars was reported," explained Louie.

"I examined all of the Engagement Letters and verified through an analysis of his bank statements when the retainers were deposited. Scherr understated his taxable income by hundreds of thousands of dollars in each year. I could go back more than three years and I'm sure I'll find the same thing was done in the prior years." And I also traced the use of the retainer amounts as having been used to pay his operating expenses like utility bills, salaries, supplies, etc."

Picking up the phone, Roger called his boss with the good news that Stanley Scherr's case warranted a criminal referral.

"Louie determined that Stanley failed to include any of the retainer fees in his taxable income. He deposited the funds in an escrow account, but used the money to pay his operating expenses. He only reported the fees that were paid after the retainers.

Stanley Scherr, whom IRS management suspected was involved in the death of one of its revenue agents, was on the IRS's radar for the past several months. Tom Collins, the Section Chief who had a number of cases in his section where Stanley was the taxpayer representative, was overjoyed with the news.

"Tell Louie I could kiss him. No, on second thought, you kiss Louie for me and make sure you give the munchkin a great big hug with that kiss," said Tom.

"What did Tom say?" asked Louie when Roger concluded his telephone call.

"He said, good job."

***

The next day, Louie had the audit files assembled and sent to the Criminal Investigation Division. Because jurisdiction was now formally transferred to CID, Louie was required to notify Stanley that his individual income tax returns were now the subject of a criminal investigation. Louie could envision Stanley going ape shit when he sees this letter.

At the present time, Stanley is under a one year suspension from practicing before the IRS. In addition, there is the possibility of a criminal charge by the Maryland Attorney General's Office for conspiracy to permit a non-lawyer to practice law in his office.

Now, the nitwit lawyer is looking at a criminal tax case for having willfully filed fraudulent tax returns. If convicted, Stanley can expect to serve several years behind bars.

While on the subject of prison, Stanley saw the article in the Baltimore Sun about his client, who has apparently gone into hiding rather than stand trial for bribery. Stanley wondered what would have happened if she allowed him to defend her against the bribery charge. In view of the fact that Stanley is not a criminal defense attorney, Mrs. Lopez would have to bribe the jury to beat the bribery charge.

In addition, the genius behind Stanley's tax evasion schemes is the subject of a lengthy feature article in the Baltimore Sun. Titled, "The Rise and Fall of a Young Billionaire," Timothy Bell is portrayed as a brilliant young man who became so consumed with his wealth that he lost focus of his legal obligation to pay taxes on his considerable earnings from his computer software businesses.

As Stanley read this article, he shook his head in dismay that someone could be so foolish to have failed to report all of his taxable income. "If only Timmy had come to me for advice, he could have avoided any tax problems," Stanley muttered to himself.

***

Stanley is on the phone with a criminal defense attorney whom he saw on a late-night cable television commercial, offering legal services to those in need. Stanley requested that as a professional courtesy to another member of the Bar, he be given a discount on the legal fees he would have to pay. When told that this lawyer does not believe in courtesies or discounts, Stanley quickly sensed that they had something in common.

Wallace Shadybrook is sixty seven years old, but looks about eighty five years of age. Wallace has leathery skin from too much sun worshipping, bloodshot eyes from too much booze and a lack of sleep, a large nose and oversize ears that make him look like a clown. Standing no more than five feet seven inches and weighing about one hundred and thirty pounds, Wallace looks like he consumes his meals through the use of an IV tube.

"What is it you need me to do?" asked Wallace.

"Make my criminal conspiracy case go away," replied Stanley.

"Umm, which criminal conspiracy case are you talking about?" asked one shady lawyer to the other shady lawyer.

"The Maryland Attorney General has charged me with criminal conspiracy because I allowed a non-lawyer to practice law in my office," said Stanley.

"Oh yeah, that case! I read about it in the newspaper. If you want my advice, plead guilty provided the State agrees to a suspended sentence. Tell them there was nothing malicious about what happened because the guy who provided the legal advice is a lot smarter than you and knew what he was talking about," said Wallace.

"But doesn't that make me look like an idiot if I've got some kid who never went to law school, offering legal advice to my clients?" asked Stanley.

"What's your point?" asked Wallace.

"That they'll think I'm incompetent," answered Stanley.

"They already know that. But you're already in a world of shit, so what difference does it make?"

CHAPTER 4

When Stanley opened his mail, he almost vomited his lunch. The letter from the IRS advised him that the Examination Division transferred jurisdiction of his case to the Criminal Investigation Division. Stanley has now been put on notice that he will be receiving a visit from the special agents assigned to the investigation. For Stanley, things had gone from really bad, to it can't get much worse.

As Stanley read Louie's letter, he now knew that the IRS had raised the stakes to the point that its chips were on the table. Whether Stanley would eventually be allowed to practice tax law was a moot point if he takes up residency in a federal prison.

While Stanley was sick to his stomach, David Holland and Caroline Kilpatrick stood in the lobby of the Federal Building, waiting their turn to pass through security. This is their first time in the Federal Building and it will be the last time they ever enter this building.

Both David and Caroline are experienced tax lawyers and have been practicing before the IRS for a number of years. David is a forty seven year old tax partner at a large downtown law firm that specializes in criminal tax defense. Caroline, who is sixteen years younger, is an associate at the same firm. Caroline formerly worked at the Justice Department as a litigator in the Civil Tax Fraud Division following graduation from law school.

David passed through security without too much trouble. He made it through the X-ray machine, The Wand and the Pat Down in no time at all. The physical examination took only a few minutes and he was given a relatively clean bill of health by the screeners, who are sub-contracted by GSA. However, David was advised that he should lose a few pounds, which could be achieved through a combination of changing his diet and walking several miles a day. David was told that he could pick up his free nutritional diet at the front desk on his way out, compliments of the federal government.

Caroline's experience with the thugs playing the role of screeners was another story. Caroline was asked to remove several articles of clothing when she passed through the X-ray machine. While The Wand was a mere formality, the goon attempting to perform a strip search on her may have done so with such enthusiasm that Caroline had to yell out, "Someone please help me, I'm being molested."

When told by a supervisor that screeners zealously perform this part of the screening process to ensure that the building is secure, Caroline responded by saying, "And how will the building be secure if I've just been sexually assaulted in the lobby?"

Anxious to get away from the screeners, David and Caroline made their way to the elevators for their 10 am meeting with Louie. When Louie greeted them in the reception area on his floor, Caroline made it a point to say, "All future meetings will be held in our law firm's office. At least our building security doesn't rape us when we enter the building."

"The screeners downstairs......?" Louie started to ask.

"Don't you mean the Neanderthals doing body cavity searches?" replied Caroline.

I'll pass your complaint along to IRS management. Someone will file a report with GSA and investigate what's going on with those guys. In the future, I can meet in your office," said Louie.

Louie thought to himself, that when he makes this trip, he should bring his merchandise catalog with him and try to generate some sales of electronic gadgets on the side.

"The first issue I want to go over with you is whether the five million dollars to acquire stock in ZanTech, constitutes a disguised corporate distribution to your client in his capacity as a shareholder. Mr. Fine is the sole shareholder of The Fine Company. Mr. Fine and a business associate identified as Richard Burns, each own fifty percent of the outstanding stock of Southpoint Corporation, which is incorporated in the Cayman Islands and later underwent a name change," stated Louie.

"In 2005, Mr. Fine contemplated a business loan of five million dollars to a foreign corporation identified as Retmex Ltd., which is a client of The Fine Company. The source of the funds used for the five million dollar loan came from the Southpoint Corporation's bank account at the Bank of Bermuda. In January of 2006, Mr. Fine instructed the Bank of Bermuda to wire transfer two million dollars to Retmex," said Louie as both lawyers nodded their heads in agreement with the facts.

"Fine and Burns owned all of the outstanding stock of TransOcean Ltd., an investment company also formed in the Cayman Islands that owns businesses throughout Asia. At the suggestion of an official at the Bank of Bermuda, it was recommended that Mr. Fine, as well as Mr. Burns, formally advise the Board of Directors of TransOcean, that they believed the loan to Retmex, would be profitable to TransOcean as justification for the loan," said Louie.

"Wait a minute, how do you know that?" interjected David.

"Because I have in my possession a copy of an undated letter to the Directors of TransOcean in which Fine and Burns recommend that TransOcean loan five million dollars to Retmex. It is stated in the letter that the purpose of the loan is to obtain a more favorable rate of return on investment not otherwise available. I also have a copy of a letter dated January 25, 2006 that memorializes the same language in the undated letter," explained Louie.

"Where did you get these letters?" asked David.

"From a confidential informant," answered Louie, with neither lawyer saying anything.

"Approximately two years after the loan was made, Mr. Fine notified his financial advisor in the Cayman Islands that he wanted to call the loan to Retmex, at which time the legal entity that would initiate demand for repayment would be Uro, a company formed in the Cayman Islands and controlled by Mr. Fine," said Louie.

"And you have documentation to support this?" asked Caroline.

"I have a copy of a fax transmittal signed by Mr. Fine. Shortly thereafter, formal notice was given to Uro that the five million dollar loan was due as of March 30, 2008. I also have a copy of this letter," said Louie.

"During this time, The Fine Company formed a joint venture with a newly created corporation in Japan to provide international financial data and news to the Japanese investment community. In order to acquire an equity interest in this venture, Mr. Fine called the five million dollar note. However, because of insufficient funds, Retmex was unable to repay the five million dollar Promissory Note by its demand date. As a consequence, Retmex had defaulted on the loan and Mr. Fine commenced legal action," explained Louie.

"In order to acquire shares in the new joint venture, Mr. Fine borrowed five million dollars from Fred Chan, a business associate in Japan who would be repaid by Mr. Fine using the repayment of the loan that was made to Retmex. Eventually, Retmex repaid the five million dollar Promissory Note and this money was wire transferred to Mr. Chan in satisfaction of Mr. Fine's debt obligation," stated the revenue agent.

"Where are you going with this Agent Lipschitz?" asked David.

"At no personal expense to Mr. Fine, he received shares of stock valued at five million dollars because the funds used to acquire these shares came from Southpoint Corporation, a foreign entity that he controlled. This conclusion is further supported by a letter prepared by Mr. Fine that was stamped 'CONFIDENTIAL,' in which Mr. Fine declared that the loan would be converted into his investment in the newly created foreign joint venture," declared Louie.

"Prior to the time you got involved in this case, another lawyer told me that Mr. Fine categorically denied borrowing five million dollars from Fred Chan. In addition, Mr. Fine claimed, through his former attorney, that he transferred all of the shares to The Fine Company," said Louie.

"Mr. Fine told us that he did not borrow the money from Fred Chan," insisted Caroline.

"I have in my possession, several documents that corroborate the five million dollar loan from Fred Chan. These documents were composed by Mr. Fine and bear his signature," said Louie.

"Where did you get these documents?" asked Caroline.

"From a confidential informant, who shall remain confidential," replied Louie.

"We would like to see these documents," said David.

"In due time," remarked Louie.

"Getting back to the issue of taxability, what is the basis for your income adjustment, Agent Lipschitz?" asked Caroline.

"Mr. Fine's acquisition of the shares of ZanTech stock was accomplished without actual cost to your client because the source of the funds used to facilitate the purchase, came from Southpoint, a company that he controlled. Any payments made by a corporation for the personal benefit of its shareholder will constitute a constructive dividend in an amount equal to the fair market value of the personal benefit," explained Louie.

After a few moments of silence, David finally asked the question, "How do you know that Mr. Fine realized an economic benefit?"

"Because the acquisition of the ZanTech stock is a personal asset of Mr. Fine's and was clearly intended to be of personal benefit to him. My conclusion is further supported by documentary evidence that Mr. Fine personally owned the shares in question," replied Louie.

"Can you show us the documentary evidence?" asked Caroline.

"It happens to be The Fine Company's corporate resolutions dated Janaury 25, 2009 in which The Fine Company agreed to purchase the shares of ZanTech stock held by Mr. Fine. And even if Mr. Fine had not realized an economic benefit, it would still be taxable to him because the transfer of stock to The Fine Company would constitute 'an outbound transfer of property' involving a US taxpayer to a controlled foreign corporation," explained Louie.

Trying not to create the impression that they will acquiesce so quickly, David asked that they be afforded an opportunity to consult with their client before conceding this issue. Ever gracious in victory, Louie consented to the request.

"The next issue involves interest with respect to the five million dollar loan. Retmex paid three hundred and twenty five thousand dollars in interest to Uro with respect to the five million dollar loan. The interest payments have been identified on Uro's bank statements. Because Mr. Fine was, in actuality, the true lender of the loan, the interest payments should be imputed to him," stated Louie.

"Wait a minute. How do you know that Uro is owned by our client?" asked Caroline.

"I have a copy of a letter addressed to Mr. Fine that states the shares of Uro are held in nominee name. In organizational charts that identify the corporate structure of companies owned by Mr. Fine, Uro is shown as a wholly owned subsidiary that is controlled by Mr. Fine," explained Louie.

"Can we have a moment, please?" asked David.

"Sure. Take all the time you need. I'll wait outside."

After about five minutes, David called Louie back into the conference room. "Caroline and I would like to confer with our client before we commit to a position on imputing interest to him. It's possible that Uro included the interest payments in its gross income and paid tax on its earnings. If that's the case, we don't see how the interest should be attributed to Mr. Fine," stated David.

"That would be a valid argument if Uro reported the interest income on its tax returns. However, I don't believe that the interest payments were reported by Uro. Mr. Fine would have to provide this information to the IRS, which he previously declined to do when asked to submit copies of Uro's tax returns," remarked Louie.

"Would you be willing to split this adjustment given the unlikely possibility we could provide Uro's tax returns to you?" asked Caroline.

"This isn't KMART. We aren't running a Manager's Special today. If your client refuses to provide Uro's tax returns, he'll have to eat the entire amount of imputed interest," responded Louie.

BRUCE BRONSTEIN

"I think we need to regroup and talk to our client. Caroline and I will get back to you and we can meet next time in our office to conclude the audit," said David.

CHAPTER 5

Over at the Department of Justice, the attorneys assigned to prosecute the case of the United States of America versus Timothy Bell, are having an informal meeting. Confident that they will prevail on most, if not all, of the criminal offenses, the lawyers are contemplating the possibility of entering into settlement discussions that will result in a plea bargain with Timothy Bell.

A plea bargain is an agreement between a prosecutor and defendant in a criminal case, whereby a concession is made with respect to either the charge or the sentence. A charge bargain allows a criminal defendant to avoid the risk of conviction at trial on the more serious charge if the defendant agrees to plead guilty to a lesser charge. A sentence bargain is when the defendant agrees to plead guilty to the original charge, with a recommendation of a lighter sentence. Usually, a sentence bargain can only be granted if approved by the trial judge.

For public defenders, plea bargaining can present a dilemma because they must choose between zealously seeking a good deal for their current client or preserving a good working relationship with the prosecutor for the benefit of criminal defendants they must represent in future cases.

Sentence bargaining typically takes place in high profile cases where the prosecutor is opposed to reducing the charges against the defendant for fear as to how the media will report this to the public. A sentence bargain may permit the prosecutor to obtain a conviction for the most serious charge, while assuring the defendant of an acceptable sentence.

BRUCE BRONSTEIN

In Timothy Bell's case, a plea bargain is advantageous to him because it provides resolution to the stress of being charged with a crime. Going to trial usually requires a much longer wait, which often results in much more stress. Given Timmy's fragile psyche, the sooner he can get this nightmare over, the better.

Debbie Macht and Gary Zimmer are the DOJ lawyers who are prosecuting Timothy Bell. Experienced, well versed in criminal procedures, and knowledgeable in matters of courtroom tactics, both Debbie and Gary have a preference for litigating high profile cases and pushed hard to be assigned this case. Yet, senior DOJ officials have intimated that it may be in the best interests of both sides to explore a plea bargain.

The principal concern on the part of DOJ officials is having Timmy disclose in open court how he structured foreign transactions to evade the payment of tax. His testimony could serve as an instruction manual to others who might be motivated to create foreign entities for the purpose of concealing assets.

Debbie and Gary are in a conference room with their new boss, the Assistant Deputy Attorney General of the Criminal Tax Division. David Harbaugh has stressed his preference that Timothy enter into a plea bargain, but serve meaningful time behind bars.

"If this little twerp wants a plea bargain, he must plead guilty to all charges. In exchange, we'll offer him a reduction in his sentence. Are we in agreement with this?" said the Assistant Deputy Attorney General who was not really asking a question, but instead, telling Debbie and Gary that this is what he expects of them.

"We concur," replied Gary, who had already discussed the matter with Debbie that a sentence bargain would be preferable to a charge bargain.

Before the meeting broke up, the Assistant Deputy Attorney General added one thing. "I also want full disclosure as to how the little twerp was able to accomplish what he did. I don't want all of the specific details as to how he systematically evaded taxes in the Plea Agreement. Instead, I want it disclosed separately and make sure it's fully disclosed as a condition of the Plea. If we don't have full disclosure from him, then he's not getting a plea bargain from us," insisted Harbaugh.

***

The Commissioner of the Internal Revenue Service is in the Federal Building today to meet with senior IRS executives. The Brain Trust is meeting in a hospitality room on Level G, where refreshments are being served to those in attendance.

Louie has been told to be on his best behavior because the commissioner, intends to speak with him. A special award is to be presented to Louie for outstanding performance. In addition, Louie will be told that he will receive a QSI, which represents an in-grade promotion. This is important because it represents an immediate salary increase as well as a greater pension amount upon retirement.

Accolades of this event will be recorded. This necessitates picture taking. Picture taking means Louie will have to look his best. This will require the services of a make-up person, a fashion consultant and whoever else the IRS can recruit to make Louie look like he didn't just stumble out of bed wearing the clothes from last night.

IRS executives are lined up to greet the Commissioner as if he were a rock star. While the Commissioner has no idea who these people are, he makes it a point to tell them how he pleased he is with the job they're doing, even if they are not doing a good job. It is like the Pope meeting with members of the clergy and offering words of encouragement such as, "Keep up the good work," even if they've been charged with sex crimes. Neither the Commissioner nor the Pope would know of their underlings, so it seems as if it is a waste of time to have the leader say something like, "You're doing a great job for me. I appreciate the effort."

The really good managers do not have to grovel for promotions, while the bad managers will do anything to get ahead in the organization. This includes backstabbing, which goes back to the days of Julius Caesar. A supervisor competing for a promotion will take advantage of the commissioner's appearance by putting a knife or possibly a number of knives in the backs of fellow managers also in line for the same promotion.

When it comes to the sexes, women can be more ruthless at backstabbing than men because they have certain skills that men do not have. Their talents stand out on their bodies. This skill set goes back to when Adam and Eve were fooling around with an apple and not much in the way of clothes. Given the advantage a female may have in the looks department, putting a competitor down for the count is not all that difficult.

The real talent lies in using different strategies and tactics to disable multiple rivals in order to be awarded more than one promotion over one's career. Sabotaging more than one rival is similar to managing a military campaign. One candidate for a promotion will attempt to destroy a rival quickly and efficiently so that person will no longer be a serious competitor. The survivor will then move on to the next target and do the same. The survivor will continue until that person has the desired job. This is what many executives in large government agencies who are not good at their jobs are predisposed to do.

Another technique to watch out for involves backstabbing co-conspirators. This strategy is seldom utilized because it requires trust and confidence in others who are simply not trustworthy. Several years ago, a female subordinate engaged in late afternoon sexual improprieties with her immediate supervisor, who had a lengthy track record of improper conduct with his subordinates in other offices. In order to eliminate the threat of possible disciplinary action, these two conspired to have this person removed from his position and demoted, thereby eliminating a perceived threat to their illicit personal relationship.

Ironically, the supervisor who received the Lewinsky treatment was eventually removed from his job by IRS executives who learned of his subsequent involvement in another sexual harassment case which he initiated against another front-line manager for personal reasons. The moral to that story is that backstabbing may work the first time, but repeated attempts may result in disaster. Therefore, a clever backstabber must be fully cognizant of the limitations to backstabbing.

Another method to be on the alert for is the triple backstab. This consists of a group of three backstabbers working in unison. All three backstabbers plot against their first victim. Acting in concert, they have the element of surprise and have covered the angles of attack. After they are victorious and have eliminated one rival, two of the co-conspirators will combine forces to eliminate their other co-conspirator from consideration. With only the two co-conspirators left, the clever one will stab the other to obtain the promotion. This rarely happens because of the degree of difficulty involved.

However, an epic triple backstabbing incident did occur many years ago and it is still remembered by those employees who witnessed the devastation.   The sneakiest of the three backstabbers eventually prevailed by trampling over the others who fell by the wayside. Of course, the last one standing didn't last long in the new job when it became obvious that the job had been given to the least qualified person.

A tactic that is popular among some backstabbers involves the planting of false rumors to destroy a rival's credibility and reputation. This also necessitates using cohorts to help destroy the main competition. In order to obtain the assistance from others, the backstabber will often make promises that he or she has no intention of keeping. This type of backstabber is on the fast track to a political career.

A backstabber may also resort to whistleblowing. This strategy is employed only when the backstabber is desperate.   The backstabber is about to be put on notice that he or she's work product does not meet acceptable standards.   To avoid disciplinary action such as a demotion or dismissal, the backstabber becomes a whistleblower. As a consequence, any disciplinary action that is taken is perceived as being vindictive by IRS management.   This can be a successful tool by the backstabber in getting IRS management demoted or fired.

A really good employee does not have to resort to these tactics. The problem is that when the commissioner does make a once in a lifetime visit, everyone plays the game. Because Louie is not a manager, he doesn't have to put on a facade. It also helps when your brother-in-law is still an influential figure with senior Treasury Department officials.

That afternoon, Louie was escorted by several Secret Service Agents to meet with the commissioner. Louie has been instructed by his bosses not to refer to the Supreme Leader as "The Commish" or "Your Royal Highness." Therefore, with those titles not available, Louie decided that he will greet him as "Sir," and say as little as possible. Louie, who is no bigger than a munchkin, will play the strong, silent type.

The commissioner carries himself as if he were the man in charge. Tall, well dressed and debonair, the man looks like he came from central casting to play the part of a senior government executive. There is a certain presence about being the commissioner and this man has the right stuff.

The entire time Louie spent with the commissioner, he had as chaperons on each side, his respective bosses, Tom Collins and Roger Smith. Both men held their breaths hoping that Louie did not say anything other than thanks for the award. They are also concerned about Louie taking a catalog out of his pocket and trying to sell electronic gadgets to the commissioner as if he were one of the guys.

Tom made it a point to briefly highlight that Louie was reassigned open cases with Stanley Scherr as the representative. When Tom got to the part about Louie having generated approximately thirty two million dollars in additional tax due with respect to the eight cases, a huge smile creased the commissioner's face. In addition, Tom advised the commissioner that Louie worked the Lopez case which later became a refund claim in District Court, to which the commissioner replied, "That's the case where there was jury misconduct?"

"Yes sir. The jury foreman accepted a bribe from Mrs. Lopez, who has apparently disappeared. The verdict has been set aside and the case has been scheduled for a new trial. With Mrs. Lopez in hiding, we doubt that it will be re-tried," said Tom.

"And, Louie has only recently completed his audit of Stanley Scherr's personal income tax returns. The Examination Division has released jurisdiction to CID for a criminal investigation," added Roger.

"Agent Lipschitz, I can see that your reputation precedes you," said the commissioner.

"Yes, Louie does have quite a reputation," interjected Tom before Louie could utter a single word.

"And, I think it's time we get back to work. Sir, if you'll excuse us," said Tom, as he and Roger made like bodyguards as they escorted Louie away from the festivities.

"Hey, I was just about to ask The Commish if he was in the market for any electronic gadgets. And you had to pull me away? Couldn't you have given me a few more minutes to make a sale?" asked Louie.

"Louie, if you had pulled a stunt like that, you would be the first IRS employee to have received a special award, a QSI and be demoted all in the same day," said Tom. "What do you say to that?"

"Just for that, I'm not going to tell you about the latest penile implant that just came out," replied Louie.

CHAPTER 6

When Stanley arrived at his office, he was told by Erin that Kim Swenson has called and would like to come in to see him. "She needs some tax advice," Erin told her idiot boss, who is the last person on the planet who should be offering tax advice.

As Stanley's problems seemed overwhelming to him, he immediately perked up when he heard Kim's name. Telling Erin to arrange the appointment for late morning, Stanley hoped to take Kim to a popular restaurant for lunch where he could be seen with a gorgeous blonde. However, having lunch with Kim is not going to happen.

Stanley attended to a few housekeeping items and then played several games of paper basketball which resulted in lots of crumpled up paper basketballs on the floor and none in the wastebasket. With his law practice imploding, Stanley can appreciate what Nero went through while Rome was burning.

Within the next hour, Kim Swenson arrived and seeing her in the flesh made Stanley's day. Looking like she just returned from a lengthy vacation in Hawaii, Stanley asked Kim what she had been doing lately.

"I just got back from an extended vacation in Hawaii. Actually, I was shooting an adult film on the islands which only took four days. So, I stayed there another three weeks," replied Kim.

Before Kim became a porn star, she was a middle school teacher who was arrested and charged with having sex with an underage student. The child's parents eventually withdrew the complaint against Kim after she paid them several hundred thousand dollars. In order to pay off the kid's parents, Kim became an adult film star.

Kim had previously sought Stanley's expert advice as to whether the two hundred thousand dollar payment was deductible. Stanley had no idea so he sought the advice of a CPA and was told that it was not deductible. Apparently, Kim was either impressed with Stanley's knowledge of taxation or she didn't know another tax professional because she has returned to this idiot for help.

Stanley is drooling over the sight of Kim sitting across from him. She is without question, Stanley's favorite client. In fact, Stanley has even instructed Erin not to bill Kim for his time or any legal work that he might do for her. The thought that he should pay her to come into his office had even crossed his mind.

Kim is showing a lot of skin today. Wearing a low-cut dress that is the size of a postage stamp, Stanley was able to see the tiny diamond piercing in Kim's belly button while the hem of Kim's dress is barely below Kim's belly button.

"How can I be of help?" Stanley finally asked after he put his eyeballs back in his head.

"Well, I've been doing really great lately. With my porno films, royalties from the sex videos, and appearance fees to attend strip clubs all over the country, I made over a half million dollars in the last eight months. I've been wondering about whether I should do some tax planning?" said Kim.

As usual, Stanley looked befuddled in Kim's presence. The thought that Kim could earn more than five hundred thousand dollars in just eight months was unbelievable.

"My cousin, the used car salesman, told me about this idea. He suggested that I form a ...., here I wrote it down," as she reached into her purse to remove a paper. "My cousin said I should look into forming a personal services corporation to save on taxes. I wanted to run this idea by you since you're the tax expert," said Kim, who had no idea that Stanley Scherr was definitely not a tax expert and would soon be out of the tax business.

"A personal services corporation?" asked Stanley, who was clearly not familiar with a PSC.

"Yeah. I didn't understand what my cousin was talking about so I asked my neighbor, the nurse I told you about, who took an accounting course in college. She told me, here it is on my notes, that it used to be popular with highly paid professional athletes and entertainers who would assign their earnings to a corporation to avoid paying tax on the entire amount and then draw a salary on only a portion of their earnings. The way my neighbor explained it, the corporation would pay tax at a lower tax rate on the earnings it retained," said Kim.

"Right," Stanley remarked as he nodded his head up and down like a trained seal.

"Well, my neighbor, seems to think it's not a good idea because the highest individual and corporate tax rates are about the same so there would be no great benefit to do so. What do you think I should do?" asked Kim.

"Did you really earn more than one half a million dollars in only eight months?" asked Stanley.

"That was no big deal. If I had really pushed it, I could have made a lot more. I turned down some film roles and chose not to do the spread for Playboy," replied Kim.

"Playboy wanted you in its magazine?"

"That's right. They offered me more than two million dollars to pose nude. They wanted to do this big layout and article about my life. How I went from schoolteacher to porn star. But I really didn't want to publicize what happened in the last sixteen months," said Kim.

"How much do you make per film?" asked Stanley who was mesmerized with Kim's earning potential.

"Ten thousand dollars per film. But it only takes like three days to shoot all the sex scenes. Getting back to my tax question?" said Kim.

"How many days a week were you working?" inquired Stanley, who was not in any hurry to answer Kim's question about the tax consequences of utilizing a PSC to save on taxes.

"I was filming like two movies a week. Between breaks, I'd do promotional work and go to strip clubs to perform. I'd also do escort work if the price was right. Stan, can we get back to my tax question?" asked Kim.

"How much did you get paid as an escort?" inquired Stanley.

"Ten thousand a night, plus dinner at a five-star restaurant."

"Jesus," Stanley said with admiration.

"My tax question," said an exasperated Kim, hoping that Stanley will stop stalling and finally give her an answer as to whether she should form a PSC.

"Kim, to be honest with you, I don't know jack shit about personal services corporations. How about I take you to lunch?" said Stanley.

Sensing that this has been a complete waste of time, Kim got up to leave and said, "I can't. I'm shooting a threesome with two other women this afternoon in some rich guy's mansion and I don't want to be late."

***

"Roger, we need to talk to you."

"Judging by your facial expressions, it doesn't sound good," remarked Roger Smith.

"Jim and I have been assigned a sensitive matter that involves one of your field agents."

Carl Roberts and Jim Webb are responsible for investigating IRS employees who are the subject of misconduct allegations. With them was Don Banks, an appeals officer.

The IRS instituted internal procedures for investigating complaints that involve employees. It is the responsibility of the Inspection Division to have its inspectors look into allegations of wrongdoing. If an employee is found guilty of misconduct, the consequences can be harsh. If misconduct has been determined, the employee can be suspended or terminated from employment.

"It's Ben Newman," said Carl.

Ben Newman's title is revenue agent. However, Ben prefers to identify himself as a CPA on all IRS stationery. This is confusing because some taxpayers may think that they were audited by a CPA rather than a revenue agent if the IRS hired public accounting firms to perform tax audits.

Roger has counseled Ben as to the importance of identifying himself as a revenue agent who is employed by the IRS. According to Roger, it is helpful that taxpayers know that their tax returns were examined by a representative of the Examination Division and not a practicing CPA. It is also important that Ben not hold himself out to be a practicing CPA because the IRS does not engage the services of practicing CPAs to conduct audits.

Roger has gone so far as to instruct Ben to cease using the symbol CPA, and instead, refer to himself as a revenue agent. Apparently, this instruction has fallen on deaf ears.

Whereas Ben may be book smart, as a field agent he is an imbecile who has no idea how to conduct an audit. Ben's workpapers often fail to properly address the issues in question. Actually, his audit workpapers consist of an almost endless litany of footnotes rather than a discussion of the facts and law.

In Ben's mind, every taxpayer is a criminal who deserves life in prison. Given this attitude, Ben believes that nothing a taxpayer says is to be believed and any documents that are submitted are to be viewed with contempt and disdain.

As a consequence, Ben's cases are usually unagreed and sent to an Appeals Office for reconsideration at the request of the taxpayer. Virtually all of these cases are eventually resolved by an appeals officer. In many of these cases, it is the appeals officer who will apologize to the taxpayer for the shoddy treatment that the taxpayer experienced during the audit.

In numerous instances, taxpayers have filed claims with the IRS to recover administrative costs and legal fees as a result of Ben Newman's actions. This is not only embarrassing but can be expensive to the government if it must reimburse taxpayers for the fees that they incurred throughout the audit process if it should be determined that Ben's actions were unreasonable and the IRS cannot establish justification for the agent's position.

features that suggest they spend their spare time competing in Iron Man competitions. Possessing lean, muscular physiques, they both have military style buzz cuts. These

"Approximately two months ago, I settled a docketed case and sent the Decision Document to Counsel for entry with the court. The trial attorney assigned to the case called to ask me how I had managed to get the petitioner to agree to the civil fraud penalty when Counsel did not approve the assertion of the civil fraud penalty in the Notice of Deficiency," Don stated.

Should a revenue agent believe that the civil fraud penalty should be asserted against a taxpayer whenever a Notice of Deficiency is to be issued, the Notice must first be approved by Counsel for legal sufficiency. This is a procedural requirement because it is Counsel that must meet its burden of persuasion when asserting fraud. If Counsel does not approve the imposition of the civil fraud penalty when it reviews the Notice, it will not defend the fraud penalty in Tax Court.

"I knew that Counsel had not approved the assertion of the civil fraud penalty. It was my understanding that Counsel did not review the Notice because it did not have sufficient time to do so. The Notice was issued on April 13, with only two days remaining on the statute," stated Don.

"There was nothing in the admin file that indicated the file had been sent to Counsel. I didn't know that when I was assigned the case," Don admitted.

"Steve Willis was the trial attorney on this case and he later told me that he had, in fact, reviewed the Notice. When Steve told me that he did not approve the civil fraud penalty, he qualified it by saying that he rejected the civil fraud penalty," Don added for clarification.

"Steve then told me that he had written a Declination Memorandum that was quite lengthy and explicit as to why the civil fraud penalty was not applicable in this case. Steve then asked me whether I had read his legal opinion which he had inserted in the administrative file," Don said.

"I don't understand. If Steve declined to approve the imposition of the civil fraud penalty in the Notice, how in the hell did the fraud penalty get into the Notice?" Roger asked Don.

"Because, Counsel's Memorandum was not in the file. In addition, all references to the case having been sent to Counsel for legal review were sanitized," Don explained.

"So, you had no knowledge of what Counsel had said in its legal review?" Roger asked Don.

"That's right. All references to Counsel's review had been deleted. The file was sanitized."

"Jesus," said Roger. "And you suspect it was Newman?"

"Who else could it have been? It was Newman's case. He was looking at a potentially blown statute if he had to prepare a new Notice. Or, maybe he just wanted to assert the civil fraud penalty against the taxpayer and figured that if he removed Counsel's Memorandum from the file, Appeals would eventually settle the case and get concessions from the taxpayer that he was unable to get," surmised Don.

"Roger, as you can guess, Jim and I have spoken to Steve and we have a copy of his legal opinion. We've gone through the admin files and we've interviewed the clerical people in Appeals and Counsel who were responsible for shipping and carding in the case. The Memorandum was removed by someone in Exam and we believe that it was Newman. We've eliminated any other person in Exam who touched the admin file. This constitutes misconduct on his part and is a punishable offense," Carl said.

"Aside from the procedural issues that we have, there is another concern and this impacts the taxpayer in this case. Newman asserted the fraud penalty when he was specifically instructed by Counsel not to do so. The taxpayer hired a lawyer to represent them. Legal fees were incurred. Perhaps legal fees did not have to be incurred had fraud not been asserted. We can't say for sure. But Newman's actions put the taxpayer in somewhat of a bind. Had Don not resolved the case, Counsel would have waived the penalty in its entirety. We're bringing this to your attention before we confront him with this charge," Carl said.

"Knowing Ben, I have no doubt that he did this because he seems to have this mindset that all taxpayers are crooks.   He does go overboard at times," Roger remarked.

"Roger, this isn't the first time with Newman.   He's been on our radar for some time," Jim acknowledged.

"This is a serious misconduct issue.   We're of the opinion that he should resign before he is terminated," added Carl.

"Who's we?"

"Our director shares this view," Jim added.

CHAPTER 7

"Look, there was really no harm in allowing a non-lawyer to offer legal advice, particularly when each law client has acknowledged that they were more than satisfied with the advice offered. In point of fact, Mr. Scherr has stated that his expertise did not include international taxation and that he was not knowledgeable in other aspects of taxation such as Termination Assessments, the rules governing foreign bank accounts and other unusual tax matters that sole practitioners generally do not see," Wallace Shadybrook argued on behalf of his idiot client.

Wallace Shadybrook, late night cable television lawyer extraordinaire, is in a pre-trial settlement conference in the office of an Assistant State's Attorney General. Wallace's goa is to convince the State of Maryland to drop its criminal conspiracy case against his client.

"The Maryland Attorney General is concerned that someone not authorized to practice law was, in fact, practicing law at the behest of your client. And now you're telling me that your client was not qualified to provide legal advice so he allowed a non-lawyer to step into his shoes and give a legal opinion which they relied upon. That doesn't speak well for Mr. Scherr's legal abilities, does it?" said Brian Kent, the Assistant Attorney General assigned to Stanley Scherr's case.

The young Assistant Attorney General graduated from law school three years ago. Still very preppy looking and studious with wire frame eyeglasses, Brian is respectful of his elders and in this case, he is showing his adversary great respect given how old Wallace appears to be.

"Would you have preferred that Mr. Scherr had given incorrect legal advice to his clients?" asked Wallace.

"Of course not."

"Then there is really no harm in this case because Mr. Scherr's clients, by all accounts, were given the correct information by Mr. Bell. I have obtained an Affidavit from another law firm with a well-respected tax practice that has reviewed the tax issues that were addressed by Mr. Bell and this law firm has confirmed that Mr. Bell's advice was technically correct. Furthermore, Mr. Scherr's clients have submitted Affidavits to your office that they were more than satisfied with the quality of Mr. Bell's advice. So, there was no real harm to any clients. Let's just pick up our toys and go home," exclaimed Wallace.

"Where is Mr. Scherr?" asked Brian.

"He is currently in his law office tending to administrative matters. Unfortunately, he lost a number of clients as a result of unfavorable publicity. The fact that one of his clients bribed a juror, and I might add, without his knowledge, has been a serious setback to a practice that was only recently thriving," said Wallace.

"Mr. Scherr has admitted that he made a serious mistake in judgment in not disclosing that Mr. Bell was not a lawyer. Mr. Scherr has confided to me that he would have been embarrassed had he disclosed this fact to his clients for fear that their perception of him would be a negative one. That is the reason why he let his clients think that Mr. Bell was a lawyer," asserted Wallace.

"Mr. Kent, let me ask you this, if I may? What purpose does it serve the citizens of Maryland if my client is sent to prison?" asked Wallace.

Before the young man could respond, Wallace said, "Before you answer that question, please consider that a prison sentence is not an appropriate penalty in this instance. Does prison life rehabilitate criminals? I think studies will show that it doesn't. And aren't our prisons supposed to house the worst criminal offenders? Of course. And would you consider Mr. Scherr's mistake so egregious that it warrants being sent to prison?" asked Wallace. "No. It does not."

"Mr. Kent, I apologize to you. I posed a question to you and then stopped you before you could answer by asking more questions," said Wallace.

"Sir, you can tell your client that the State of Maryland will not prosecute him on the conspiracy charge. He's free to continue to practice law," said Brian as he stood to shake the hand of a defense attorney who looked old enough to be his great grandfather.

***

Erin Schlaffer has returned to her job at the FBI. On her last day in Stanley's office, the nitwit lawyer wished Erin well but neglected to take her to lunch. Erin, in turn, wished that she had found more incriminating documents needed to charge Stanley with facilitating a tax evasion scheme for his clients.

"Without incriminating documents that establish there was a conspiracy to defraud the government, we can't charge him with a criminal offense," said Erin's boss at the FBI. "I know you did your best, but we need to move on to other cases."

"I think it's ironic that while I was undercover in Stanley Scherr's office, we had a team of agents doing surveillance work on the outside, with neither of us aware of the other. It's like the right hand doesn't know what the left hand is doing," said Erin.

"It's not the first time the FBI has done this and it probably won't be the last time," replied Erin's supervisor. "Just don't advertise this fact to anyone."

***

Stanley received the good news from Wallace that the State of Maryland has dropped the criminal conspiracy charge against him and is now anxious to get back to business, provided he can find a client.

Stanley is still barred from appearing before the IRS in any administrative capacity. He can, however, appear in court to litigate a case. However, litigation is something that Stanley does not do well, unless of course, he can find a jury that can be bought.

If Timothy Bell was not in a federal correctional facility, Stanley envisioned the young man working side-by-side with him as a research assistant. Stanley has decided that it is time he visit his protégé in lockup. This should make for an interesting reunion.

***

"Holy shit. What in the hell was he thinking?" Tom Collins shook his head in disbelief at the stupidity of what one of his field agents has done.

"I have no idea what the dumb shit was thinking," Roger answered with a shrug of his shoulders.

"Newman's actions have undermined the integrity of our tax system. What Newman did was stack the playing field in his favor by arbitrarily asserting a civil fraud penalty which was improper," Tom argued.

"I know," acknowledged Roger.

"I want his resignation on my desk before the close of business. Tell him that if he doesn't resign today, I'll terminate his employment," declared Tom.

"You do realize that the union will file a grievance against you for wrongful termination, don't you?" said Roger.

"The union doesn't have much of a case. Newman sabotaged a taxpayer's file. He's guilty of insubordination since he intentionally disregarded legal advice from Counsel. He either deleted entries on a Case Activity Record or he deliberately failed to record these entries. I think we have a serious case of misconduct," Tom exclaimed.

"Newman strikes me as the type of employee who will not resign. What if we transfer him to another function?" Roger suggested as an alternative.

"Rog, I'm not running an employment agency. The last time I checked, I was supposed to be supervising my front-line managers who are supposed to be supervising their field agents. That's what we do here. And besides, who would possibly want Newman? He's the most incompetent agent we've had in Baltimore in the last twenty five years. He doesn't have anything to offer another function. Besides, if we look in the other direction when something like this happens, what does it say about us? We are, in essence, sending a message that we failed to take disciplinary action when action was necessary. Can you imagine what kind of a precedent this would set?" Tom asked Roger.

"I was just thinking out loud. Before I sit down with Newman, our friends in Inspection are going to grill him. I can't imagine that's going to be pleasant," Roger said.

"It certainly won't be pleasant. If Newman shoves a cyanide pill down his throat, I don't want him doing it in a government office building," Tom remarked.

***

Ben Newman sat across the large conference room table from Carl Roberts and Jim Webb. Ben has been told that he can have his union representative with him for the duration of this meeting and as a precautionary measure, Ben has asked his union representative to attend.

Union representatives are generally those employees who have the most seniority. Most shop stewards in the union devote the majority of their time to union matters and very little time to actual IRS work. The person attending this meeting is seventy eight years old, hard of hearing and frequently falls asleep during work hours.

Sam Goldman looks every bit one hundred and seventy eight years old and then some. In fact, if Hollywood were casting someone to play Methuselah, Sam would get the part based on his physical appearance. Sam was about to doze off when Ben nudged his forearm to get his attention.

"For the next twenty minutes, Carl and Jim recited the facts just as Don Banks had explained the facts to Roger Smith in the previous meeting. When Carl and Jim had finished, they locked eyes on Ben.

"We know you sanitized the admin file. Why did you do it?" asked Carl.

Ben sat there for a moment without saying a word. Finally, Sam perked up as if he had just awoken from a nap and advised, "You don't have to answer that question."

"If you're going to decline to answer our questions, we'll conclude our inquiry now. We're prepared to recommend that you be dismissed from government service. You'll be served with papers by the close of business today," Jim said.

Holding up his hands as if he were about to be robbed, Sam said, "Wait a minute fellas. Let's back up a second."

"We aren't here to play games. If you're willing to answer questions, we can proceed. Otherwise, we're done here," Jim said.

Sam turned to Ben and whispered in his ear. In response, Ben then whispered in Sam's ear. This continued for several moments as if these two are teenagers who have secrets to tell each other.

Disgusted that this is now a waste of their time, the Inspectors told the two whisperers that the interview is over and they are free to leave. After they left, Jim called Roger with the news.

When Ben returned to the eighth floor, he was told to report to Roger's office. Entering Roger's office is like walking into the lion's den. What Ben did has made Roger look like a supervisor who failed to properly supervise a subordinate who clearly required close supervision.

Roger's inability to closely monitor Ben also reflects poorly on Tom. However, there is some plausible deniability because management would have no way of knowing that an employee has deliberately sanitized an admin file.

"You wanted to see me, Roger?" said Ben as he walked into Roger's office as if he expected to be asked to lead a tax auditing workshop for junior field agents.

"Have a seat. We need to talk. I just got off the phone with Jim Webb and Carl Roberts. They intend to recommend that you be dismissed from your job for misconduct," Roger said.

"I can explain that," insisted Ben.

"Ben, you were given an opportunity to explain and you declined to do so," Roger remarked.

"But I was caught off guard and not prepared to answer their questions," Ben replied.

"You had your shop steward with you and I'm told the two of you were whispering back and forth like a couple of schoolgirls. I want your resignation now or I'll process your termination papers and seek your dismissal, effective immediately. Having been fired by the federal government will not look good on your Resume if you intend to seek a new job," Roger replied.

Upon hearing this, Ben began to sob. Within seconds, tears flowed down Ben's cheeks as he started to stammer his words. Sensing Ben's fragile emotional state of mind, Roger allowed him a few moments to compose himself.

"I did it because I felt I had to do something. Counsel's legal opinion was all wrong. That trial attorney didn't know what he was talking about. He totally missed the boat. I assumed the appeals officer would agree with me and sustain the fraud penalty," pleaded Ben.

"First, the legal advice that you were given was not wrong. This was not a fraud case. In fact, the appeals officer agreed with Counsel that the fraud penalty was not applicable. Second, you do not have the authority to disregard a legal opinion by Counsel. We have an attorney-client relationship with Counsel and we are bound by Counsel's advice. Third, you intentionally removed Counsel's work product from the admin file. And fourth, you deliberately sanitized the admin file by excluding any record of the file having been sent to Counsel for approval of the Notice," Roger exclaimed.

"But Don Banks settled the case with the taxpayers agreeing to the civil fraud penalty. So, in a sense, I was vindicated by the Appeals settlement," argued Ben.

"Not exactly. What Don did was propose that the penalty amount be equivalent to the negligence penalty. While it is true that the agreement referred to the civil fraud penalty, Don did this only to avoid the inconvenience of having Counsel file a motion for an increased deficiency and then have to prepare a different agreement," explained Roger.

"Look Roger, most of us view fraud differently. It just so happens that I take a very aggressive pro-government stance on issues and others don't. Is that wrong?" Ben asked.

"What's wrong is your stacking the deck against a taxpayer who is entitled to be treated fairly. You tilted the playing field in your favor. How would you feel if you were the taxpayer in this case and it was done to you?" Roger asked.

"But taxpayers and representatives do this sort of thing all the time. They withhold incriminating information from us, they intentionally mislead us, they submit false documents and lie. It goes on all the time," Ben argued in response.

"Just because this does happen in limited instances doesn't mean that we have to be underhanded and deceitful. We have internal procedures in place that we're expected to follow. There's also a Code of Ethics that you're required to adhere to, and in this specific instance, your conduct does not meet the standard of conduct expected of you," asserted Roger.

"What are my options?"

"It's almost 3 o'clock. Go back to your desk. Type your letter of resignation and e-mail it to me. I want it in the next fifteen minutes. If I don't see it by then, you'll be given your termination papers by 4 pm," said Roger.

"Isn't there something you can do for me? I love this job. I love auditing taxpayers. This is something that I was born to do. Please don't take this away from me," pleaded Ben.

"I'm sorry Ben. You'd better get started with your letter of resignation. Time is running out."

When Ben Newman returned to his desk several minutes later, he placed a phone call to Sam Goldman. Sam had fallen asleep and was still somewhat groggy when Ben explained what he was being told to do.

"It sounds like they're serious," said Sam.

"What should I do?" asked Ben.

"Ben, if you resign, you can't file a grievance. If you force them to fire you, we can file a grievance and go through the grievance procedures," Sam advised Ben.

"How long would that take and can I get my job back?" Ben asked his shop steward.

"It could take forever and a day for a decision. And I have no idea if you could be re-hired. Look, if management were to allege that you were incompetent, that's tough to prove and we would stand a good chance of winning. But with a misconduct charge like this, it's so factual. They pretty much are holding your nuts in their hands," proclaimed Sam.

Ben decided to let Methuselah go back to sleep. He then proceeded to type his letter of resignation and e-mailed it to Roger. After Roger received the e-mail, he walked over to Ben's desk and instructed him to turn in his IRS credentials including his pocket commission, his office key, cabinet keys, and swipe card. Roger asked Ben to leave his desktop computer on and provide him with a list of all security passwords for accessing his files and programs. Ben was then told he had ten minutes to clean out his desk and remove his personal items.

Once Ben had signed his resignation papers, he was escorted out of the building by several Inspectors. This was a rather un-ceremonial exit. There was no farewell party, no gifts, and no hugs and handshakes from his co-workers. There was a definite chill in the air as if someone had turned the A/C setting on the office thermostat to the lowest temperature.

Ben compared this moment to when suspects are arrested and taken away in handcuffs, with their heads covered by coats so they won't be recognized. Ben felt that he had been tossed to the curb and run over by a bus driven by IRS management who did not appreciate his many skills. After Ben left, Roger stopped by Tom's office to chat.

"I'm not happy about forcing him out. The man has a wife and two young kids to support," said Roger.

"I know. I'm not happy with the result either. Newman wasn't much of an agent, but I admired his spunk in defending the IRS. I suspect he's going to have a tough time finding a job in the private sector so I took the liberty of putting a call into a friend at the Maryland Comptroller's Office. In a few months there will be a position opening up for a Sales Tax Examiner. He'll make the same amount of money that he was making here and the work will be better. He's more suited to sales tax issues because its compliance oriented. I asked that someone in the state government discretely notify Newman of the position and encourage him to apply for the job. If he applies for it, he stands a good chance of being hired," predicted Tom.

"Don't you think we should tell him?"

"No. I don't want Newman to think that we pulled strings so that he could get another job. It's important to his psyche that he think he was selected for the position because of his qualifications," remarked Tom.

CHAPTER 8

Stanley made the drive in approximately two hours to the federal correctional facility where Timmy is staying. In order to be admitted, Stanley must pass through several security points. Stanley is very familiar with this process.

The first stage required that Stanley remove his personal items and pass through an electronic scanner that pales in comparison to the diagnostic X-ray machine used in the Federal Building. Next, Stanley got "The Wand" treatment. However, when Stanley was not given "The Pat Down" treatment, he asked, "Don't you guys want to frisk me or something?" In response to this question, Stanley was told to move it along.

When Stanley was escorted to a waiting room where Timmy would soon be brought, he thought back to his experiences in the Federal Building. Mumbling to himself, Stanley said, "Jeez, they didn't even offer me any nutritional or fitness tips. In the future, if I want my bladder and prostate checked, I'll have to make a visit to the Federal Building."

After Timmy was brought into the meeting room, Stanley greeted him with a firm handshake. Timmy was clearly pleased to see Stanley and inquired as to how he is doing.

"I've got some issues I'm dealing with, but all things considered, not bad," said Stanley. "How are you doing in here?"

"I'm okay. By the way, my parents were in to see me the other day." Upon mentioning his parents, Timmy was about to break down and cry.

Stanley allowed Timmy a few moments to compose his thoughts. The sight of Timmy starting to unravel like this is disconcerting to Stanley.

Stanley finally said, "My lawyer convinced the Maryland Attorney General's Office to drop its criminal conspiracy case against me. The lawyer who represented me in the pre-trial settlement conference is a criminal defense attorney by the name of Wallace Shadybrook. He's an old fart but really knows his shit. Do you want me to ask him to assist in your defense?"

"Will he take the case?" asked Timmy.

"Are you kidding me? Timmy, every criminal defense attorney in the country would agree to take your case. Your case is on every news channel at all hours of the day. You're getting more press than the president. Every lawyer in America would kill to represent you," Stanley proclaimed.

"Stan, I can't be selective with my legal representation because a really good law firm will want big bucks to handle my case which means I'll have to get the money from an overseas bank account. Either the IRS or the FBI will find out about this, trace the funds and find where I've stashed billions of dollars. The government will then seize the bank accounts and then file more criminal charges against me. It's too risky," explained Timmy.

"I see your dilemma," said Stanley.

"This Wallace Shady….whatever. Is he good?" inquired Timmy.

"I think so. I saw his ad on a late-night cable show. He's a little cranky and he wouldn't cut me any slack on his legal fees, so I saw something in him that I admired. Greed," admitted Stanley.

"How am I going to pay him? I can't ask my parents for money."

"Don't worry. I'll front the money and you can pay me back later when you get out of here," said Stanley.

"What about my Public Defender?" asked Timmy.

"You'll still need the Public Defender until Wallace is on board. Once you have Wallace, you won't need the Public Defender."

Stanley and Timmy continued to chat and catch up on current events. Timmy listened with rapt attention when Stanley told him about his one year suspension to practice before the IRS and having lost so many clients. Stanley also told Timmy that Mrs. Lopez has probably fled the country and without her, there will be no retrial of her refund claim. In addition, Stanley let Timmy know that Agent Lipschitz discovered substantial unreported income which he believes warrants a criminal investigation into Stanley's tax returns. This means Stanley is now a candidate for an adjacent prison cell in a federal prison.

"Wow," said Timmy. "I had no idea that you could be in trouble for tax evasion. Anything I can do to help? Wait a minute, what was I thinking? I'm in a jail cell with no place to go and I'm asking you if you need my help?" exclaimed Timmy.

"Actually, I will need your help when you get out of here, assuming I'm not in prison. I've decided to change from a tax representation firm to a firm that does tax planning. I can use your research skills to advise clients on tax planning techniques. Of course, you'll be introduced to all clients as my research assistant who is not a lawyer. So, as long as you're not giving legal advice, we can be a team again. How does that sound?" asked Stanley.

"Swell," replied Timmy as if he just swallowed an entire bottle of Milk of Magnesia. The very last thing Timmy needs is to be seen associating with Stanley Scherr who may soon be convicted felon doing hard time in a federal prison for tax evasion.

***

After Stanley returned to his office, he called Wallace Shadybrook on Timmy's behalf. When Stanley explained Timmy's unfortunate situation to him, Wallace responded by saying, "I'll need a fifty thousand dollar retainer before this goes any further, plus I'll be charging four hundred and fifty dollars an hour for my time, whether it's legal or non-legal."

"What's legal or non-legal mean?"

"Stan, legal means my time is spent on legal work, while non-legal means commute time, time spent photocopying, typing, that kind of stuff."

"Don't you have a secretary who handles your administrative work?" asked Stanley.

"Nope."

"Four hundred dollars an hour to type a letter?" asked Stanley.

"No. That's four hundred and fifty dollars an hour to type a letter. No discounts, no courtesies, no bullshit. You want me to represent your friend, that's my price. Take it or leave it," said Wallace.

"And you would charge four hundred and fifty dollars an hour in litigation?" asked Stanley.

"No."

"It would be more to go to trial?" asked Stanley.

"No."

"Then what is it?" asked Stanley, who felt like he was playing a game of cat and mouse with this shyster.

"There is no litigation cost because I don't litigate," answered Wallace.

"I don't understand."

"I don't go to court. I don't try cases. Litigation is not what I do," replied Wallace.

"But you're a criminal defense attorney," said a puzzled Stanley.

"Right. And what I do is represent criminal defendants throughout the judicial process. I make every effort to plea bargain their cases. I will settle every case prior to trial so that I don't have to go to court. That's because I don't go to court. Now do you understand?" asked Wallace.

There was silence on the other end of the telephone line. Wallace finally broke the silence by saying, "Litigation is difficult for a man my age and certainly in my state of health. Juries don't like me. Judges don't care for me. And opposing counsel? Let's just say the prosecutors who know me, know what to expect from me. I work cases fast but I get results. In the end, I'll save the client money because I won't drag out my time and have the client incur unnecessary legal fees."

"If you were to represent my friend......?"

"The case does not go to trial. He'll take a plea," said Wallace.

"And if the plea bargain is not acceptable to him?" "He'll take the

plea," repeated Wallace.

"Perhaps my friend might be better represented by the Public Defender," countered Stanley.

"He can always go that route. You get what you pay for," said the shyster to Stanley.

"I'll get back to you," said Stanley, knowing full well that he wasn't going to get back to Wallace.

***

Louie made himself comfortable in the reception area of a very nice downtown law firm. The accommodations are much nicer than the Federal Building. Louie has even been offered refreshments by the lovely receptionist. Taking in the view of the Inner Harbor from the tenth floor of the Trade Center Building, Louie wouldn't mind spending the day here. In contrast, the two lawyers he is to meet with would prefer that he not spend the day in their office.

Caroline was the first out of the gate to greet Louie, followed by her law partner. She did so in a professional tone of voice and with respect. This is a tacit acknowledgment that Louie is a formidable adversary. Both David and Caroline have conceded that they underestimated Louie for the first meeting. The lawyers are determined not to make the same mistake again.

Louie began the conference by asking his hosts where the client stands with respect to the first two issues.

David answered by saying, "We've recommended that he agree to the five million dollar disguised dividend and ask that you agree to an allocation of the imputed interest adjustment."

"What sort of allocation?" asked Louie.

"We thought a fifty/fifty split would be fair," answered David.

"I don't think a split is feasible when your client failed to provide the IRS with copies of Uro's tax returns that would identify interest income being reported," replied Louie.

"Our client has told us that he can't provide these tax returns," said Caroline.

"He will not or cannot?" asked Louie.

"We didn't press him on that point. Apparently, it's a sensitive subject with the client," admitted Caroline.

"With that being the case, I can't split the adjustment," replied Louie.

"Can't or won't?" asked David.

"The answer is yes to both," responded Louie.

"Well, we should get started on your other adjustments. We would like to address the two hundred and forty thousand dollar adjustment that you've characterized as a transfer of corporate funds into Mr. Fine's personal bank account," said David who paused for a moment to pass the baton to his law partner.

"Caroline, why don't you clarify the facts for Agent Lipschitz," suggested David.

"There seems to be some ambiguity with some of the underlying facts in this issue. Southpoint underwent a name change after its incorporation to Latham Industries. Following the name change, there appeared to be discrepancies as to who actually owned stock in Latham," said Caroline.

"We've uncovered documents that indicate Mr. Fine owned fifty percent of the outstanding stock of Southpoint and that later, he and a gentleman by the name of Fred Kelly each owned fifty percent of the stock of Latham. We believe that our client's ownership interest is only fifty percent. Here are copies of the Memorandums of Understanding that were entered into by the respective parties," said Caroline as she handed the documents to Louie.

Louie glanced at the documents and then opened a folder to retrieve his set of documents. "In a series of letters written by Mr. Fine, your client claimed that he owned all of the stock of Latham. These letters are addressed to loan officers at Chase Bank, Bank of America and the Bank of Bermuda. You'll note that these letters are dated after the dates that appear on your copies of the Memorandums of Understanding," said Louie.

As the letters were shown to David and Caroline, the complexion of their skin turned a lighter color.

"I would also like to point out that I have in my possession, various documents that list the companies owned by Mr. Fine. In each organizational chart, Latham Industries is shown as a wholly owned subsidiary of TransOcean, which we know is a controlled subsidiary of Mr. Fine's corporate structure," said Louie.

"And, I might also add that Fred Kelly has provided me with a letter signed under a 'penalty under perjury' declaration that he did not have an ownership interest in Latham," said Louie who presented it to Caroline who quickly read the letter and handed it to David.

After examining Louie's documents, David asked, "Where are you getting your information, Agent Lipschitz?"

"From a confidential informant, whose identity will remain confidential."

"Now that we know Mr. Fine is the owner of Latham, there shouldn't be any mystery as to the merit of the two hundred and forty thousand dollar income adjustment. In a series of wire transfers, a total of two hundred and forty thousand dollars was deposited into Mr. Fine's personal bank account at the Bank of Bermuda. When I first questioned Mr. Fine, he stated that the two hundred and forty thousand dollars represented reimbursement for his having purchased a total of four horses on behalf of Latham," said Louie.

"That's our understanding also," responded Caroline.

"Two days after the horses were purchased from a ranch in New Mexico, Mr. Fine submitted the Bill of Sale to Fred Kelly in care of Latham. The two hundred and forty thousand dollars included the purchase price of the horses, plus shipping fees from New Mexico to Bermuda," stated Louie.

"So, what is the problem that you have?" asked David.

"I interviewed Fred Kelly. According to my notes from this interview, he did not own any horses in Bermuda. I had previously asked Mr. Fine to provide me with the name of the shipping company and copies of the invoices to verify the shipment of the horses from New Mexico to Bermuda. In response to this request, your client told me that the shipping records could not be located," said Louie.

"Oh shit," exclaimed David.

"I don't believe that the horses even exist, and if they do exist, I don't think they were transported to Bermuda. At the end of the day, Mr. Fine has two hundred and forty thousand dollars in his personal bank account. Do you still want to challenge the validity of this adjustment?" asked Louie.

"Can you give us a moment?" asked David, as he turned to Caroline to whisper in her ear.

"Agent Lipschitz, could we impose upon you to allow us to discuss this in private. We shouldn't be more than a few minutes," pleaded Caroline.

"Sure, it's no problem at all. Take your time. I'll wait outside your conference room. Just let me know when you're ready for me."

After Louie left the conference room, Caroline exclaimed, "David, he's killing us."

"Don't I know it! It seems like he keeps pulling rabbits out of a hat. By the time he's finished, the client's going to fire us," acknowledged David.

"Look, our client's a liar and a thief. We can't defend what he's done," said Caroline.

"We have an obligation to our client to provide the best defense possible," countered David.

"What defense? Our client committed perjury and submitted false documents. Not only did he lie, but he had others lie for him. Now we're talking about obstruction. I don't want to be a party to this. I used to work at Justice. I'm not going to sacrifice my career for a slime ball client," exclaimed Caroline who was starting to get upset.

"What are you proposing we do? Throw in the towel?" asked David.

"Yes. Let's concede it now and move on to the other issues. If we agree to this adjustment, it's possible he may go easy on us with the remaining issues," said Caroline.

"You don't honestly believe that do you?" asked David.

"No."

CHAPTER 9

Louie has returned to the conference room, reasonably confident that the lawyers will concede this issue which they quickly did. It is just a matter of time until they concede the entire case. Louie made a mental note to ask them if they need any of the latest electronic gadgets for themselves or for family and friends.

"There are more bank deposits that I found. There's a seven hundred and eighty thousand dollar deposit to a Hong Kong bank account that was maintained by Latham," said Louie.

"Oh God," muttered Caroline.

"Excuse me?" said Louie. "Did you say something?"

"No. Please continue with what you were saying," said Caroline.

"In the early stages of the audit, Mr. Fine refused to cooperate with the IRS by disclosing his ownership of foreign bank accounts. After I discovered his ownership of foreign bank accounts, he refused to provide me with account statements. The account statements were eventually obtained through summons enforcement," remarked Louie.

"According to the bank statements, there were quite a few cash deposits made on a regular basis. Virtually all of the deposits were just under ten thousand dollars. However, because many of the transfers were coming from US banks, the deposits were reported to the Treasury Department as suspicious activity and Currency Transaction Reports were filed. I have a computerized listing of the CTR's and the information reported in this document is set forth in my report," explained Louie.

"Do you know if Mr. Fine had access to the seven hundred and eighty thousand dollars?" asked David.

"I've identified how he spent seven hundred and fifty thousand dollars. One year following the deposits, the same sum of money was withdrawn from his personal bank account in Hong Kong and deposited into his personal bank account in Bermuda. Several weeks later, these funds were transferred to a bank in the Cayman Islands. One day after this transfer, Mr. Fine purchased shares of stock in an IPO at a cost of seven hundred and fifty thousand dollars. This raised a question as why someone who is about to purchase shares of stock would engage in the systematic transfer of funds in different foreign banks and pay bank service charges on each transaction? It didn't make sense to me, but what do I know?" said Louie.

"We're prepared to concede this adjustment as well," said David.

"Darn," said Louie. "You didn't even give me a chance to tell you about the fax transmittals that I have which describe your client's desire to conceal his ownership of certain entities from the IRS. When I get to the civil fraud penalty, I'll have to come back to this."

"Oh Jesus," muttered Caroline.

Glancing up from his audit workpapers, Louie asked, "I'm sorry, Caroline. Did you say something?"

"No. Please continue."

"Let's proceed with the five hundred and twenty five thousand dollars in payments to contractors. Mr. Fine purchased approximately one hundred acres of land in Puerto Rico and had a new residence built on the property site. I have the specifications to construct the new dwelling unit on the property so I know what the original cost proposals were. The construction contract stipulated payments would be made as specific work was started and completed," said Louie.

"Agent Lipschitz, excuse me for interjecting here, but Mr. Fine did not deduct the construction costs on his tax returns and the costs for construction were paid by him. It's our understanding that no funds came from any of the corporations that he controlled," said David.

"So, this should not be an audit issue as far as we can see," added Caroline.

"That's right," chimed in David, as if a two to one vote would bar Louie from addressing this issue.

"I happen to disagree. Payment for all of the construction work was handled through Mr. Fine's financial advisor in the Cayman Islands. Payment was authorized by your client and communicated by fax transmittals to your client's financial advisor, who has been identified as a Barry Leftwich. Mr. Leftwich then issued checks from Uro's bank account at CIBC Bank & Trust Company in the Cayman Islands. I have all of the letters in this file, if you care to see them. I also have copies of Uro's bank statements," declared Louie.

"It's our understanding that there are memo entries on the checks that designated the funds were advanced as shareholder loans. Isn't that correct?" asked Caroline.

"While it is a correct statement that there were memo entries on the checks that designate the funds were advanced as shareholder loans, it is not a true statement," responded the revenue agent.

"Huh?" said David. "How can it not be true?"

"Because in fax transmittals sent by Mr. Fine to Mr. Leftwich, your client made it very explicit that these funds were not to be treated as shareholder loans. Mr. Fine went on to say that the memo entries would designate the money as loans but he had no plan or intention of ever repaying any of the amounts. With no reasonable expectation of repayment, you can't make an argument that the funds constituted bona fide debt," explained Louie.

"I'd like to see those fax transmittals," said David.

Louie then opened another folder and removed the memorandums written by their client. After providing David and Caroline with copies, he waited a few moments for their response.

When David was finished reading the letters, he turned to Caroline and asked her if she needed a moment to consult with him before responding to their now unwelcome guest.

"Agent Lipschitz, could David and I have a few minutes to discuss this, please?"

"Sure. I'll be outside again."

After Louie left the room, Caroline said, "He's killing us. Where the hell is he getting all this information? He knows a lot more about our client than we do. In fact, he seems to know everything."

"Calm down, Caroline. It's just one case. And besides, our client has done this to himself. When this is over, I'll talk to Howard about our client. We'll have to concede this issue also."

"David, why don't we just concede the entire case and save ourselves the misery of being tortured like this?" asked Caroline.

When Louie was asked to come back in the room, David and Caroline announced that they would recommend to their client that he agree to all of the audit adjustments, including the imposition of the civil fraud penalty. What they had also agreed upon but could not disclose to the agent, was that if the client doesn't agree to this, they would resign from further representation.

***

Immediately following his dismissal by the IRS, Ben sent Resumes to every accounting firm in Baltimore. No job offers were extended. As a matter of fact, very few firms even offered Ben the courtesy of an interview. As a last resort, Ben swallowed his pride and sent his Resume to H&R Block.

Told that they had no interest in his services, Ben was despondent. Desperate to line up a job, Ben answered an ad for a tax return preparer at AAA Tax Accounting and was offered a job at minimum wage.

AAA Tax Accounting is located in a small office between a rundown bowling alley and a greasy pizza parlor. The name AAA Tax Accounting was selected by the firm's owner so that it would appear first in the Yellow Pages. Other than that, there was nothing first rate about this business.

AAA Tax Accounting prepared tax returns for walk-ins while they were either going to the bowling alley or eating pizza. The manager of AAA Tax Accounting's office was a twenty two year old high school drop-out who didn't know tax from tacks.

The firm's owner instituted a rule that two employees should always be available to prepare tax returns for walk-in customers. The problem that the owner had was that he was down to only two employees who could prepare tax returns.

The senior return preparer was a seventy seven year old immigrant from Thailand who had a total of six weeks on the job. The other return preparer had immigrated from Mexico last month. Because Pedro did not speak English, he had to attend a Berlitz class at night.

Ben was told to report for work a few minutes before 10 am so that he could receive new employee training. Actually, the orientation consisted of being given directions to the bathroom at the bowling alley and given a document to read. The document contained the following words: THE CUSTOMER IS ALWAYS RIGHT.

At 10:35 am, a customer arrived to have her tax return prepared. When Ben opened the shoebox containing her records, he attempted to ask her a few questions. Asking questions did not go over well with the office manager.

Gwen Smith is responsible for supervising the tax return preparers. Gwen has a serious Gothic look that suggested she may either practice witchcraft during her smoking breaks or she enjoys sleeping in a coffin. With a pale complexion and heavy mascara, Gwen has the perfect look if Halloween took place every day of the year.

"What are you doing?" Gwen practically snarled at Ben.

"I'm attempting to verify that Mrs. Porter, who earns twelve thousand and five hundred dollars per year as a teacher's assistant is eligible to claim sixteen children as dependents," Ben answered.

"We don't verify. If the client tells us she provided support for sixteen children, she provided support for sixteen children," Gwen replied.

"But that's impossible. How could someone earning less than thirteen thousand dollars a year provide for the financial support of sixteen children? And who are these children? And where do they live? According to Mrs. Porter, she lives in a one bedroom apartment with only one bathroom. Don't you see the problem?" asked Ben.

"No. That's because there is no problem. We are in business to provide a service to our customers. This is no different than ordering a burger at a fast food burger joint. We do it the way the customer wants it prepared. It's called customer service. Now, prepare the tax return the way she wants it prepared. If you can't do it, I'll give it to Pedro. He knows better than to ask stupid questions," said Gwen.

"How can he ask questions? He doesn't even speak English," Ben responded.

"That's why Pedro is my top producer. He cranks out more tax returns than anyone else," said Gwen.

With that said, Ben walked out without bothering to submit his resignation. Ben Newman was now in search of another job.

CHAPTER 10

Timothy Bell received formal notification that the Maryland Bar Association will be conducting a hearing to determine whether he will be charged with a criminal offense. The complaint filed by the FBI has been assigned to a hearing panel and the case is scheduled to be heard in two weeks. Timmy will be unable to attend.

Stanley has told Timmy that Wallace is not a suitable candidate to handle his criminal defense because Wallace seems to have a problem with litigation. Therefore, Timmy must rely on the Public Defender for legal representation.

In the meantime, Stanley has offered to represent Timmy in the Bar Association's administrative hearing and has agreed to do so for free. While Timmy is fully cognizant of Stanley's many limitations, he has accepted Stanley's offer. To assist in his defense, Timmy intends to research the hearing process and formulate a strategy that Stanley can use. In essence, Timmy will do all the work.

***

Louie is in the office of Ted Gibbons, whose client is none other than the famous fortune teller, Madame Googalak who would prefer to be known as a spiritual psychic advisor. The distinction is approximately forty dollars because a spiritual psychic advisor can charge forty dollars more per consultation than a fortune teller.

Madame Googalak, whose real name is Maxine Kaminski, is neither a fortune teller nor a spiritual psychic advisor. In actuality, Maxine is a fraud who preys on idiots willing to pay her to tell them what they want to hear. Maxine is a capitalist who knows how to capitalize.

After Maxine Kaminski graduated from high school, she went to work as a telemarketer. Maxine was paid twenty five cents for every phone call that resulted in a subscription to National Geographic. After making more one thousand telephone calls in her first week on the job, Maxine earned a total of twenty five cents in commissions which didn't set the world on fire.

Maxine's next job involved walking dogs. While this paid more than twenty five cents for the week, it was not what Maxine wanted to do for the rest of her life. After two weeks spent walking dogs, Maxine decided to switch careers.

Maxine's next job took her to McDonald's. There, Maxine worked as one of the assistants to the head chef, an eighteen year old kid who could barely speak English and whose job involved flipping burgers. The fries were prepared by the associate head chef and the milkshakes were the responsibility of the assistant to the head chef.

Maxine's skills as a psychic were starting to take shape during her employment at McDonald's. It didn't take long to see that her mobility at McDonald's was blocked by the many employees with seniority. Maxine did not need a fortune teller to predict her future.

Sensing that she had special skills, Maxine determined that her true calling was in the field of psychic readings. Maxine started her business by placing an advertisement in the Yellow Pages as a psychic, using a local telephone number.

The following year, Maxine became a psychic advisor with a toll free 800 telephone number. The next year, Maxine was a spiritual psychic advisor to hundreds of thousands of people throughout the country. Of course, as business picked up, Maxine needed to employ more and more psychic readers or simply enough people to answer the phone.

Maxine needed to train her employees in the art of psychic readings. Actually, Maxine couldn't really train anyone because she didn't know anything about psychic readings other than it paid really well. To navigate around this problem, Maxine provided each phone operator with a script, which was the equivalent of a Bible. It was imperative that every phone operator follow the script. Failure to follow the script resulted in termination.

Maxine operated her business out of a low-rent office building in Baltimore County. Although her office was a dump, Maxine generated substantial revenue from this scam.

Ted Gibbons and Maxine Kaminski sat across the conference table from Louie. When Louie glanced up from his audit workpapers, he said to Maxine, "I see you have a large number of deductions on your corporate tax returns. Let's talk about some of these items. Would you like to guess where I'm going to start?"

Maxine shook her head sideways, which Louie interpreted as no.

"Office supplies," announced Louie.

Ted quickly interjected by saying, "My client operates an office building that includes administrative staff. She incurs a variety of expenses needed to operate an ongoing business activity that is quite successful."

"Thank you for clarifying that with me, Ted. However, I have a number of questionable items that comprise office supplies," declared Louie.

"Such as?" asked Ted.

"Frosted Flakes cereal," said Louie.

"What?" asked a clearly puzzled representative.

"I'd like an explanation as to how one hundred and twenty six dollars of Frosted Flakes cereal constitutes an ordinary and necessary expense incurred in connection with carrying on a trade or business?" said Louie.

"I don't know anything about Frosted Flakes," admitted Ted.

Turning to Maxine, Louie asked, "Ms. or Madame, whatever, I need to know how the cost of one hundred and twenty six dollars of Frosted Flakes cereal qualifies as a business expense."

"My children eat Frosted Flakes. I think my accountant took this expense and somehow charged it to the business by mistake," said Maxine.

"And hot dogs, potato chips, Oreo cookies, crayons, diapers, bicycles, kids' clothes, dolls, DVDs, a baseball bat and glove. It's a fairly long list and it would take hours to go over each specific item. These items were also charged to the business," stated Louie.

At this point, Ted covered his eyes with his hands and began to moan as if he was having a migraine headache.

"Can you see where I'm going with this" asked Louie.

Maxine shook her head no.

"Ted, here's my report. Get back to me by the end of this week," Louie announced as he got up and walked out.

When Ted glanced down at the proposed deficiency amount, he swallowed twice and told his client what she owed.

"A half a million dollars?" screamed Maxine.

A half of a million dollars plus interest and penalties," Ted corrected her.

"I never saw that coming," responded the phony spiritual psychic advisor.

***

Today is the day that Stanley had hoped would not come to fruition. Two special agents are in his office to interview him in the matter of his criminal investigation.

Richard Lewis and Mike Hankin introduced themselves, presented their IRS credentials and badges and informed Stanley that his cooperation will be viewed in a favorable light, at which point the disgraced lawyer started to sweat.

Lewis placed a cassette player on the table to record the interview. As Stanley was advised in advance that this session would be recorded, he had the right to also record the interview. Stanley had apparently forgotten about this and didn't bother to do so.

Lewis began by asking Stanley to provide background information on tax courses he took in law school, his affiliation with various tax groups or other professional associations, his professional work experience in the field of taxation, and so forth.

When Stanley inquired as to the relevance of this information, he was told by Hankin that they ask the questions for a reason and that this will be clear to Stanley before the interview is over.

It was soon evident that Stanley had an unremarkable biography. Stanley was then asked if he has always prepared his own tax returns, to which he answered in the affirmative.

Eventually, Hankin asked Stanley about his bookkeeping system and had the lawyer explain how he recorded the retainer fees.

Stanley immediately answered by saying, "All retainer fees are recorded on the General Ledger. I have copies of the checks placed in each client's file so that we know the retainer has been paid."

"Who is we?" asked Lewis.

"That would be me and the secretary who was working here," replied Stanley. "At this time, I do not have a secretary."

"Show us your General Ledgers for each of the tax years. We'd like to see how you classified the retainer fees on your books," said Hankin.

"Sure. Just give me a few minutes to get it for you," said Stanley as he got up to retrieve his books and records.

Stanley had no idea that before special agents conduct interviews, they obtain extensive background information from a variety of sources. Special agents have the benefit of reviewing the audit files and have access to information and files otherwise not available to revenue agents. With unlimited resources at their disposal, special agents can dig deep into cases. Special agents also have the authority to pretty much scare the shit out of people. This is a wonderful thing for investigators to have when building a case for possible criminal prosecution.

When Stanley left the room, the agents turned off the tape recorder and chuckled. "What an imbecile," said Lewis."

"Hey, Rich, did you see the sweat on his shirt?" asked his partner.

"Did I? How could I miss it? That knucklehead was soaked in sweat like he just finished running a marathon," replied Lewis.

Stanley returned with his General Ledgers, which he placed in front of the agents who then turned on the tape recorder. Upon seeing the amount of retainer fees recorded on the first General Ledger, Lewis turned to Hankin and pointed at the numbers. The agents then looked at the other two General Ledgers and verified the amounts recorded as retainer fees.

The agents then placed Stanley's tax returns on the table and pointed to the amount of gross income as shown on the returns.

The amounts as shown on the tax returns are less than the retainer fees as recorded on the General Ledgers.

The agents let that sink in for a moment. It has now registered with Stanley as he is drenched in sweat.

"Mr. Scherr, are you aware of the fact that retainer fees are includible in your taxable income?" asked Lewis.

"I think part of the confusion is that my secretary may have considered the retainer fees to be something that goes into an escrow account," replied Stanley who was clearly attempting to shift the blame on Estelle Schwartz.

"Your answer was not responsive to my question," said Lewis. "I specifically asked you if you knew that retainer fees must be reported in your taxable income."

"Umm, yes."

"And you created this escrow account, is that correct?" asked Lewis.

"That's correct."

"And you have already admitted to us that you personally prepared your own tax returns. Do you recall this admission?" asked Hankin.

"Yes."

"Only a moment ago, you attempted to blame your former secretary for your failure to report the retainer fees in your taxable income. My partner and I interviewed Ms. Schwartz and we have an Affidavit that she signed under penalties of perjury, in which she attested to having absolutely nothing whatsoever to do with the entries recorded on your General Ledgers. According to Ms. Schwartz's Affidavit, her duties and responsibilities were to answer the phone, type a few letters, do some filing, and make coffee," said Lewis.

As Stanley pulled a handkerchief out of his pocket to mop up the sweat on his face, he responded by saying, "I hereby invoke my Fifth Amendment right against self-incrimination. I'll be seeking the services of a lawyer from this point on," said Stanley.

CHAPTER 11

Richard Lewis and Mike Hankin have returned to their office to prepare a memorandum to memorialize their meeting with Stanley. This memorandum will be an integral part of the special agent's report.

The special agent's report, or more commonly referred to as SAR, contains a detailed account of the investigation. The SAR includes the special agent's recommendation and is reviewed by the special agent's immediate supervisor. After the supervisory special agent has reviewed the SAR, it is reviewed by the Quality Review Team before it is given to the assistant special agent in charge. After the assistant special agent in charge has reviewed the SAR, it is presented to the special agent in charge for final approval within CID.

Before the case can be referred to the Justice Department, it must be reviewed and approved by the Associate Area Chief Counsel for Criminal Tax. Counsel's criminal tax attorney will prepare a Criminal Enforcement Memorandum that discusses the nature of the crime for which the special agent has recommended prosecution, the evidence relied upon to prove the crime, technical or legal issues, anticipated problems in prosecution and the special agent's recommendation. Once Counsel's criminal tax attorney has concurred with the recommendation that the case should be prosecuted, it is referred to the Department of Justice.

The work product in all criminal cases sent to the Justice Department must be first-rate because it serves as the foundation for a criminal prosecution if accepted by the Justice Department.

After preparing the memorandum, the agents worked together on the SAR. When the SAR was completed, the special agents assembled their files, including copies of the General Ledgers. By the next day, the case was on its way through the lengthy review process within CID.

After all required signatures appear on the closing documents, Stanley's case will be sent to the Department of Justice. If the Justice Department accepts the case for prosecution, Stanley will be charged with having committed a criminal offense.

In light of the lengthy review process, it could take several months before the DOJ makes a decision as to whether it will accept the case for criminal prosecution. In the meantime, Stanley must wait to learn his fate.

***

BRUCE BRONSTEIN

Timmy has spent the past few days doing legal research in the matter of his pending hearing for impersonating a lawyer. Timmy decided to compose a letter in the form of a formal declaration and stipulate to certain admissions so as to show remorse on his part in order to persuade the members of the hearing panel that he should not be prosecuted for impersonating a lawyer.

Timmy carefully crafted the letter on one of the computers in the correctional facility's library. He started by declaring that it was his intention to help those who were seeking tax advice and that he only provided guidance in matters in which he knew the answer. Furthermore, he stressed that he did not receive any compensation for the guidance that he provided.

Timmy then declared that he now understands that to offer guidance when he was not licensed to do so was wrong and promised that it is a mistake that he will never repeat again. This admission is important to the hearing panel.

Timmy further stated that his offense was neither malicious nor harmful because the clients to whom he provided guidance were satisfied with his analysis and recommendations. Indeed, the advice that they relied upon was determined to have been the correct advice. Thus, there were no adverse consequences to them.

Timmy also noted that he was asked to offer guidance to only a few of Stanley's clients. Thus, there was no overt pattern of reckless behavior because only three or four clients were given advice by Timmy.

Finally, Timmy agreed to sign a Cease and Desist Affidavit promising that he will never impersonate an attorney again. Timmy concluded his appeal by imploring the hearing panel not refer his case to the Maryland Attorney General's Office for criminal prosecution.

While hopeful that the complaint filed against him will be dismissed, Timmy is not overly confident that he will talk his way out of a criminal trial.

After the members of the panel read Timmy's letter, they were pleased with its content. Satisfied that Timmy is remorseful and will refrain from practicing law should he be unlicensed, they voted to dismiss the complaint that was filed by the FBI.

***

Stanley doesn't have much to do since his law practice imploded. Most days, Stanley comes into the office and sleeps at his desk until it is time to either go to lunch or go home, where he has nothing to do.

This morning, Stanley dozed off at his desk and dreamt that he is standing on the edge of a plank awaiting word that he has been indicted for criminal tax fraud. When the indictment was announced, Stanley saw himself being pushed off the plank, sinking to the bottom of the ocean and devoured by hungry sharks. As Stanley is being eaten by the sharks, the people aboard the boat applaud their approval. This dream will be repeated later again today.

Stanley was startled when the phone on his desk rang. Anxious to hear a client's voice, Stanley grabbed the phone. It is the voice of a prospective client and at this stage of Stanley's career, he is in dire need of a client who can pay for legal work.

"Mr. Scherr, a friend of mine suggested that I give you a call. A federal tax lien has been placed on my house and my car. I have a bank account that has been seized and my refund checks for both my federal and state taxes have been applied to the taxes that I owe. I really could use your help," said the individual on the other end of the phone.

"To whom am I speaking?" asked Stanley.

"I'm sorry. My name's Lazlo Krull. Maybe you've heard of me?"

"I don't think so," replied Stanley.

"Can I stop by your office sometime soon and see you? I guess you're pretty busy and all, but I need to talk to a tax lawyer real soon and I was told that you know all about solving IRS collection problems, you know what I mean?" said Lazlo Krull.

Although Stanley was barred from appearing before the IRS as a representative, there was no prohibition against him doing advisory work for clients. And in Stanley's mind, this case could fall within the scope of advisory work.

"I can see you at 2 pm today, Mr. Krull. I just had a cancellation so you were fortunate to call when you did," said the shyster who was back to his old tricks.

***

Ben Newman has had a "come to Jesus meeting" with his wife, Nancy. After pretending to go to work for several weeks, Ben told Nancy that he is now among the unemployed and looking for work. Nancy has accepted this admission like a good soldier who doesn't ask a lot of questions.

Nancy is a soft spoken librarian who is supportive of her husband. Rather than criticize his faults, Nancy prefers to look at his positive traits. Ben has never been arrested for drunk driving, he has never committed a violent crime and he is a big fan of the Law & Order and CSI shows. These are important attributes to Nancy.

Ben is very attentive to his two young sons, Zach who is five years old and Brady, who has just turned three. Ben has always made an effort to help out with the kids as soon as he comes home from work because he views spending as much time with his family as moments to be cherished. On weekends, Ben devotes all of his time to Nancy and the kids. While Ben would never be a candidate for employee of the month, he might be a serious contender for Father of the Year.

Ben and Nancy have a mortgage, student loans that remain unpaid, and a variety of other debts. In view of the fact that Nancy earns less than forty thousand dollars a year as a librarian, they are unable to pay their household expenses with Ben not working. Given this problem, Ben told Nancy of his plan to earn a living.

Ben announced that he will start his own tax practice and that he will open a virtual office at minimal expense and recruit clients through mass marketing. Ben intends to create a website in which he will promote himself as, "The Tax Man," and this will all be accomplished by dipping into their personal savings account.

Upon hearing this, Nancy gulped. "Our personal savings account? Is that really a good idea?" she asked her unemployed husband.

"Honey, I looked everywhere to find a job. No CPA firm in the area would even talk to me. I couldn't even get hired by H&R Block. Can you believe that? The one firm that did employ me for all of ten minutes had a vampire running the office and my two co-workers were refugees who didn't even speak English. If I had to go to the restroom, I needed to go next door to the bowling alley which looked like a hangout for members of Hells Angels. And the pizza parlor next door was a dump. If the Health Department ever inspected the premises, it would be condemned. The rats inside were the size of buffaloes," complained Ben.

"Oh sweetie, I'm so sorry. What about the State of Maryland? Did you try there?" inquired Nancy.

"According to its website, there are no openings. Apparently, there doesn't appear to be anything for me with the state government," replied Ben.

What Ben didn't know was that the call that Tom Collins had arranged, would not be forthcoming for several months because of a temporary hiring freeze.

***

At precisely 2 pm, Lazlo Krull made his grand entrance. Stanley, who is without a receptionist ever since Erin quit, made it a point to stand by the front desk as if he were placing client files on the desk for some invisible person to file.

Lazlo Krull is dressed as if he just came from Pimlico Racetrack, which he probably did. Wearing a plaid sport coat, striped shirt and polka dot tie, Lazlo is covered in colors, none of which match. His slacks are a fire engine red color and the hat he is wearing is a bright pink. This man will never be on the cover of GQ.

Lazlo's wardrobe looks even more ridiculous given his physique. Lazlo is tall and gangly, with incredibly long arms and legs. If Lazlo had more than two arms and two legs, he would resemble an octopus.

Lazlo followed Stanley to the small first floor conference room facing the back of the building. This meeting room is the size of a closet and was probably used as a closet by the family who originally lived in this building. Once Lazlo has taken a seat at the table, he reconfigured his legs to somehow fit under the table. In truth, Lazlo's lower body is crunched up like a pretzel. It is one of these miracles that can be performed only once in a lifetime. No matter how many times someone attempts to re-create something that appears to be impossible to do, it cannot be accomplished a second time. This is a Kodak moment that Stanley should preserve for history.

Before Stanley could say a word, Lazlo started in by pontificating, "The IRS came after me real hard like I was the most notorious public enemy in the history of civilization. You know what I'm saying?"

"Yes. I believe I do," replied Stanley who knows only all too well.

"Here's what happened. I sell used cars during the evening shift. During the day, I like to gamble, you know what I mean? So, I went up to Atlantic City one day to gamble and I hit it big playing blackjack. I won over sixty thousand dollars that day. The casino gave me a 1099 for my winnings, but I also lost some money gambling, which the IRS never gave me credit for, you know what I'm saying?" exclaimed Lazlo.

"A couple of months later, I'm playing the horses at Pimlico and I hit it big again. Another forty G's. This also gets reported to Uncle Sam. Now I got a hundred big ones to put on my tax return, except I don't have the money to pay what I owe. Shit, there's nothing there because I probably wound up losing most of it, you know what I'm saying?" said Lazlo.

If Stanley hears Lazlo ask if he knows what he's saying one more time, he intends to take the phone on the conference room table and use it to perform a colonoscopy on Lazlo.

"You said something on the phone about tax liens?" asked a perturbed Stanley.

"Right. So, the IRS went ahead and increased my income by a hundred gazillion dollars, and I get this tax bill for like twenty five large ones. That's bullshit. So, I told the IRS that's bullshit and I keep telling them its bullshit. They don't know from bullshit so I got this stupid deficiency notice and I wind up telling them its bullshit," said Lazlo.

"Anyhow, I didn't challenge this in Tax Court because, what am I going to tell the judge? It's bullshit. Except, those IRS lawyers are sneaky and don't play fair. So, I know I'll lose. Then I got this bill for like thirty six thousand dollars, which I can't pay. Next thing I know, I got these letters telling me that if I don't pay, the IRS will start filing tax liens and seize my assets, you know what I'm saying?" said Lazlo.

"Now I got tax liens coming out of my ass. I got no money to gamble, and let me tell you something, selling used cars is one tough mother, you know what I'm saying?" said Lazlo.

It has suddenly dawned on Stanley that his new client is a deadbeat with no visible means of being able to pay him. Even if Stanley could limit the fees to five hundred dollars, the likelihood is he would not be paid. And Stanley's mantra is, "make sure you get paid before any shit gets done."

CHAPTER 12

"Rog, are you trying to set me up?" Louie exclaimed when he saw the case that his boss assigned to him.

"Louie, what the hell are you talking about?"

"You assigned this tax return to me," Louie said as he held the tax return over his hand as if he were providing parking instructions to an airline pilot.

"And whose return is that?" asked Roger.

"Martha O'Connell, whose professional name is Trixsee," replied Louie.

"Oh, that."

"Is there something I should know?" asked Louie.

"That assignment is a gift. You'll enjoy doing the examination. You can even do it in her place of business. But make sure you clear it with your wife first. In the meantime, come with me," said Roger.

"Where are we going?" inquired Louie.

"Tom's office."

When Louie and Roger reached Tom's office, they had to wait outside because the Chief of the Examination Division was in the middle of a conversation that he was having with himself. When the Chief wanted to discuss something with others, he usually did all of the talking. This rule is applicable with respect to subordinates. When the Chief wanted to discuss something with someone who outranked him, the Chief generally allowed that person the privilege of talking.

When the Chief was finished talking, he left Tom's office without bothering to look at Roger and Louie who sat down and waited for Tom to say something.

"I take it you've looked at your new case assignments?"

"You are very perceptive, My Master," replied Louie.

"Try not to leave your fingerprints on Trixsee when you've completed the examination," said Tom.

"Okay, what's going on?" asked Louie.

After a few moments of silence, Tom said, "I wanted you to have Trixsee, not in the biblical sense of course, but to make up for what I'm about to do to you," answered Tom.

"And what is it that you're going to do to me, Glorious Leader?"

"You are about to be assigned the tax returns of a former President of the United States of America. I'm still going over the returns before it's assigned to you. Louie, this is going to be a very messy case. He's still a prominent figure in world affairs. The issues that I'm sure you're going to raise are sensitive. It could result in substantial tax due, maybe even serious penalties. His representatives, whoever they are, will be top notch. They are going to be head and shoulders above anyone you've dealt with before. This case could also become very political if he doesn't like what you are doing. In other words, he and his lawyers won't hesitate to go over your head if this gets ugly, which I expect it will. Just so you understand," said Tom.

"I'll work it like any other case. If the former president doesn't like it, that's his problem," said Louie.

"That's my boy. You have our support on this case. Keep Roger up to speed as to what you're doing and make sure both of you keep me in the loop. If the lawyers give you a hard time, make sure you let me know. I want everything documented in your Case Activity Record. Furthermore, you are not to discuss the case with anyone other than Roger, myself and Counsel, if you require legal assistance," said Tom.

"Just one more thing, Louie," as he and Roger turned to leave. "This case could be toxic," added Tom.

"Toxic for who?" replied Louie as he and his boss left Tom's office.

When Louie returned to his desk, he was asked by one of his fellow agents if he knew the difference between an exotic dancer and a stripper.

"Why?

"Because Trixsee is an exotic dancer and you may offend her if you call her a stripper," replied the agent.

"Good point," said Louie as he turned around to leave for lunch.

When Roger returned to his office, he buzzed Tom and asked, "How bad are the tax returns?"

"Worse than bad."

"And how do you think this is going to play out?" asked Roger.

"My money is still on Louie."

***

Timmy's parents drove to Washington, D.C. to meet with the prosecutors in their son's upcoming trial. The Bells have asked for this meeting so that they can sit down with the prosecutors and tell them about their son and hopefully convince them that he is not the criminal mastermind that they believe him to be.

After waiting in a reception area for what seemed like an eternity but was only five minutes, the Bells were greeted by Debbie Macht and Gary Zimmer, who were courteous and polite to them. The Bells were escorted to a conference room and offered refreshments, which they politely declined.

The Bells began by thanking the DOJ lawyers for taking the time to meet with them. Ella Bell asked if she could speak first, which the lawyers agreed to with a nod that let her know that she has the floor.

"Our son Timothy, well we call him Timmy, has always been a wonderful child. He is our only child and we love him dearly. As a youngster, Timmy was such a good student that he was asked to be a substitute teacher whenever the classroom teacher was unable to teach. This started when Timmy was around nine years old," said Mrs. Bell.

"Timmy skipped several grades in school because he was so advanced intellectually. However, he was always willing to tutor others for free and helped many of his classmates with their schoolwork. Timmy never cheated in school and never took shortcuts.

"Timmy graduated from high school and college at a very young age and started a small business in which he employed people who needed jobs. It didn't take long for his business to become very successful.

"When Timmy became wealthy, he gave us a check for two hundred and fifty thousand dollars and told us that we could do anything we wanted with the money. Aaron and I chose to donate all of the money to various charitable organizations that were in dire need of money. After we donated all of the money, Timmy then matched our donations by giving another two hundred and fifty thousand dollars to the same charities.

"Our son succeeded with his business operations through hard work and by playing by the rules," said Mrs. Bell.

"Excuse me, Mrs. Bell. The Justice Department is not prosecuting your son because it believes that he was employing dishonest means to earn money. No such allegation has been made. He is being prosecuted for crimes that relate to the concealment of assets to defraud the government and tax evasion. All of the criminal charges relate specifically to tax crimes," explained Debbie.

"My husband and I understand. I was just trying to provide you with an insight into Timmy's childhood and as a young adult. When Timmy became a billionaire, he became fixated on preserving his wealth. We don't know what caused this change in him. Aaron and I were never consumed with having money.

Aaron is a college professor so we don't live lavishly," said Mrs. Bell, who started to sob.

"Dear, let me finish," offered Aaron, as he gently put his arm around his wife's shoulder. "Our son genuinely cares about others. He tried to offer guidance to those in need of tax advice when they came to see the lawyer that Timmy had asked for help. Timmy never asked for money and, in fact, never received money for the guidance that he gave.

"Our son has the potential to do so many wonderful things for the world. Putting him in prison will deny him that opportunity. We feel he is deserving of a second chance. Can you see it in your hearts to give him that second chance?" asked Mr. Bell.

"Mr. and Mrs. Bell, we appreciate your sincerity and we certainly are sympathetic with your situation. I would feel the same way if it were my child. However, we're talking about tax crimes where your son made a voluntary decision to not pay taxes where he was legally obligated to do so. His behavior in this regard was reckless," explained Gary.

"The criminal statutes mandate prosecution for such reckless behavior. And that is the responsibility of the Justice Department. Whether he is found guilty or not is a matter for a judge or a jury," said Gary.

"Is a trial necessary?" asked Mrs. Bell.

"We are preparing your son's case for trial unless he intends to change his plea from not guilty to guilty," replied Debbie.

"Would you be willing to let him plead guilty without going to prison?" asked Mr. Bell.

"If your son changes his plea to guilty, he would have to agree to a prison sentence," said Debbie.

"What about a reduced prison sentence?" asked Mr. Bell.

"Unfortunately, we cannot discuss the terms of sentencing with you. We can only enter into negotiations with your son and his attorney. I'm sorry. If your son is interested in discussing a plea bargain, he should have his attorney contact us," said Debbie.

After spending a few more minutes with the Bells and wishing them a safe drive home, Debbie and Gary walked back to their respective offices.

"Deb, I suspect their son is going to want to talk to us about a plea bargain," said Gary.

"Yep."

CHAPTER 13

Louie has not wasted any time. He notified Martha O'Connell that he is examining her tax returns for the past two years and will need to meet with her. As a revenue agent, Louie is expected to conduct audits outside his office. Therefore, the interview will be held at The Pussycat Club where Martha O'Connell, aka Trixsee, is considered the star attraction.

Two weeks after sending out the appointment letter, Louie is on his way to The Pussycat Club. A cover charge of ten dollars is collected from all patrons before entering the premises. This is supposed to keep undesirables from entering the club, but if an undesirable individual has ten dollars, then its objective hasn't been met. It will enrich the club's owner, though.

Louie wondered how the ten dollar cover charge is being treated for federal income tax reporting purposes. He is tempted to pose this question to the behemoth stationed alongside the front door.

Louie walked over to the employee in charge of collecting the ten dollar cover charge. Standing close to seven feet tall and weighing well over three hundred pounds, the behemoth who was the size of Godzilla, put his hand out. Without saying a word, he is essentially telling Louie that he must fork over the ten dollars before he will be allowed inside.

In response, Louie produced his IRS credentials and announced that he was here on official government business. Godzilla inquired as to whether Louie was here to see him and when told no, allowed the munchkin to enter without making the obligatory ten dollar payment.

When Louie walked into The Pussycat Club, he was immediately overwhelmed by the loud music and naked women, only not necessarily in that order. Louie asked the bartender where he can find Martha O'Connell.

"Who?" asked the bartender.

"How about Trixsee?"

"You want to see Trixsee?" asked the bartender.

"No, I really want to talk to Martha O'Connell, but I'll settle for Trixsee," replied Louie.

"And you are?"

Once Louie showed the bartender his IRS credentials, he was told Trixsee is with some of the other dancers in one of the dressing rooms and that the munchkin is free to go back there to see her.

While making his way to one of the dressing rooms, Louie was wondering why a nude dancer would need to change her clothes if she is performing in the nude. Louie is very thoughtful and seemed to think that this is an apparent contradiction.

Louie entered the first dressing area, and soon thereafter, accidentally bumped into a naked woman. As a matter of fact, there are a number of voluptuous naked women in various stages of applying their make-up. None of them really seemed to care that a munchkin holding a briefcase is standing there.

"Sweetie, are you here to perform?" asked one of the nude dancers.

"No. I'm here to see Trixsee," answered Louie.

"Hey, you're kind of cute. How about performing with me? I could use a munchkin in my act," exclaimed another stripper.

"Do you know where I can find Trixsee?" said Louie, who was anxious to get the audit started.

"Trixsee's in the next room," said another dancer who was nodding with her head in the direction of the other dressing area.

Louie got another dose of naked bodies when he entered the next dressing area. By this time, Louie had completely forgotten his wife's first name. In a few more minutes, Louie will probably have forgotten the reason for his visit.

"I'm here to see Trixsee," announced Louie, who was pretending not to check out the naked women in his presence. However, these ladies were not that stupid.

"I'm Trixsee," said the attractive redhead who walked over to Louie and extended her hand. "I'm really Martha O'Connell and I take it you're Agent Lipschitz?"

After shaking hands, Louie showed her his IRS credentials and asked if there was a place they could talk in private. Trixsee thought it might be a good idea to put some clothes on so she got dressed in her bra and panties for the audit.

Trixsee escorted Louie to another room where they found some chairs and a table. Apparently, the dancers used this area to munch on food during their breaks.

"Ms. O'Connell, I've performed a preliminary examination of your tax returns for the past two years. There are several issues that I need to address with you. Can we do it, here?" asked Louie.

"Sure. Did I screw up my tax returns, Agent Lipschitz? I used one of those software programs that you see advertised on TV for free. I guess it wasn't so great after all," said Trixsee.

"No. There are just a few things that I have questions about. I noticed that your travel and entertainment expenses are substantial. I need to see your records and explanations with respect to these expenditures. You also claimed substantial deductions for medical expenses. I'll need to see documentation and explanations for this," said Louie.

"Well, my travel expenses came to a lot because I had to drive to clubs in DC, Virginia and Pennsylvania when I wasn't working here. Management treats the girls here like independent contractors so there are times when we have to line up work at other clubs. Nobody reimburses us for our travel expenses and it does cost a lot to drive out of state. I can get you statements from the owners of the clubs outside of Maryland where I performed that will verify all this," offered Trixsee.

"That would be a good idea. And your medical expenses?" asked Louie.

"Hmm. Maybe I put that down on the wrong line. I want to show you my breasts," said Trixsee as she began to take off her bra.

"That's not really necessary, Ms. O"Connell," said Louie.

"But it is, Agent Lipschitz. You see, that's where the money went," said Trixsee.

"A boob job?"

"I like to refer to it as breast augmentation," replied Trixsee.

"I can see they're very nice."

"Aren't my boobs spectacular? I went from a 34B to a 36DD and its made all the difference in the world in my ..... occupation as an exotic dancer. Well, I really like to think of myself as an entertainer like a performance artist and not just a stripper," explained Trixsee.

"Of course. For income tax reporting purposes, you must show that the surgical procedure was an ordinary and necessary expense incurred in connection with your employment or trade or business activity, with the underlying premise that it was motivated for profit," said Louie.

"Can you help me out with what you just said?" pleaded Trixsee in a playful tone of voice.

"The breast enhancement has to be related to your profession or instrumental in the production of income. Does that help?" asked Louie.

"Thank you. Before I got my new boobs, I was just another nude dancer. Now, I'm making more than twice what I was earning before," said Trixsee.

"Are you referring to tips as your earnings?" asked Louie. "Yes."

"And, I assume that you report all your tips?" inquired Louie.

"Of course. I keep very accurate records each night. I'll put all of my tips in a box and when I get home, I'll count the money and record the total in my journal. At the end of each month, I'll add the earnings for that month and record that amount. I'll then compare my earnings to see which months are better. If the winter months are slow at The Pussycat Club because of the weather, I'm thinking about going down to Florida for the winter and performing at a club where I can make more money," remarked Trixsee.

"Do you derive personal enjoyment from your new, umm boobs?" inquired Louie.

"Sure. Why do you ask?" asked Trixsee.

"With medical procedures such as cosmetic surgery, you'll find insurance companies will not pay any part of the cost because the procedure is considered elective. A boob job is not an expense that insurance would cover. As such, it is not deemed to be ordinary and necessary to a business activity," said Louie.

"But, Agent Lipschitz. I'm making so much more money now because of my new boobs. Can't you look at it as being a money maker? If it allows me to be more profitable, then it should be deductible. Doesn't that make sense?" asked Trixsee.

"There is still the personal enjoyment factor," said Louie.

"Are you saying that because I derive some personal enjoyment from having a boob job, that it is not tax deductible?" asked Trixsee. "That just doesn't seem fair."

Martha O'Connell is sitting topless across from Louie. As she intentionally adjusted her voluptuous body in the chair, Louie could see her breasts gently sway side to side. Trixsee's strategy was brilliant and her timing was impeccable. Apparently, revenue agents have not been trained how to defend themselves against gorgeous women who are naked during an audit.

Louie looked up for a second so Martha wouldn't think he was mesmerized by her magnificent breasts. Louie could see Martha's lips quiver as if she were about to cry. At this point, Louie's mind was starting to turn to mush as the little guy had lost his focus. Is this the same Louie Lipschitz who is the most feared tax examiner on the planet?

"Ms. O'Connell, you have done what no other person has been able to do to me in my entire career at the IRS. I'm going to issue a 'No Change Letter' to you," said Louie.

"What does that mean?"

"It means that your tax returns have been accepted as filed. I will not make any audit adjustments. But make sure you still send me the Affidavits with regard to your out-of-state travel. I'll have to include that in your file before I can issue the No Change Letter."

As Martha O'Connell stood, she extended her hand and then stepped closer to Louie and gave him a warm hug that caught him off guard. Louie's head was caught between her magnificent breasts for a moment in time that Louie was hoping would last longer than a moment.

When Louie had recovered enough so that he could walk, he made a hasty retreat out of The Pussycat Club. On the walk back to the Federal Building, Louie knew he would be asked how the interview went and he dreaded having to explain his audit result to Roger, whom he knew would tell Tom. If they had been in his shoes, Martha O'Connell would probably be getting sizable refunds for each of the past few years.

CHAPTER 14

Timmy has been told by his parents about their meeting with the prosecutors and has asked that his Public Defender stop by the correctional facility to meet with him. Timmy is now prepared to propose a plea bargain in which he pleads guilty to all offenses for a reduced prison sentence.

Derick Mason is pleased with Timmy's decision. He is of the opinion that this is the most viable option available to Timmy. It is now a question as to how many months the prosecutors are willing to reduce on sentencing.

Timmy has been informed that, if convicted, he should expect a minimum sixty month prison sentence. With a plea agreement, his sentence may be reduced to thirty six months in a federal prison, with time off for good behavior and a credit allowed for time served.

While this is hardly good news, Timmy is emotionally prepared to accept this offer, if made available to him by the prosecutors.

***

"A No Change Letter? Am I hearing this right?" asked Roger.

"There is nothing wrong with your hearing, boss," replied Louie.

"What the hell went on in that club? Did you do anything inappropriate?" asked Roger.

"Nothing went on and I didn't do anything inappropriate," answered Louie.

"Did you solicit her?" asked Roger.

"What?"

"I don't mean that. I'm referring to that catalog crap you sell during official government work hours and on government property," said Roger.

"Jesus, I forgot to take my catalog with me."

"Was she wearing any clothes during this interview?" asked Louie's boss.

"Yes."

She was fully clothed?" asked Roger.

"Umm .... not exactly."

"What exactly?" asked Roger.

"She was partially clothed," acknowledged Louie.

"Define partially clothed."

"She was wearing panties," answered Louie.

Roger rolled his eyes upon hearing what Trixsee was wearing during the audit. "How did Martha look?" he asked Louie.

"Her boobs were truly magnificent."

"I suspected as much. Now I want you to expend the same zeal to your next assignment which happens to be former President Alexander Talbot's tax returns. The tax returns are in several boxes by your desk."

"Several boxes? How many are several?" asked Louie.

"Either four or seven good size boxes. You'd better get started," said Roger

Within minutes, Louie has already performed a preliminary review of the former president's tax returns. Tom was right when he said that this case could get messy.

Alexander Franklin Talbot, Jr., was without question, the most controversial president in history. His cabinet consisted of his buddies from Alpha Beta Kappa, the first national college fraternity whose charter was revoked due to a number of criminal infractions on campus.

Alex Talbot was a star football player in college and was good enough to have been drafted to play in the NFL. Alex played professional football for fifteen years, of which the last seven years were spent holding a clipboard while standing on the sidelines away from the action.

When his football career ended, Alex accepted a job as a broadcaster for CBS. While Alex was a marginal NFL quarterback, he was a star as a broadcast analyst. Alex worked at CBS for three years and when his contract was up, Alex left the network for a larger stage.

Alex Talbot was good at looking good. Tall with a lean, muscular physique and always sporting a bronze tan, Alex Talbot could have been a movie star, except for one minor problem. Alex did not have the time or desire to memorize lines from a movie script. Alex's talent was improvisation. Unfortunately, the movie industry prefers that its actors recite exactly what is written in the script. That's probably why there are screenwriters in Hollywood.

Alex decided his next job should be in politics. As a former NFL quarterback who played on several championship teams, Alex was popular with the citizens of his state and became a US Senator in his first attempt at public office.

Alex enjoyed being a member of the Senate. The many perks which were made available to him as a member of the Senate were nice. However, the many perks available to the person in the Oval Office were nicer. Indeed, the perks of being president were so attractive that after two terms in the Senate, Alex Talbot decided to run for the Office of President of the United States.

The truth is Alex Talbot won the presidency because every woman eligible to vote, cast her vote for him. Men, on the other hand, still thought of him as a backup quarterback who looked good holding a clipboard while wearing a baseball cap. However, winning one more vote than your opponent was good enough for Alex. When the election was over, no one really cared about the margin of victory. In Alex Talbot's mind, his team scored the winning touchdown on the last play of the game, which is all that counts.

During Alex Talbot's only term in office, he could count his presidential accomplishments using only two fingers on one hand. At least the world did not come to an end with President Talbot sitting in the Oval Office with his hand somewhere near a red button. Alex Talbot viewed his presidency as a stepping stone to a higher calling. That is, to make a gazillion dollars for himself and his fraternity brothers. This was one of Alex Talbot's two accomplishments.

While Alex Talbot did not send US troops into overseas wars and did not piss off foreign nations, he simply didn't do anything of consequence as President of the United States to make America a better country. Alex's four years in the White House were spent playing flag football on the White House grounds whenever he was in D.C., which wasn't often. Of course, Alex's team always won. Being president has its privileges.

When Alex was not staying at the White House, he spent his waking hours going to sporting events all over the country and when he wasn't doing that, he took lots of vacations to exotic destinations to relieve the stress of his job. Gambling on college and professional football games, major league baseball, college basketball as well as NBA games can be stressful.

Alex assumed that with all the politicians and federal employees in the country, somebody would be doing what needed to be done. Meddling in the day-to-day operations of the federal government was something that neither appealed to, nor interested, him.

Alex's first year out of office was relatively uneventful. The former commander-in-chief had a book published about his life. While the former president is technically the author of the book, it is generally known by all that the book was written by his assistants.

The next year in civilian life was more exciting. The ex-president was an active speaker on the cocktail circuit and commanded top dollar to speak. Needless to say, all of his speeches were written by his assistants, presumably the same assistants who wrote his book.

By the third year, Alex Talbot was up to his eyeballs in business deals. The former president negotiated deals where he was paid sizable advisory fees in advance. He also was astute enough to structure deals where he received consulting fees for a period of twenty four months and an exit fee if he resigned from any venture or was asked to leave by his business associates.

After being out of office for the past four years, Alex Talbot has been involved in numerous business deals and has accumulated substantial wealth. In addition, many of Alex's college friends have done well with Alex's assistance.

Alex Talbot claimed to be an author, business consultant, venture capitalist and deal-maker who did not earn any revenue of significance. Louie was not sure what an unpaid deal-maker is, but will look into these various activities in order to ascertain that these are bona fide business activities operated for profit, particularly when none of the Schedule C activities showed a net profit for any of the years in issue.

While the tax returns indicate numerous sources of earnings, the deductions claimed are so substantial that net operating losses have resulted from the Schedule C activities. The former president has carried back these losses to prior tax years and has sought refunds. The most recent return was flagged by the Service Center, and as a result, the prior years were pulled from storage and associated with this return. Altogether, Louie has the past three years and two carryback years.

"Jesus, he claimed deductions for toothpaste, haircuts and body massages," complained Louie before he turned around to find Tom standing behind him.

"Are you talking to yourself?" inquired Tom.

"How long have you been standing there, lurking over my shoulder?" responded Louie.

"Having fun with El Presidente?" Tom asked while ignoring the question.

"No."

"It looks ugly, doesn't it?" asked Tom.

"Yep."

"There could be fallout from this," said Tom.

"I know."

"Do you want help? I could assign another agent or two and make it a team project," offered Tom.

"No thanks. I prefer to work it by myself."

"Okay, but the offer is on the table in case you change your mind. By the way, what are you going to do about the statutes?"

"Let them expire."

"Very funny," said Tom. "If that should happen, you'll be joining Ben Newman."

BRUCE BRONSTEIN

CHAPTER 15

Louie sent an appointment letter to the former president along with a shopping list of documents that he wanted to review prior to the first meeting. Louie requested bank statements for all bank accounts as well as all brokerage account statements for all of the tax years in issue. This should generate a phone call.

Less than one week after mailing his letter to the former president, Louie received a phone call from Alex Talbot's attorneys who had faxed their Power of Attorney to Louie prior to the phone call. The former president has retained Donnelly & Smith, a politically prominent Washington, D.C. law firm whose tax attorneys are among the very best in the country.

The two senior partners in Donnelly & Smith who will be representing the former president are Edward Smith, a former IRS Chief Counsel, and Larry Donnelly, a former senior executive at Treasury. The lawyers have placed a call to Louie to discuss his letter.

Polite and professional, the lawyers spent a few minutes chatting with Louie, attempting to size the little guy up for themselves. In fact, they have already made a few telephone calls to tax lawyers in Baltimore to find out about Louie's reputation. They have been told by Trent Stratford and Joel Abramowitz, among others, that Louie Lipschitz may come in a small package but he is the very best at what he does and that they should not underestimate him.

The lawyers are pleased that Louie Lipschitz is a worthy adversary. They will soon discover how proficient the little guy is when they talk to him.

The first matter of business is the venue. The lawyers are curious as to why the audit is being handled by an agent in Baltimore when the taxpayer and his lawyers are located in the District of Columbia. Louie easily parried this by saying that it is within the discretion of IRS management as to which field office is assigned cases and it could be any number of reasons why this case was assigned to Baltimore as opposed to Washington.

Smith and Donnelly believe they know why the case was assigned to Louie. If a representative does not want a certain agent to perform the examination, that representative will request that the case be reassigned. In this case, the lawyers could push for a reassignment to an agent in Washington as a matter of convenience to the taxpayer and the taxpayer's representatives.

The lawyers raised the possibility as to whether the case can be transferred to Washington for reassignment because it would be more convenient for all involved. Once again, Louie parried this by saying it is within the discretion of IRS management to transfer cases to other offices. Louie then offered to hold all meetings in their office as a matter of convenience to them.

By offering to travel to their office, Louie has effectively eliminated the transfer of the case to Washington, D.C. The lawyers must now deal with Louie, which is what they had anticipated from the outset.

Next up for discussion is the potential statute problem that Louie has addressed in his letter to their client. While there is almost one year remaining on the statute of limitations, Louie has solicited a consent agreement that would allow the statute for all years to remain open indefinitely at this time. The lawyers have asserted that this is unacceptable and have told Louie that their client has agreed to sign a consent agreement to give the IRS an additional four months beyond the current statute to conclude the audit.

Louie expected as much and countered by saying, "This audit could take well over a year just to reach an agreement on the issues, let alone re-compute the tax liabilities given net operating losses. An extension of only four more months doesn't give me much time."

"Our client is hopeful that you will be able to expedite his case and work through all of the issues as promptly as possible. He is interested in having a definitive answer as soon as possible because your findings may impact future tax years. Needless to say, we would want to avoid a repetitive audit, if at all possible," said Smith.

"My boss has asked me to give this case expeditious treatment so I intend to perform the audit as soon as possible. However, there is a lot of work to do in just reviewing the tax returns, examining your client's books and records, working through the issues, and reaching an accord on my findings. Of course, additional time is needed just to process everything for closing. As you may know, I cannot close a case with less than ninety days left on the statute," explained Louie.

"We're familiar with your ninety day administrative procedure, so I think we can convince our client to agree to a six month extension beyond the current statute," offered Donnelly.

BRUCE BRONSTEIN

"I would like to point out that your client has sought millions of dollars in refunds as a result of his net operating loss carrybacks. If my audit findings reflect sizable refunds, the issuance of the refunds must be approved by the Joint Committee on Taxation," replied Louie.

For a few moments, neither of the lawyers said a word. The thought of having the Joint Committee on Taxation, which reports its findings to Congress, involved in the former President of the United States' tax returns was not something that Alex Talbot would be happy about.

Finally, one of the lawyers asked, "Based on your experience, how much longer would the Joint Committee review and approval process take?"

"I have no idea," answered Louie, which was a truthful answer. "But as you probably know, if Joint Committee approval is required, it will take considerably longer from an administrative standpoint to prepare the case for closing."

The lawyers were not happy that this could potentially be a Joint Committee case. Having the Joint Committee review the case would take an undetermined amount of time and concerns could be raised by the Joint Committee that might preclude Louie's findings from being accepted. Upon hearing this, Smith asked Louie, "What do you suggest?"

"Suppose your client agrees to an additional one year statute extension and we'll see how the audit progresses. If the case requires Joint Committee approval, your client will agree to sign an 872A before I send it to the Joint Committee," offered Louie.

"Agreed," the lawyers said in unison.

***

Stanley's criminal case has sailed through the review and approval process within the IRS and has been sent to the Department of Justice for acceptance as a criminal prosecution. The case has been assigned to Debbie Macht for approval.

After reading the report prepared by the special agents, Debbie called Jennifer Lee and asked her if she wanted to get together for lunch. When Debbie explained what she had on her desk, Jennifer readily agreed to meet her for lunch.

Sitting outside a delicatessen that was hardly reminiscent of the delis in New York City, Debbie asked Jennifer what she thought of Stanley Scherr.

After swallowing the last bite of a corned beef sandwich, Jennifer said, "He's a terrible lawyer who happens to be unethical, unprincipled, unscrupulous and underhanded. And I don't think he's very bright."

"Okay, I got the picture."

"How strong is the report?" asked Jennifer.

"It's really strong. I think we have an excellent case for a criminal conviction. There's a consistent pattern of substantial unreported income in each year. Scherr deposited his retainer fees into an escrow account but excluded the fees from income. I have no idea what his rationale was for treating the retainer fees as non-taxable. Whatever his justification, it doesn't matter. He's supposed to be a tax lawyer, right?" said Debbie.

"You could have fooled me. I got the sense that someone told him what to say and he just acted out his role in court," said Jennifer.

"Let's assume Scherr plays dumb and admits that he didn't know he had to include his retainer fees in his taxable income," said Debbie.

"I don't think he has to play dumb. I think he is dumb. But here's his problem. If he comes across as a dummy, that would be an admission that he's incompetent. His ego won't allow him to do that. Also, he'll be opening himself up to potential lawsuits by anyone who was given legal advice that turned out to be blatantly wrong. His exposure to legal liability might necessitate returning legal fees to his clients. I think he'll argue that it was something his secretary messed up on. The fees were inadvertently misclassified on the General Ledger and it was the secretary's fault. He'll then say he was preoccupied with his law practice and relied on a bookkeeper or an accountant to reconcile his books at the end of the year," said Jennifer.

"Okay, what you just said makes sense. However, Scherr didn't use a bookkeeper or an accountant to prepare his tax returns. He stated that he prepared his own tax returns and his former secretary claimed that he made the entries on his General Ledger. Also, he kept a record of the retainer fees in each client's legal file so whenever he opened the client's legal file, he saw the amount of the retainer. When he prepared his tax returns, he had to know that the gross income from his law practice was substantially understated," said Debbie.

"Sounds like you have a slam dunk case for tax evasion," said Jennifer, as she held up an outstretched arm to get the waiter's attention.

"Yep. Sounds good to me."

CHAPTER 16

Aaron and Ella Bell have told Timmy about their meeting with the DOJ prosecutors. While it is Timmy's decision, they have encouraged him to consider a plea bargain. To Timmy's credit, he was willing to do so to avoid putting them through the stress of a trial. Timmy has discussed the matter with his Public Defender, who shared the same view. Apparently, no one wants to see this go to trial.

"When you enter into a Plea Agreement, you've relinquished your right to a trial. The judge will then ask you questions in order to determine whether you understand the consequences of your guilty plea. You've made an admission of guilt so the judge must determine whether the plea is voluntarily made or whether threats or promises were made to pressure you into pleading guilty. The judge must also ensure that you understand the charges against you and the corresponding sentences or fines," Derick explained while Timmy nodded his head that he understood.

"And finally, the judge must ascertain the factual basis of the plea to make sure that there is proof that you actually engaged in the conduct with which you have been charged. In other words, you have to explain in court what you did," said Derick.

"I have to make a full disclosure?" asked Timmy.

"That's correct," replied Derick.

***

Louie has received copies of Alex Talbot's voluminous financial records for the past three years. It has taken Louie more than two days to analyze these documents.

In order to ascertain whether Alex Talbot understated his taxable income, Louie had to perform a bank deposit analysis. This involves reviewing the activity in the various bank accounts and identifying the source of the deposits to determine its taxability.

Because Alex Talbot maintained a total of seven checking and savings accounts at four different banks, Louie had to identify any deposits and corresponding withdrawals from one bank account to another bank account. Thus, transfers between bank accounts were taken into account in his bank deposit analysis. This is a very tedious and time consuming process which requires the patience of a saint.

It was late in the day when Louie discovered a "memo reference" with respect to the transfer of five thousand dollars to another bank account on one of the bank statements. Louie guessed that it might have been a bank account that belonged to Alex Talbot's wife. Because each spouse elected to file separately, her tax returns were not part of this examination. Louie made a note to inquire into the ownership of this account. An explanation will be sought from the former president in a formal Information Document Request.

An Information Document Request or IDR is used to identify specific information that is needed during the preliminary stage of the audit. If documents such as bank statements are not voluntarily submitted upon request, the IRS may initiate summons enforcement to obtain these materials.

Ever persistent, Louie decided to tackle the brokerage account statements before leaving the office. After reviewing the brokerage account statements, Louie discovered the transfer of five thousand dollars to a bank account that is not one of the seven bank accounts he was told the former president owned. Louie compared this bank account to the other undisclosed account and found that the two accounts are the same. Because the disbursement was not made by check, it was a transfer from one account to another account. Louie will also inquire about this account transfer in his IDR.

***

One week after Louie's IDR was sent to Alex Talbot and his lawyers, he received a telephone call from Edward Smith. The day before Smith called Louie, he spoke with his client concerning the undisclosed bank account.

Edward Smith was selected to be the Chief Counsel of the IRS by President Alex Talbot. The Chief Counsel, whose function is to provide legal advice, reports directly to the Commissioner. It is one of the most prestigious executive positions in the federal government. As such, it is normal to assume that one might feel a sense of gratitude when selected by a sitting president to serve in such a capacity.

When a new administration replaced Talbot, Smith left government service and started his own law firm with a colleague who was an executive at the Department of the Treasury.

"Alex, the IRS agent has questioned a bank account that was previously not disclosed. He seems to think that you may have an interest in this account based on the fact that there is the term, 'memo reference,' on several of your financial statements. What can you tell me about this?" asked the lawyer.

"Nothing. I don't know anything about an undisclosed bank account," said Talbot.

"Alex, are you absolutely certain?" asked Smith.

"Yes."

"And you're comfortable with my telling Agent Lipschitz that you have no knowledge whatsoever of this account, and that you have fully disclosed all bank accounts per the IDR?" asked Smith.

"Yes. I've provided the agent with all of my banking and brokerage account records."

"Okay, I'll put in a call to Agent Lipschitz tomorrow morning. But I have to warn you, the agent will insist on knowing the identity of the owner of the undisclosed account," stated the lawyer.

"Ed, if that's the case, give him any name you want. Just don't give him my name."

***

"Agent Lipschitz, I spoke with Alex Talbot yesterday as to ownership of a bank account that was referenced on one of his bank statements. Additionally, you've raised a similar question concerning the same account, which is referenced by the same term, 'memo reference,' on the account statement. My client has told me that he has no knowledge of this bank account," declared Edward Smith.

"I'll need to know who owns this account," replied Louie.

"We can't help you with that. My client told me he doesn't know and we're concerned about respecting the privacy of the owner or owners of the account. I'm sure you can appreciate the importance of maintaining confidentiality to all concerned," said the lawyer.

Louie ignored the comment and replied, "I'm inclined to think that the account is either owned or controlled by your client."

"My client has voluntarily disclosed his ownership of all bank accounts. He claims to have no knowledge of any other accounts. For your information, this client is a former president and member of the United States Senate," said Smith.

"That's my point exactly," replied Louie.

***

Louie informed Roger of his most recent conversation with one half of Alex Talbot's prestigious legal team.

"I think we need to issue a summons to find out who owns this bank account. My guess is that this is a foreign bank account and my next guess is that the owner of this account is a nominee," predicted Louie.

"You suspect foreign ownership?" asked Roger

"Yeah. I think there could be even more than this one account and they could all be under his control," proclaimed Louie.

"Jesus Christ! Do you know what you're saying?" asked Roger

"Yeah. I think we need to see Tom."

When Louie and Roger walked into Tom's office, he was just saying goodbye on the phone to his boss, who had received a phone call from the commissioner only moments before.

"Before you two say anything, guess who that was?" asked Tom.

"I'll go with the commissioner. What have I won?" asked Louie.

"That was my boss. He's the one who got the call from the commissioner. And you just won the privilege to go back to work," said Tom.

"I don't know what you said to Talbot's lawyers, but you certainly hit a nerve. When the commissioner got the call from Talbot himself, he remembered you from his visit to Baltimore last month. The commissioner happened to mention to Talbot that you were the recipient of some awards for recognition as the IRS's best agent in the history of this agency. He played it up pretty good, even if it wasn't true. Talbot was not happy with that and asked that the case be assigned to another revenue agent. Our Glorious Leader passed the request on to my boss who rejected the idea. I suspect Talbot's lawyers will tell him to refrain from making any more phone calls to senior government executives and let them do their jobs," said Tom.

"Tom, you were right about the fallout and it didn't take Louie long to provoke Talbot."

"It's a skill," Louie said with pride.

"No, it's not a skill. You just have some kind of a mental defect that allows you to piss off people," Tom replied.

CHAPTER 17

The following day, a summons was issued to one of Alex Talbot's banks and a second summons was issued to his brokerage firm.

The IRS has broad investigatory authority and it is the intent of Congress that the IRS have the authority to issue an administrative summons in order to compel a taxpayer or a third party to produce information in the form of documents and/or testimony for use in its investigation. Congress clearly wanted effective tax investigations by allowing the IRS expansive information gathering authority.

Before issuing the summons, Tom notified the Chief of Exam, who informed the commissioner, who informed the Secretary of the Treasury. Courtesy calls were also placed with the chief of staff in the Oval Office by the Secretary of the Treasury so that the White House was aware of the situation just in case Alex Talbot decided to work the phones again.

Although the summons was issued to Morgan Stanley and Bank of America, the IRS is also required by statute to provide the taxpayer with a copy of each summons. When Alex Talbot received his copy of each summons, he made a personal visit to see his lawyers at Donnelly & Smith.

The receptionist who greeted the former president was quite surprised when he walked into the lobby unannounced and without an appointment to meet with his lawyers. The former president told the receptionist that he needed to see the firm's senior partners and that whatever they are currently doing was of no consequence because he needed to see them immediately.

When asked if he cared for coffee or tea while waiting for his lawyers, Alex Talbot said, "I'll take a scotch on the rocks."

"I'm sorry sir, but I don't believe we have alcoholic beverages in the office," replied the receptionist.

"Never mind." Looking to his left, he saw the first member of his legal team and then the second attorney walking towards him.

"Fellas, let's huddle up. We need to go over our playbook," Alex said to his lawyers as if they were about to take the field.

His lawyers looked at each other for a few seconds before they escorted their anxious client to a conference room.

"Alex, what brought you in to see us without calling first?" asked Larry Donnelly.

Ignoring the lawyer's apparent annoyance that he barged in to see them without the courtesy of an advance phone call, Alex replied, "This piece of shit," as he waved his copy of each summons over his head, before tossing it on the conference table for his lawyers to see.

"That is something we expected the IRS to do when you said you had no knowledge as to who owned the bank account in which funds were transferred," said Edward Smith.

"I happen to be a former president and a former senator. Can't the IRS just accept my word as the truth?" asked Alex.

"I'm afraid it doesn't work that way," replied Donnelly.

"Well make it work that way," Talbott practically screamed.

"The IRS is responsible for the administration and enforcement of the tax laws. As a former US Senator and President of the United States, you should know this, and you should have known that Agent Lipschitz would initiate this action to discover who owns the bank account in question," said Donnelly.

"There must be a way to put a stop to this, isn't there?" asked Talbot.

"In the case of the bank and the brokerage firm, neither can bring a proceeding to quash the summons, but in the case of a third party, you can," said Smith.

"Good. Then do it," ordered the former president.

"Wait a minute. There are things you should know. When a petition to quash a summons is filed, the government will file a motion to dismiss for lack of jurisdiction, file a motion for summary denial, or even file a counterclaim for enforcement. Most summons enforcement proceedings should be decided on the papers and the government almost always prevails. We're confident that the government would prevail in this instance," added Smith.

"Why do you say that?" asked Talbot.

"The Department of Justice can bring an enforcement proceeding seeking a court order directing compliance with the summons. Although the government bears the burden of persuasion, it only has the initial burden of making a prima facie showing that the summons is valid. A declaration from the investigating agent is considered sufficient," said Smith.

"Alex, the IRS is required to meet four criteria. That the summons was issued for a legitimate purpose; seeks information that may be relevant to that purpose; seeks information that is not already in its possession and satisfies all administrative steps," added Donnelly.

"But the information the agent wants to see relates to a bank account that received a total of ten thousand dollars. How relevant is that to the audit?" asked Alex.

"The government must establish that there is a realistic expectation that the summoned information may be relevant to its investigation," answered Donnelly. "There is no legal requirement that it be definitive."

"Then what?" asked the disgruntled client.

"Once the government makes its prima facie case, the burden is on us to show that enforcement would be an abuse of process. We must introduce specific facts and evidence to support your allegations. This is a heavy burden to overcome," replied Smith.

"You think I'll lose?" asked the depressed client.

"Yes, without question," concluded Smith.

"What if you were to file a motion just as a delaying tactic? How much time would I have before the information is made available to the IRS?"

"You have up to twenty days after given notice of the summons to file a petition to quash. The government then files a counterclaim for enforcement or a motion whenever a petition to quash a summons has been filed.   Then it's a matter for the court," answered Donnelly.

"This is bullshit. This is nothing more than a fishing expedition," exclaimed Alex.

"As long as the IRS has identified the documents it wishes to inspect, it is not considered a fishing expedition," replied Smith.

"So, we'll lose on the summons. Can the decision be appealed?" asked Talbot, who was hoping the answer is yes.

"As a general rule, it is not appealable because it's so factual. Even if it were appealed, the courts are not likely to grant a stay pending appeal of a summons enforcement order," responded Donnelly.

"Jesus Christ! So, what you're telling me is this is a lost cause," said the former president.

"It could be worse. Look on the bright side," said Donnelly.

"What's that?"

"The IRS cannot issue a summons if it has already made an institutional decision to refer your case to the Department of Justice for criminal prosecution," said Donnelly.

"That's great news," said the former president with a touch of cynicism in his voice as he got up to leave.

***

"Okay, that wasn't half bad. Let's try it for real this time. Ready, set, action," yelled the set director.

"Hi folks. My name is Benjamin Newman."

Ben sat behind an executive desk as if he was about to address the nation. Wearing a dark blue business suit, white button down cotton dress shirt and a bright red silk tie, Ben looked the part of the President of the United States.

Actually, Ben looks like the typical guy next door. Ben is of average height and weight, average build and average looks. Striving for a clean cut look and speaking in a warm, friendly tone of voice per his director's instructions, Ben is very average, which is a good thing for a tax accountant.

"For those of you who have been previously audited by the IRS and are in fear of having your tax returns examined again, help is here. For those of you who patronize gypsy type tax return preparers every year, help is here. For those of you who would like to have tax planning advice to save on your taxes, help is here. As a CPA and former IRS agent, I have the experience to offer sophisticated tax planning opportunities to those seeking tax advice, as well as prepare your tax returns correctly so that you can sleep at night knowing that the IRS will not come after you," Ben said.

Turning to look in the direction of the camera on the other side of the set pursuant to the set director's instruction, Ben continued with his scripted speech.

"I can recite IRS rules and procedures in my sleep. Having worked for the IRS, I know how tax returns are selected for audit. Let me help you avoid having your tax returns examined by the IRS. Call me today so that I can help you. The 800 number will appear at the bottom of your screen in five seconds. Don't hesitate. Call today," Ben said.

BRUCE BRONSTEIN

"That's a wrap everybody. Ben, you were great. We should have the tape ready for production by tomorrow morning," exclaimed the set director, who looked like a Viking with his tall, lean muscular physique and long blond hair and beard.

"Thanks Lars."

CHAPTER 18

Stanley Scherr has been indicted for tax evasion. Words to this effect appear in the Baltimore Sun. If Stanley is given a copy of the newspaper while he sits in a jail cell, he can read all about his arrest and his pending criminal trial.

Actually, Stanley only learned of this wonderful news when he heard the loud knock on the front door of his residence at 6:30 am by armed special agents who promptly took him into custody as if he was one of the most wanted suspects in the nation. The sight of Stanley being led away in handcuffs was not one of the highlights to his underwhelming career as a lawyer who would stand up to the IRS and bust its balls as he so boldly claimed.

Stanley has been read the charges and his rights. When he was told he can keep his mouth shut, he obediently did so. At this point in time, Stanley was thinking about hiring Wallace Shadybrook, a criminal defense attorney who doesn't do litigation. At the very least, Stanley thought he could use Wallace to negotiate a plea bargain with very little prison time. This is what is called, wishful thinking.

At the first opportunity Stanley had in which to make his one phone call, he called Wallace. When Wallace was told by Stanley that he is in a holding cell awaiting arraignment on tax evasion charges, Stanley was given more good news. As of this morning, Wallace has increased his hourly fee from four hundred and fifty dollars to five hundred dollars.

"Are you still there, Stan?" inquired Wallace after a few moments of silence.

"Where else am I going to be? They have me locked up in a jail," complained Stanley.

"Are you okay with my new hourly fee?" asked Wallace.

"Do I have a choice?"

"We all have choices. But I can assure you that you'll actually be saving money because I won't be spending much time on your case. And you understand that even though I'm going to have you plead guilty, I'll try to get you the best prison sentence I can. Remember, you only get what you pay for and I'll get you what you deserve," promised Wallace.

"That's what I'm afraid of," remarked Stanley as Wallace had already hung up on him.

***

Just outside Washington, D.C., the Public Defender has met with the prosecutors in Timmy's tax evasion case and a tentative agreement has been reached. In exchange for a plea of guilty to all charges, the prosecutors will recommend a prison sentence of twelve years, with time off for good behavior and credit given for time spent in the federal correctional facility. In addition, Timmy must make full disclosure as to how he structured transactions that involved money laundering, conflicts of interest, bribery and gratuities.   While Timmy will be required to make these admissions in a Statement of Facts to the court as part of his Plea Agreement, he must provide the Department of Justice with a more detailed stipulation of facts in a full disclosure of all financial improprieties that he committed.

Although Timmy is not thrilled with the prospect of being imprisoned for up to twelve years, he stoically accepted his fate. He thanked Derick for his efforts and extended his appreciation to the prosecutors for their professionalism.

Debbie was somewhat stunned at such kind words coming from someone who is being sent to prison for up to twelve years. Gary was also surprised at Timmy's respect for them. As Derick walked out of the room with Debbie and Gary, he assured them that Timmy was sincere in what he said.

The prosecutors advised Timmy that he needed to draft a comprehensive version of the Statement of Facts that encompasses everything that he did. The prosecutors will compare this version with the Statement of Facts as prepared by the special agents. Once the prosecutors have reviewed both statements, they will draft the Plea Agreement. After Timmy has signed the Plea Agreement, a court date will be set to conclude the proceeding, at which time Timmy will be required to allocute to his crimes in open court.

***

Alex Talbot placed a telephone call to his financial advisor in order to discuss his investment portfolio.

"Alex, your portfolio is in great shape. The mutual funds are outperforming the S&P. Your tax-exempt bonds continue to pay a terrific return and your stock portfolio continues to appreciate in value. Your investments are doing very well and should continue to prosper given the market's projections," said Ralph Adler.

"Ralph, that's great news. However, I wanted to talk to you about an item that popped up on one of my account statements. It's a five thousand dollar transfer to another account. Do you remember this?" asked the former president.

"No, that's not something I recall."

"There's a designation on the account statement that it's a 'memo reference.' Does that jog your memory?" asked the former president.

"I'm sorry, it doesn't ring a bell. You'll have to give me more information than that," replied Ralph.

"Jesus Christ. Just pull up the damn statement on your computer screen and look at it. The date of the statement is August of 2008," said Talbot.

It took the broker a few moments to pull up Talbot's account statement for that month. "Okay, I've got it up on my screen. Now I'm searching for the transfer from your account...... Okay, I see it now. What about it?" Ralph asked.

"Can you make it go away?" asked Alex.

"Can I what?" was the response.

"Can you make it look like something other than an account transfer? How about if you create some documents to show that the five thousand dollars was used to purchase worthless stock options? And when the IRS questions this, you'll explain that the transfer reference on my account statement is an error. There was no transfer. Can you do that for me?" asked Talbot.

"Alex, you're asking me to create false documents to cover up an insignificant five thousand dollar transfer to another bank account? I can't do that. I could lose my broker's license, my job, even be charged with securities fraud for doing that. And you want me to lie to the IRS on top of securities fraud? Are you kidding me?" said Ralph.

"Could you do it for one million dollars?" asked Alex.

"I don't see why not."

***

As Stanley contemplated his fate, he thought back to his childhood. When Stanley was a young tyke, he bullied smaller children his age who forked over their lunch money to Stanley's posse of eight year old punks. Stanley's role model must have been Don Corleone because Stanley practically made a career out of collecting money from people just because this was something he wanted to do.

Stanley thought back to the summer when he couldn't return to camp and instead, operated a newspaper delivery service. Stanley smiled when he recalled how he manipulated a younger boy into doing all the work and accepting less than his promised fifty/fifty split down the middle.

One of the highlights in Stanley's storied career as a cheater was when he recruited someone to take the LSAT for him so that he could attend law school. Cheating to gain admission to law school was one thing. Having the same person take the Bar Exam for him was another and Stanley managed to pull this off after several previous attempts to cheat on the Bar Exam had resulted in failures. Once he became a lawyer, Stanley now had a license to cheat. Stanley made it a practice to overcharge clients for work that was never done. When it came to overbilling, Stanley did so with great skill.

When Stanley wasn't overbilling his clients, he lied to them. He misrepresented himself as a tax lawyer who could resolve tax disputes when he couldn't. He promised favorable results on audits and collection cases and lost every case. And in spite of all this, he continued to overcharge clients for shoddy work.

Stanley now understood how it felt to be the getting the shaft. Wallace was merely returning the favor that Stanley had done to so many of his clients by charging him five hundred dollars an hour to do essentially nothing. In return for the extravagant legal fees Stanley will pay to a hack who will not represent him in court, he will go to prison.

Stanley wondered how things could have gone south for him so quickly. Sometimes in life, things come around full circle. In Stanley's case, he finally accepted his lot in life that his legal career was over and that he would be spending the next few years hanging out with the dregs of society, making license plates and chairs for government offices.

CHAPTER 19

Louie returned to his other cases while waiting for the summoned documents to be sent to him. Carrying a full workload of cases, the little guy was anxious to close a few of the cases that have languished in his inventory longer than his normal processing time. Today is the day Louie will wrap up one such case.

"Agent Lipschitz from the IRS is here to see you sir," buzzed the lovely young receptionist to the senior tax partner at the law firm of Howe & Moore.

"Mr. Howe will be with you shortly." After having said that, the young lady apologized to Louie. "I'm so sorry. I should not have used the word, shortly."

"I'm not offended. What's your social security number?" joked Louie.

With a worried look on her face, the receptionist asked, "Are you going to audit my tax returns?"

"I'm just kidding," said Louie, who has been called a lot worse by a lot of people.

"Agent Lipschitz, it hasn't been long enough," said Mark Howe as he walked over to shake hands with his adversary.

"Don't you like me?" asked Louie, as he shook hands with the law firm's senior tax partner.

"I'd like you a lot more if I didn't have to deal with you," replied the lawyer.

Mark Howe started his own law practice almost thirty years ago with a colleague. They were working at a large downtown law firm with several hundred attorneys and decided to start their own practice, which eventually grew into a mid-size firm that specialized in estate planning, business law and taxation. Mark preferred to handle tax controversy work and dealt with federal and state tax issues. Dealing with Louie Lipschitz was another matter. In all the cases that Mark Howe had with Louie, Mark never came close to prevailing on any issues of consequence.

Mark Howe was almost sixty years old but looked good for his age. Well dressed and physically fit, he always made a nice appearance. Tan and relaxed from playing golf for the past two weeks in Florida where he maintained a second home, Mark looked like he didn't have a care in the world. Until now.

"Agent Lipschitz, thanks for coming to my office today. I'm very much relieved that I didn't have to endure another body cavity search in your building," said the lawyer, as he escorted Louie to a nearby conference room.

"You don't enjoy rectal exams in front of strangers?" asked Louie.

"I wouldn't call it an exam. It's more like sexual assault. One of my associates, a beautiful female attorney who was hired several years ago, had to endure an awful lot from some of your screeners when she met with an agent several months ago. When she returned to the office later that day, she informed me that she will never set foot in the Federal Building again unless she is personally accompanied by a SWAT Team," replied Mark.

"Granted, our screeners do get a little carried away at times."

"A little carried away? The poor girl had considered going straight to the Emergency Room at Mercy Hospital for treatment. Her thighs were black and blue with bruises. I wouldn't be the least bit surprised if the police could get fingerprints off her ass. Those goons shouldn't be working in a Federal Building. Their talents are wasted there. Instead, they belong at Gitmo, waterboarding prisoners," declared the attorney.

"Did you want to discuss the Milo Cervantes case or continue with your stand-up comedy act?" asked Louie.

"Let's talk about Milo's case. I can't believe you're proposing to reclassify his business deductions as charitable contributions. I sense that this is my first case with you as the examining agent that I'll win. If I could take you to lunch afterwards to celebrate, I would," Mark said.

"Confidence is good. I like that. It makes losing that much harder to accept," replied Louie.

"You think I'm going to lose?" asked the lawyer.

"I do."

Clearing his throat, Mark Howe said, "Perhaps it would be helpful if I first gave you some background information about Milo Cervantes. Mr. Cervantes immigrated to the United States when he was only five years old from his native Greece and dropped out of school at age sixteen to help his parents run a small grocery store. When Milo turned twenty one, he had saved up enough money to purchase a row house which he converted into rental property. By the age of twenty four, Milo had already acquired more than forty low-income apartment buildings in downtown Baltimore.

"Eventually, Milo sold off his apartment buildings and used the proceeds to build high-rise structures throughout Baltimore. My client's construction company has grown to be very successful over the years. This success is due in large part because Mr. Cervantes is actively involved in numerous real estate development projects which complement his construction business," Mark added.

"My client's construction company has been involved in various construction projects throughout the Baltimore area. These projects have involved luxury apartment buildings along the waterfront, hotels, office complexes, hospitals, universities and shopping malls. Many of these contracts are the direct result of my client's real estate development projects in his individual capacity," said the lawyer.

"How so?" asked Louie.

"Milo is a well-known developer. His reputation is such that businesses want to do business with his construction company. His company does quality work and meets its construction deadlines. In construction, your reputation is everything," replied the lawyer.

"Mr. Cervantes is engaged in the business of developing community projects. He made payments to numerous charitable organizations which were made with a reasonable expectation of commensurate financial return. These payments bore a direct relationship to his business. As such, these payments constitute deductible business expenses," argued the attorney.

Deductions claimed as a business expense by a taxpayer who is engaged in a trade or business are deductible without limitations. However, charitable contributions are subject to statutory limitations based on a taxpayer's adjusted gross income. Thus, charitable contributions not otherwise deductible in the year claimed are subject to carryover to the next available taxable year. This can be an important distinction in characterizing a payment as a business expense as opposed to a charitable contribution.

"We're talking about payments that were made to a number of charitable organizations. Typically, payments made to charitable organizations are treated for tax reporting purposes as contributions," declared Louie.

"Typically, yes. I'm in complete agreement with you, Agent Lipschitz. However, this case is distinguishable from the general rule because my client reasonably expected to derive business by making these payments."

"No, he didn't personally expect to derive financial gain. It was his construction company that theoretically would have benefited through additional business," argued Louie.

"My client is synonymous with his construction company. They are one and the same," argued the lawyer.

"Then why didn't his construction company make contributions to the charities?" asked Louie.

"Had the construction company made the payments, it might be considered a charitable contribution," replied Mark.

"Exactly. And that's my point," concluded Louie.

The lawyer sensed that Louie had boxed him into a corner. He then said, "My client believes that he had a moral obligation to allow the City of Baltimore to share in the success he enjoys as a community business leader. That is why it is important that the payments come from him and not his construction business."

"Do you honestly believe what you just said," replied Louie.

"Umm…..... yes."

"Counselor, these are my thoughts. Payments made to a charitable organization which bear a direct relationship to a taxpayer's trade or business and which are made with a reasonable expectation of financial return commensurate with the payment may constitute a business expense," acknowledged Louie.

With that admission, Mark Howe smiled. However, the smile may have been premature.

"In view of the fact that your client did not receive income directly related to the payments on his individual tax returns in years concurrent with the payments, the expectation of financial return is too remote or prospective," explained Louie.

That comment took the smile off the lawyer's face.

"I would also like to add that the statute governing charitable contributions overrides the code section governing business expenses by reason of the fact that the donee charitable organizations were not under a legally binding obligation to provide your client with a specific economic benefit which otherwise might not be forthcoming," remarked Louie.

With that, the lawyer took a gulp.

"I have interviewed a number of officials at these donee charitable organizations and no one admitted there was a 'quid pro quo' arrangement," said Louie.

Mark gulped again.

"And before I forget, I'd like to leave these newspaper articles with you," said Louie.

"What newspaper articles are you talking about?" asked Mark.

"I came across these newspaper articles in which your client was interviewed about his business activities and prominence as a community leader. In the interviews, he talked at length about his belief that those individuals who have prospered doing business in Baltimore City should give back to the community. Specifically, he cited the fact that he has personally donated substantial sums of money to various charities and does so solely for humanitarian purposes. He further added that he strongly believes it is his civic and moral obligation to do so. When asked about the fact that he generously donates to charitable organizations, he insisted that he does so without any expectation of deriving future business. Until I had read these articles, I had no idea your client was a humanitarian," said Louie.

As Mark Howe read the newspaper articles, his blood started to boil. When he finished reading the newspaper articles, the lawyer looked at Louie and said, "I wish to hell that he had kept his big mouth shut. Why did he have to make these statements to the press?"

"I have no idea. When you tell him how it went today, you can remind him that he should still feel good about himself," Louie exclaimed.

"And why should he feel good about himself when he's missed out on the business deduction?"

"Because he's a humanitarian who donates money to charities for strictly charitable reasons," said Louie.

CHAPTER 20

Ralph Adler is staying late at the office. In order to earn his one million dollar fee, Ralph must create a false purchase order that shows Alex Talbot invested five thousand dollars in the market and lost his entire investment shortly after the date of the money was transferred. Ralph reviewed the trading activity at that time and determined that an investment in corn futures will produce the desired result. Accordingly, Ralph created a false invoice that showed Alex Talbot purchased a five thousand dollar contract for corn futures and that the investment was worthless twenty days later. Ralph then mailed a copy of the newly created statement to Talbot.

Ralph knew that the IRS will be given the official records that are in the Back Office files of Morgan Stanley. The official records will contradict his client's claim that the transfer appears as a mistake on his statement. Ralph is hopeful that Alex Talbot is able to convince the IRS that the brokerage firm simply recorded the transfer on the wrong account statement.

Ralph believes the explanation that a mistake was made by the brokerage firm is plausible. As such, it is possible that the IRS may accept this explanation. However, there is tremendous risk that if the brokerage firm's Compliance Officer conducts an investigation, it will be discovered that he created false documents at the behest of his client.

If it is determined that he intentionally created a false document, Ralph could be dismissed and the infraction could constitute a crime. In addition, the IRS could charge him with obstruction, which is a felony.

While Ralph decided that for one million dollars, it's worth the risk, Alex Talbot was busy working the phones. In fact, Talbot has never worked harder. If only he had applied himself with this kind of zeal earlier in his NFL career, Talbot might have been a star quarterback.

Alex Talbot concluded that the IRS will eventually learn the identity of the bank account's owner. The bank account in question is at Banque SCS Alliance SA in Geneva, Switzerland. The owner of the foreign bank account is a shell company identified as International Business Solutions, which was incorporated in Switzerland. The principal corporate officers and directors of this company are Hans Schumann and Klaus Bergmeister, who are listed on its corporate records as residents of Switzerland.

Talbot is of the opinion that there is insufficient documentation that would enable the IRS to attribute ownership of this Swiss bank account to him. Yet, he did not want to underestimate the IRS. He is well aware of what an ambitious agent can do, particularly when he once pressured an IRS official to initiate an audit of one of his enemies when he was President of the United States.

***

Stanley Scherr is standing before the Honorable William Smulyan and has been asked how he pleads. In fact, he is asked several times before he finally snapped out of his funk and said, "Not guilty, Your Majesty."

Looking down from the bench at Stanley, Judge Smulyan remarked, "Mr. Scherr, no one has ever mistaken me for royalty.

Not my wife, my children or my grandchildren. You may refer to me as Judge, Your Honor or Sir."

"Yes sir, Your Honor, sir," answered Stanley as if he were addressing an officer in boot camp.

With bail set at one hundred thousand dollars, Stanley has made arrangements with a local bail bondsman to post a cash bond. Within twenty four hours, Stanley is out on bail and walking the streets of downtown Baltimore. Stanley has tentatively lined up Wallace to negotiate a plea bargain which is good for Wallace and bad for him. In light of this predicament, Stanley would much prefer hiring another criminal defense lawyer who charges less than five hundred dollars per hour and can make an effort to actually appear in court to argue his case.

Stanley stopped by the law office of Roger Rice, a noted criminal defense attorney. Roger, who goes by the nickname, "Roger the Dodger," agreed to see Stanley without an appointment.

"What can I do for you Mr. Scherr," asked Roger.

"I've been indicted for tax evasion. I'm out on bail and I need someone to represent me in court," said Stanley.

"Wait a minute. Aren't you that 'Tax Man' character who claims that he kicks the IRS's ass?" asked Roger.

"Umm…. yes." It took Stanley a moment to actually say yes and it was said with little pride or enthusiasm.

"Well, I'll be damned. The Tax Man has been charged with tax evasion. Wait until my wife hears about this," exclaimed Roger, as Stanley was starting to cringe at the thought of all this unwanted publicity.

"You do criminal defense work, right?" asked Stanley.

"Yes, I do," Roger said with an impish grin. Roger's reputation as a preeminent criminal defense attorney was such that everyone in the legal community knew of him.

"Stan, I should tell you that I'm not accepting new clients given my current workload. You should try Gloria Jackson. Her office is two blocks down the street. She's really good with white collar crimes," said Roger as he stood to shake hands with Stanley and wished him well as he escorted him out of his office.

It took almost two hours until Stanley got to see Gloria Jackson. When Stanley asked her if she would accept him as a client, he didn't expect her to say, "I can't at this time. I was just asked by the mayor to defend some members of his administrative staff in a corruption case brought by the US Attorney. That case alone will take at least six to eight months of my time. If you're looking for a good white collar criminal defense lawyer, I recommend you see Crazy Al Simone."

"Who?"

"Al Simone. We call him Crazy Al because he's crazy. But he's an awfully good lawyer and if anyone can help you, it's him," said Gloria. "His office is one block south of mine."

Stanley felt as if he were a mouse scampering along a maze. At least he didn't have far to go.

When Stanley entered the reception area of Crazy Al Simone's office, he had to quickly step out of the way of the FBI agents who were escorting Crazy Al out in handcuffs. After the authorities took Crazy Al away, Stanley asked the receptionist what that was all about.

"Gee. I really don't know," was the reply.

Stanley called Roger Rice to let him know that Gloria Jackson was unable to take his case and that the attorney she recommended would also be unavailable. When he relayed Crazy Al's arrest by the FBI, Roger said, "Crazy Al has a lot of high-profile clients and some of them are believed to be mobsters. It wouldn't surprise me if Crazy Al was corrupted by them."

"Is there someone else you can recommend?" asked Stanley.

"You might try Joel Abramowitz's firm. They do mostly civil tax litigation, but I'm sure they have some lawyers who can do criminal tax work," said Roger the Dodger.

"Do you know Wallace Shadybrook?" asked Stanley.

"Sure. It seems as if Wally has been practicing for a hundred years. He's good, as long as he doesn't have to argue your case in court," said Roger who was anxious to get back to work.

"Right. He does plea bargains. Does he get good deals for his clients?" asked Stanley.

"That depends on what kind of a prison sentence you consider to be good," said Roger.

BRUCE BRONSTEIN

CHAPTER 21

Louie was getting ready to put his case files away when he was told that he, Roger and Tom would be meeting with the Chief of Exam in three minutes. After everyone assembled in the Exam Chief's conference room, Louie was asked to provide a status report on the Alex Talbot audit.

"As you all know, I've issued a summons to one of his banks and his brokerage firm in order to discover the identity or identities of the owner or owners of the bank account which was not initially disclosed. We must wait at least twenty days so that Talbot can challenge our right to the summoned information. If he challenges the summons, then it's going to delay the audit," said Louie.

"It's my guess that his lawyers will discourage him from challenging the summons. They have to know we'll eventually obtain the summoned information. I don't think they'll want to start a fight over something they can't win early in the audit. I think they'll want to pick and choose their battles when it is appropriate to do so," stated Louie.

"Where do you stand on the other issues?" asked the Exam Chief.

"It seems as if he's claimed a deduction for every personal living expense imaginable. If he owned a dog, I'm sure a dependency exemption would have been claimed," exclaimed Louie.

"What makes you think he doesn't own a dog?" asked Tom.

He has a high-rise condo in the District, a horse farm in Virginia, and a penthouse apartment in New York. The homeowner's association rules prohibit pets in the DC condo and the New York apartment. That suggests there is no dog," said Louie.

"But he could keep the dog on his horse farm," surmised Roger.

"Who gives a shit about a dog? It doesn't have anything to do with this case. What else do I need to know about this case so that when the commissioner calls me, I can sound reasonably intelligent?" shouted the Chief.

"You can tell him the examination is progressing on schedule, even with summons enforcement. If he asks, we are following our audit rules and procedures. This one is being played strictly by-the-book," announced Louie.

Wallace Shadybrook has asked Stanley to send him all materials in his possession that relate to the tax evasion case. However, Wallace has no intention of actually reading these materials. He only wants Stanley to think that he has read these documents so that he can pad his billable hours. Finally, there is an attorney out there who is now doing to Stanley, what Stanley has done to his clients.

David Harbaugh remembers Stanley Scherr. Indeed, the Assistant Deputy Attorney General, who is now running the Criminal Tax Division, remembers Stanley Scherr all too well. As far as the DOJ boss is concerned, Stanley Scherr was in bed with the woman who bribed a juror in a case that the DOJ should have won.

The DOJ boss has passed along words of wisdom to Debbie Macht. His words of wisdom are, "If this imbecile wants a plea bargain, the answer is a definitive, NO. We are not cutting any deals with him."

Debbie is of the opinion that she will win at trial and that Stanley will be sentenced to at least thirty six months in prison based on federal sentencing guidelines followed in tax evasion cases. However, Debbie would like to recommend a thirty three month sentence pursuant to a plea bargain. Debbie is willing to offer a three month concession so that she doesn't have to waste time on this case.

Debbie eventually prevailed on her new boss to take one month off the recommended sentence if Stanley pleads guilty for all tax years. This means that Stanley would have to accept a thirty five month prison sentence.

Wallace has notified Debbie that he will be representing Stanley and wants to discuss terms for a plea. Incredibly, Wallace is prepared to negotiate now.

"Go ahead," said Debbie.

"My client will plead guilty to all tax years in exchange for a one year sentence," offered Wallace.

"I'll see you in court, counselor."

"Wait. "I think I may be able to convince my client to agree to eighteen months," said Wallace.

"Do you know where the courthouse is located?" replied Debbie.

"C'mon, you're sending him to prison time for a non-violent crime. Can't you show some compassion for my client?" pleaded Wallace.

"Make sure you allow extra time for DC traffic. It can be a real bitch," said Debbie.

And so can you, thought Wallace. "My client will agree to twenty four months. And not another day," said Wallace.

"I suggest that you also allow extra time for passing through security in the courthouse," said Debbie.

"What are your federal guidelines for tax evasion? Three years?" asked Wallace.

"That's right."

"Okay. Bottom line, what are you willing to knock off?" inquired Wallace.

"One month."

"I'm sorry. For a second there I thought you said one month," said Wallace.

"I did."

"C'mon, can't you give me more than one month off? Look, I have to sell this to my client. How can I sell this to him when you're not giving him an incentive to plead?" said Wallace.

"Quite frankly, I really don't care whether he takes the plea or not. You see, I have a very strong case that I expect to easily win, unless your client bribes the jury. And, it's a tax lawyer who goes by the name, 'The Tax Man,' who is on trial for tax evasion. And, last but not least, look at what he did. He intentionally excluded more than eighty five percent of his legal fees from income. Now, how do you think that's going to play out in court before either a jury or a judge?" asked Debbie.

Wallace is in shock. He can't believe that the prosecutor won't budge. Unfortunately for his client, he has no leverage because he will not litigate this case.

"Is that your final answer?" asked Wallace, as if he were participating in a popular television game show.

"The offer today is one month off sentencing. The offer expires after twenty four hours. I suggest you get in touch with your client and let him know that he has until tomorrow to accept the plea bargain. Otherwise, I'll see him and you in court," said Debbie, who was not aware of Wallace's aversion to appearing in court.

***

"What did you say she offered?" asked Stanley, who couldn't believe what he just heard.

"You heard me right. Ten years," Wallace lied.

"Ten years?" Stanley cried out, as if he had been sentenced to death.

"Relax, Stan. I negotiated it down to less than three years. It wasn't easy, but that's why you're paying me five hundred bucks an hour."

"I'm practically paying you a king's ransom and the best you could do was get me three years in the slammer?" exclaimed an irate Stanley.

"Stan, it's technically less than three years. But the important thing is, I didn't just get you a deal. I've presented you with a gift. I got you an offer that with time off for good behavior, you'll be out in less than two years," replied Wallace.

Stanley reconsidered the offer and concluded that it really wasn't that bad. With time off for good behavior, he'll be out in a couple of years as opposed to rotting away in a federal prison for the next decade.

"Make the call. I'll take the offer," Stanley told Wallace, whom he now regarded as a brilliant negotiator.

***

The day after Ben Newman's infomercial appeared on cable television, he received more than three hundred telephone calls from potential clients who required his services. After running the infomercial over a three day period, Ben had almost one thousand potential clients. In total, Ben was asked to prepare more than seven hundred tax returns, represent almost one hundred clients in pending tax audits and collection disputes, and provide tax planning advice to more than a hundred others.

Ben did not expect this kind of a response so soon. In light of this reaction to his infomercial, there was no way Ben could handle this volume of work by himself. Now, "The New Tax Man" in town had to hire qualified associates. This meant Ben needed to retain a search firm to interview prospective candidates.

In the meantime, Ben decided to start preparing tax returns until he could hire some assistants to perform this function. When Ben told Nancy about how much work he needed to do, she immediately reminded him that he no longer worked for the IRS and did not have to grill every client about every little aspect of their lives. In other words, not everyone is a crook.

"And honey, try to keep this in mind. The clients who are paying you to help them, deserve the benefit of the doubt."

Ben is now taking this sage advice to heart.

CHAPTER 22

Wallace didn't waste any time calling Debbie Macht. Wallace decided that with the clock ticking away, he needed to act quickly so Stanley doesn't have a change of heart. Wallace has learned his lesson that allowing clients to think on their own is not a good idea.

Approximately ten years ago, Wallace had a client who was told that the prosecutor would accept a guilty plea that would mandate a prison sentence of thirteen years.

The client had second thoughts about accepting a plea bargain and rejected the offer as he was willing to take his chances at trial. Since Wallace finds litigation to be a nuisance, he faked an illness so that he would not have to appear in court. In court, the client waived his right to counsel and before the jury was chosen, had managed to convince the prosecutor to offer a term of eleven years. The prosecutor agreed to do so since he was actually willing to offer a ten year sentence had Wallace asked for ten years.

Debbie prepared the Plea Agreement and a copy has been faxed to Wallace, who called Stanley into his office so that he can read it in its entirety. Stanley has been told he must sign the faxed copy and return it by fax to Debbie by 3 pm that day. The originals have been mailed out and should be received in the next few days.

As Stanley read the Plea Agreement, Wallace cautioned him to pay careful attention to the Statement of Facts. When Stanley completed his reading assignment, Wallace instructed him to read the declaration before signing the Plea Agreement. Stanley read the declaration aloud for Wallace's benefit even though Wallace has already committed the language to memory.

"I have read this agreement and carefully reviewed every part of it with my attorney. I understand it and I voluntarily agree to it. Specifically, I have reviewed the Factual and Advisory Guidelines Stipulation with my attorney, and I do not wish to change any part of it. I understand this Plea Agreement, and I voluntarily agree to it. I am completely satisfied with the representation of my attorney," Stanley read aloud.

After Stanley signed the Plea Agreement, Wallace signed his name under the declaration that read, "To my knowledge, his decision to enter into this agreement is an informed and voluntary one."

"Stan, you've made a wise decision," said Wallace, who had already collected his legal fee in advance.

"When do I have to appear in court?" asked Stanley.

"I would think in the next week or so. Then, you'll have some time before you actually have to surrender to the authorities. In the meantime, I suggest you get your affairs in order to make the transition as smooth as possible," advised Wallace.

"And what happens to my law license?" asked Stanley.

"You can flush it down the toilet. You won't be practicing law ever again," replied Wallace.

"What can I do to earn a living when I get out of prison?" asked Stanley who was thinking long term and not focusing on spending the next three years of his life in a prison cell.

"You got lots of time to plan for that, pal."

***

Alex Talbot is celebrating his fifty eighth birthday by enjoying a night out on the town with his attractive wife, Karen. Alex and Karen have been married for twenty years and by all accounts, it is a perfect marriage. Star college quarterback married the college team's prettiest cheerleader and went on to become the president.

The marriage is a storybook tale of tremendous personal accomplishment and good fortune. While Alex pursued a highly successful political career after football, Karen has established a reputation as one of the most popular interior decorators in the Washington metropolitan area. In fact, Karen is in such demand by clients that it is often easier to get an appointment to meet with the former president.

The Talbots have three children who have planned professional careers in law and medicine. With multiple residences, many friends to entertain and a jet set lifestyle that keeps them busy, the Talbots are constantly on the move.

When Karen excused herself to powder her nose, Alex made a phone call to Ralph Adler. "Were you able to take care of that favor for me?"

"It's done. I've mailed you a copy of the statement that shows you purchased corn futures. If questions arise, you can say the firm inadvertently failed to record this on your account statement and instead, mistakenly showed it as a transfer to an incorrect account," said Ralph.

"Good work, Ralph. Your check is in the mail. Make sure you deposit the money in an overseas account under a nominee. You don't want the IRS to be able to trace the money to you or me," said Alex.

"I'm more worried about the SEC if my Compliance Department finds out what I've done."

"Ralph. Listen to me. Your compliance people won't know anything about it because you haven't changed my account. As long as the agent doesn't talk to your compliance people, you're safe," replied Alex. "Karen's coming back. We'll talk later," said the former president as he terminated the call.

In actuality, Alex's wife was not returning to their table at that exact moment. Instead, Alex placed another call on his cell phone and said, "I need you to take care of a problem for me."

When Karen returned to the table in time for dessert, she asked her husband, "Everything okay?"

"Couldn't be better, sweetheart."

***

Trent Stratford, III is considered to be one of the best tax lawyers in Baltimore. As a former Acting Chief Counsel of the IRS and currently the senior tax partner in his law firm, Trent Stratford is well known and highly respected by members of the tax community.

Indeed, Trent Stratford is a senior statesman among local tax lawyers. Tonight, Trent is burning the midnight oil because he must represent a client in a tax audit tomorrow morning. The reason why Trent is putting in long hours is because the agent in question is Louie Lipschitz.

Louie has had a number of cases with Trent Stratford. None of the audits turned out well for the lawyer's clients. Cognizant of this fact, this prolific lawyer intends to be fully prepared for the little guy.

Unable to continue with the Alex Talbot case until the summoned information has been given to him, Louie has set aside this case for the time being. The next case in his inventory for immediate disposition is a case that Louie has considered to be a waste of his valuable time.

Louie informed Trent that he intends to address the sizable cash donations made by Jeff Waldman to the University of Maryland. Trent is puzzled that Louie seemed concerned about the donations because the five million dollar pledge was paid in a timely manner.

Trent has verified that the University of Maryland is a qualifying charitable organization in accordance with section 501(c)(3) of the Internal Revenue Code. Trent has also verified that the funds were used for the charitable purpose for which it was designated. Thus, Trent is unsure where Louie intends to take this but knows from past experience with the agent that if the munchkin intends to question something, there is a problem.

When Louie arrives for the meeting at 9 am, he was made to feel right at home by the office staff. Louie has already turned down offers of refreshments and lap dances from the secretaries but was anxious to generate some orders from his merchandise catalogue. However, he sensed that this may not be the right time to solicit sales, particularly if the audit does not go well for the lawyer.

Trent greeted Louie as if they were long lost friends. Clearly, Trent is not a long lost friend. While polite and professional to Louie, it is no secret that Trent feels uncomfortable in the presence of an IRS agent who has crushed his nuts in every one of his cases.

Trent decided to assert himself by saying, "Agent Lipschitz, I understand that you have expressed concerns as to the validity of the five million dollar contribution that Mr. Waldman made to the University of Maryland. What seems to be the problem with the donation?"

"A charitable contribution is synonymous with the term 'gift' and by that, we are talking about a voluntary transfer of property made with no expectation of a 'quid pro quo' arrangement," said Louie.

"Your definition is correct. And I am not aware that there was a 'quid pro quo' arrangement," replied the lawyer. "Are you suggesting that there was a 'quid pro quo' arrangement?"

"I believe that the facts indicate there was a 'quid pro quo' arrangement," replied Louie.

Trent has now placed his fingertips on his forehead as if he is exorcising a migraine headache to vacate his head. He finally looked over to Louie and said, "Please tell me how this is possible."

"Mr. Waldman negotiated several features in a side agreement when he pledged the five million dollars. One, he insisted on having his name placed on a new football stadium that is currently under construction. Two, he had the college pay him an annual fee of fifty thousand dollars for advisory services provided by a public relations firm that he owns. Third, the college is required to purchase athletic clothing from a sports apparel company that he owns," said the munchkin.

Upon hearing this, Trent looked ill.

"Are you okay?" asked Louie.

"I'm just a little surprised that I'm hearing this for the first time. My client did not reveal any of this to me," said the lawyer who looked sick to his stomach.

"I sense that he negotiated the terms of these side deals on his own. University officials have intimated this to me," said Louie.

"Are all of the donations to be disallowed?" asked the lawyer, who was clearly perturbed upon learning what his client did without his knowledge.

"What I am willing to do is allow a deduction as a business expense for the amounts equal to the financial benefit derived from the payment. Thus, the allowable deduction will be equal to the advisory fees and revenue from the sports apparel. The charitable donation is out," said Louie.

"That's a big hit. He'll lose out on the charitable contribution and get very little benefit on the business side. But my client has no one to blame but himself," replied the lawyer.

"My sentiments exactly, counselor."

***

The same morning, Edward Smith stopped by his partner's office to chat.

"Larry, you looked troubled," said Smith. "Is it the Alex Talbot case?"

"It's more like the Alex Talbot mess," replied Donnelly.

"Let's not be too harsh on him. It's entirely possible there's nothing to this business with the two transfers of five thousand dollars each," said Smith.

"Do you honestly believe that? You saw his reaction when he learned of the summons. He went ape shit. Why would he react that way if the undisclosed account wasn't his?" asked Donnelly.

"I know. It does seem a bit odd."

"Have you heard from Alex since we last advised him not to challenge the summons?" asked Donnelly.

"No. We have a few more days to go before the time period for filing a petition lapses. He's been advised of the deadline to file. I suggest we wait. Once the deadline for filing has expired, the summoned information will have to be submitted to the IRS. Then Agent Lipschitz will let us know whether there's a problem. If the bank account belongs to Alex, he has a lot of explaining to do," declared Smith.

"Why the worried look on your face?" Donnelly asked his law partner.

"Why did he have to appoint me Chief Counsel?"

"Don't forget that he sent a lot of prominent clients to us when we started this firm. Alex was instrumental in our success, in case you forgot," exclaimed Donnelly.

"And that's what bothers me. He's been almost like a Godfather to us," said Smith.

"Let's hope I don't wake up tomorrow and find a dead horse's head in my bed," remarked Donnelly.

"Or find ourselves buried in concrete," added Smith.

CHAPTER 23

The following day, The Washington Post reported that Ralph Adler, a financial advisor at Morgan Stanley was killed in a car accident. Upon seeing the article in the newspaper, Alex Talbot called out to Karen who was making a pot of coffee.

"Honey, do you remember Ralph Adler, my financial advisor over at Morgan Stanley?" said Alex.

"Of course. I've met him several times. I even know his wife, Evelyn. Why?"

"According to The Post, he was killed yesterday morning on his way to the office," replied Alex.

"Oh my God," exclaimed Karen. "What happened?"

"From what The Post is reporting, the accident took place approximately two miles from Ralph's residence as he was leaving for work that morning. Apparently, the braking system in the car failed as witnesses reported seeing the car swerve into a tree. According to the news account, he later died while being transported to Washington General Hospital," said Alex.

"That's terrible. I think we ought to send a condolence card to his family and call a caterer to have some meals sent to his family's home. Does the paper say when the funeral service will be held"" asked Karen.

"No."

"I'll call and find out. I think we should both plan on attending the funeral," said Karen.

"Of course. It's the very least we can do," said Alex, who hadn't even bothered to send his late friend the one million dollars he was promised

***

Later that day, Alex Talbot took a nap. Alex enjoyed taking afternoon naps because it gave him an opportunity to think before he dozed off. With Ralph Adler either not around to explain the discrepancies in the firm's records or eventually confess that he was asked by the former president to create a false statement to conceal Alex Talbot's ownership of a secret foreign bank account, Alex felt as if a huge boulder was taken off of his shoulder.

Alex knew his Bank of America account was still a potential problem. Alex considered calling a friend at Bank of America who could bail him out by having documents created to explain the mistake on his account statement. Although hesitant to use the same excuse that it was a mistake by a financial institution, the former president felt that he had no other choice.

"Gary, how are you? It's Alex Talbot."

"Alex, it's good to hear your voice. How have you been?" asked Gary Mandel.

"Great. How about you and your family?"

"Good. We're all good. I haven't talked to you in almost a year. You still flying all over the world doing business deals?" asked Gary.

Not like I used to do. I just turned fifty eight and I'm slowing down. Karen thinks I'm ready for a retirement home. Maybe she's thinking about trading me in for a new model with less mileage," replied the former president.

"I seriously doubt that. Anyhow, what can I do for you?" asked Gary. Gary Mandel was a Senior Vice President at Bank of America and a longtime friend of Alex Talbot.

"Gary, I have a very sensitive problem that I need help with and I'm hoping you can help. Of course, I don't want to do anything that can cause problems for you so if you feel that this may be a hardship for you, please say so," said Alex.

"Alex, what is it?" asked Gary who was concerned that his friend had a problem.

"One of my account statements references a transfer to another bank account. It happens to be a foreign bank account that is not in my name, but which I have an interest in and did not disclose to the IRS. This is embarrassing for me because I should have known better. An IRS agent has issued a summons to your bank and wants to know the identity of the owner of the foreign bank," said Alex.

"I see."

"According to my lawyers, the bank is required to disclose this information to the investigating agent," said Alex.

"That's correct. The bank must comply with the summons."

"And I want the bank to comply. However, what I was hoping you could do for me, as a personal favor, would be to create a statement that acknowledges your bank made an error on my account statement by showing the transfer of funds from my checking account," said Alex.

"I don't understand," said the banker.

"It's important that the IRS not know that I had an interest in a foreign bank account. If you could have the bank provide me with some kind of statement that acknowledges the transfer as being a mistake on my bank account, I think I can square it with the IRS," explained the former president.

"Alex, you're not suggesting that Bank of America participate in a plan to deceive the IRS, are you? We could be charged with obstruction of justice or conspiracy," exclaimed the banker.

"Listen to me Gary. I would never put you in a position of personal risk. If you are uncomfortable with this, I understand. So, forget I said anything about this to you," said Alex.

"Alex, I'm really sorry I can't help you," said Gary, who had no idea how sorry he was about to be.

"Gary, forget it. It's not a problem you need to worry about. I apologize for bothering you with this problem."

After Alex hung up the phone, he placed a call to someone in his employ whose specialty is dealing with sensitive problems. This was a phone call Alex was not particularly happy about because it meant that a friend would have to be dealt with in an unkind manner. In addition, there would be a sizable fee for the execution of this problem. Alex explained the problem and asked for a second favor, which his underling agreed to do.

"I want you to make arrangements with someone whom you trust to have false documents prepared for me that will show the transfer was a mistake on my account statement. You'll have to deposit five thousand dollars back into my account going back to the same month. Then, you'll have to withdraw the same five thousand dollars at the same time. Show it as if I had purchased a CD or something, and after you've done it, I'll give you the five thousand dollars back," said Alex. "You're a former Secret Service Agent. Call in a favor with someone you trust at the bank and make sure that person is discrete and can be trusted," explained Alex Talbot.

"Next, I want Gary Mandel fired from his job on charges of sexual harassment of a female subordinate. As soon as he's terminated, make it appear that he committed suicide in disgrace. I want this to happen by next week, so get moving on this now," ordered the former president.

***

Debbie Macht has moved quickly on Stanley's Plea Agreement, which has been entered with the court and a date has been set for the parties to appear. Stanley Scherr is now one step closer to taking up residency at a federal prison.

Timothy Bell's Plea Agreement is also in the pipeline. However, due to its factual complexity, Timmy's plea bargain will take time to conclude.

IRS and Justice Department officials are ecstatic that these two felons are going off to prison for tax evasion. While these officials are doing victory laps in the hallways, Louie Lipschitz is plugging away at the Alex Talbot case.

By now, Louie has completed his preliminary review of the deductions claimed as business expenses by Alex Talbot. Louie has set up the largest deductions as audit issues on the basis that these expenses are not ordinary and necessary in connection with carrying on a trade or business for profit. Louie has noted that none of the activities claimed as businesses appear to be viable entities motivated by profit given the fact that little or no income has been reported.

The total deductions being disallowed are in excess of five million dollars for the three years in issue. This will significantly impact the net operating loss deductions being claimed and will reduce the refund claims sought by Alex Talbot.

Needless to say, neither Alex Talbot nor his lawyers will be pleased with Louie's tentative findings. The first conference to review these adjustments should be spirited.

***

Word has gotten out about Ben Newman's tax practice.

Roger Smith was having a conversation with Tom Collins when Dave Belz happened to pass by the office. "Have you guys heard the latest?" Belz asked Roger and Tom.

"What's that?" Tom asked one of his managers.

"Ben Newman has opened a tax practice," remarked Belz.

"Yeah, we know," replied Roger.

"Did you know that he reportedly has more than one thousand clients?" replied Belz.

"How is that possible?" responded Tom.

"I have no idea. And the word on the street is that he just hired three CPAs from other accounting firms to handle the compliance work and is now interviewing tax lawyers to fill several other positions for tax planning work," said Belz.

"What!" exclaimed Roger.

"This practice of his has taken off like you wouldn't believe. He filmed this infomercial for late night cable and right away, he has clients up to his eyeballs," replied Belz.

"Jesus. Who knew? Well, I'm glad he was able to land on his feet so soon," said Tom.

"Well, I don't want to sound like Nostradamus, but I see problems down the road with Newman. He claimed in his infomercial that he has all this institutional knowledge and knows how to circumvent the audit process. I have this feeling in the pit of my stomach that Ben Newman is someday going to morph into Stanley Scherr," predicted Belz.

"Jesus, that's all we need. The second coming of Stanley Scherr," Tom complained to his managers.

***

Stanley Scherr has finally told his mother that he is getting ready to go to prison.

"To visit a client?" asked Mrs. Scherr.

"No."

"To see a new client?" asked Mrs. Scherr.

"No."

"Then why would you be making a visit to prison?"

"Mom, I'm not making a visit to prison. I'm going to prison," said Stanley.

"Huh? Stan, what are you talking about?"

"I'm in the process of going off to prison," said Stanley.

"Okay. How long is your trip going to take?" asked Mrs. Scherr.

"About three years."

"That's some trip."

CHAPTER 24

Today Stanley Scherr must appear in United States District Court to formally enter his guilty plea to tax evasion charges. The Plea Agreement has been entered with the court and the judge has reviewed the agreement. Before the judge approves the plea bargain, he will ask Stanley a few questions.

"Mr. Scherr, do you understand the implications to entering a guilty plea?" asked the judge.

"Yes, Your Honor."

"And your plea is made voluntarily?" asked the judge.

"Yes."

"Were threats or promises made that forced you to enter a guilty plea?" asked the judge.

"No, Your Honor."

"Have you been under the influence of drugs or alcohol that would impair your ability to make an informed decision?" asked the judge.

"No sir."

"And you fully understand the charges alleged against you?" asked the judge.

"Yes sir."

"And you understand that your sentence will be thirty five months in prison and you will be liable for paying a court imposed fine of five hundred dollars?" asked the judge.

"Yes."

"You also understand that one of the terms and conditions of the Plea Agreement specifically provides that you must cooperate with the IRS and you will be required to satisfy all civil tax liabilities the IRS determines you owe with respect to these tax years?" asked the judge.

"Yes, Your Honor."

"Please state the factual basis of your plea for the court," said the judge.

At this point of the proceeding, Judge Harold Leon Patton is about to give Stanley the opportunity to describe how he systematically engineered a tax evasion scheme that he knew was illegal. Judge Patton is a soft spoken, elderly District Court Judge who is sometimes sympathetic to defendants about to be sentenced.

However, Judge Patton has carefully reviewed the file and is well aware of the specific facts in this case. If Stanley is hopeful of deriving sympathy from Judge Patton, he is looking at the wrong judge.

For the next ten minutes, Stanley Scherr rambled on about how he intentionally recorded retainer fees in an escrow account and excluded the fees from his taxable income. Finally, Stanley admitted that his behavior was reckless and inexcusable, a confession that was especially painful for Stanley. By the time

Stanley was finished with his admission of guilt, the reporter for the Baltimore Sun who was sitting in a back row, had enough material for a featured story titled, "The Rise and Fall of The Tax Man."

With the proceeding over, Stanley was taken into custody by the US Marshals. Not a single member of Stanley's family was in court to see him escorted out of the courtroom for processing.

Wallace made a rare appearance in court only because he didn't have to argue the case. Wallace said very little and made it a point to shake hands with Debbie and to congratulate her on a hard fought case, which Debbie thought was odd considering there was nothing hard fought about this case. Wallace then offered a handshake and pat on the back to Stanley, wishing him well in his future endeavors.

Apparently, Wallace has missed his calling. With the kind words, handshakes to all, a pat on the back and well wishes to go around, Wallace should be either a UN Ambassador or television game show host rather than a criminal defense lawyer who prefers not to have to appear in court.

***

The summoned information has finally been provided to the IRS. Louie has been waiting more than one month for the information and now he has the names of the owner of the mysterious Swiss bank account.

"What the hell is International Business Solutions and who the hell are Hans Schumann and Klaus Bergmeister?" wondered Louie.

"That's what Bank of America and Morgan Stanley reported?" asked Roger.

"Yeah. Take a look," Louie said as he passed the documents to his boss who had walked by the work table where Louie had taken up residency.

"What do you make of this?" asked Roger.

"I'll need to look into this further before I come to any conclusions," said Louie.

"Louie, I don't have a problem with you conducting an investigation. Just don't get your brother-in-law involved in whatever you plan to do," Roger.

"Hey. Give me some credit. I happen to know some people over at Treasury and the FBI. Maybe I'll hit pay dirt."

"And maybe you'll get struck by lightning," Roger cautioned him.

***

Louie has a lot of contacts at Treasury and the FBI. After making a few phone calls to some of his contacts to get information about International Business Solutions and its principal officers, Louie went back to doing more investigative work from his end. Louie has learned that this company does not file federal income tax returns and its corporate officers do not file federal tax returns either.

After waiting several days, the only information that Louie's contacts discovered is that International Business Solutions is a

Swiss corporation that is engaged in the business of brokering deals with foreign governments.

Louie then went back to Alex Talbot's tax returns to see if there is a connection to International Business Solutions. Unfortunately, there is no connection whatsoever.

Louie then requested more IRS transcripts. Louie has now asked for every transcript that can cross reference 1099 information. Again, there is nothing that ties Alex Talbot to International Business Solutions.

Curious as to why a transaction appears on Alex Talbot's bank statement that connects him to International Business Solutions, Louie decided to contact Bank of America and requested clarification as to the memo reference on Alex Talbot's bank statement. Specifically, Louie asked for any and all documentation that pertains to the transfer of funds from Alex Talbot's bank account to International Business Solutions' bank account. Louie then sought the same information from Morgan Stanley.

***

It has taken several weeks for Louie to receive replies from Morgan Stanley and Bank of America. In order to respond to the IRS's request for information, both Morgan Stanley and Bank of America had to retrieve this information from its official administrative files that were created when the accounts were opened by Alex Talbot. Unfortunately for Louie, there was not a lot of information that was available in these files.

According to Morgan Stanley, it was Alex Talbot who authorized the transfer of five thousand dollars to International Business

Solutions. In addition, Bank of America determined that it was Alex Talbot who authorized the transfer of the same amount to International Business Solutions.

The next step for Louie is to bring this to the attention of Alex Talbot's legal representatives. A conference has been scheduled later in the week to discuss the discrepancies.

It was now time for Louie, Roger and Tom to see the Chief of the Examination Division for another status report.

"Louie, where do we stand on the Alex Talbot audit?" asked the Chief of Exam, who was looking forward to hearing his best revenue agent say, "I'm almost finished with the audit."

"According to Bank of America and Morgan Stanley, it was Alex Talbot who authorized the account transfers. However, the summoned information shows that the owner of the Swiss bank account is a Swiss corporation that has no apparent connection to Talbot. Its principal officers are Swiss citizens. My IDRS research has come up empty on cross referencing everything we have on file. That's all I have for you," explained Louie.

"When do you meet next with the lawyers?" asked the Exam Chief.

"In a few days."

"Keep me posted," said the Exam Chief, who, with a nod of his head, let them know that the meeting was adjourned.

As Roger and Tom left with Louie, they each wondered where this case was going.

***

Today is the first time that Louie will have met with Alex Talbot's lawyers. When Louie arrived at the office of Donnelly & Smith, he was immediately impressed. The office is tastefully decorated with furniture that you would never see in a federal government office building. Louie was warmly greeted by an attractive and pleasant receptionist with a charming English accent. This is also something you will never find in a federal government office building.

Louie has been offered coffee, tea, hot chocolate, pastries, bagels, and fruit. Had the little guy asked for a back rub, the law firm probably had someone on call who could give him a massage.

Louie would like to bring this to the attention of IRS management because these are amenities that are not being offered in the Examination Division. Louie can just imagine the response from Tom, who might say, "If you want these amenities, go to work for Donnelly & Smith."

The lawyers did not keep Louie waiting, which is an indication of the respect that they had for the munchkin.

When they first saw Louie hop off the sofa, they were surprised at the little guy's lack of size. Looking down at the revenue agent, they let him know that it was good to finally meet him and they looked forward to working with him throughout the audit.

Louie fully expects the two lawyers will be a challenge for him. The lawyers are extremely knowledgeable in the field of taxation and will zealously defend their client to the best of their abilities. This audit will not be easy.

When everyone was seated in the conference room, Louie inquired if Alex Talbot had planned to attend. Smith informed Louie that while the former president had wanted to, he was unable to set aside time for the meeting because of other long-standing commitments.

Louie started the conference by disclosing the content of the summoned information. In response, the lawyers provided Louie with documents given to them by their client.

"Agent Lipschitz, we were only recently given these documents by Alex. Alex has told us that when he reviewed his brokerage account statement as well as his bank statement and saw the two transactions that you have questioned, he contacted his stockbroker and his banker to inquire about the two transactions," explained Donnelly.

"These documents offer confirmation that the transactions were mistakes on the part of Morgan Stanley and Bank of America. In all honesty, we don't know the particulars as to how the errors evolved. I suppose you may want to investigate further if you feel it's necessary," said Smith.

In light of these documents, Louie felt as if he had been punched in the stomach with brass knuckles. With both institutions now asserting the transfers were errors, Louie had to rethink his case.

"I may want to follow up with your client's financial advisor and banker before I make a final decision," replied Louie.

Only Louie didn't know that both men were dead.

CHAPTER 25

The remaining issues involved adjustments that the lawyers were happy to talk about. Louie addressed concerns that the alleged business activities were not operated with the requisite profit motive. Thus, Louie asserted that the losses claimed are not permissible.

In contrast, the lawyers argued that their client was, in fact, actively involved in different business activities and was now earning substantial fees. Thus, the initial expenses that he incurred were ordinary and necessary in operating the businesses. At the minimum, the deductions should be allowed, even if allowed in a subsequent tax year.

The lawyers told Louie that they will obtain additional information from their client and submit a Brief on the subject.

After Louie left to return to Baltimore, the lawyers walked back to their respective offices. Before Donnelly reached his office, he turned to his partner and said, "I'm not sure about those documents."

"Me too," said Smith. "I didn't get a chance to carefully review his account statements. I'm relying on one of our associates who looked everything over and felt that Talbot's explanation may be legitimate. If Lipschitz discovers that our client gave us bogus documents, our credibility with him is shot."

"Ed, our client is a former senator and president. That should carry some weight," said Donnelly.

"Larry, with his record, he's got serious credibility issues," warned Smith.

Shortly after Louie sent a letter to Ralph Adler, he received a reply letter from Ira Haynes, who was the Branch Manager of the Morgan Stanley branch office where the late Ralph Adler had once worked. When Louie got to the part of the letter where Ralph Adler had died in a car accident, he immediately sensed something was wrong.

Louie called Ira Haynes to discuss the Morgan Stanley document that he was given by Alex Talbot's lawyers. Without discussing any tax matters or disclosing anything that pertained to the audit, Louie asked Haynes if he had a duplicate copy of this document either in the client's file or Back Office file.

"Let me check, Agent Lipschitz and I will call you right back," said the Branch Manager.

After about thirty minutes had passed, Louie heard back from Ira Haynes.

"Agent Lipschitz, I do not have a copy in the Back Office file, which is the client's official file. However, I did find in Ralph's files, a duplicate copy of the same document you faxed to me," said Ira.

"Why wouldn't it be in the Back Office files?" asked Louie.

"I don't know. That's the official office file."

"Okay, let's talk about the transfer. If it was an error, would it have been handled this way?" asked Louie.

"Not really. The mistake would be corrected by a reversal in order to cancel it out. That cancellation would be done as soon as possible so that the transaction does not appear on the client's account statement," explained Haynes.

"That's what I thought. So, the five thousand dollars was re-deposited?" asked Louie.

"No. I don't see the re-deposit."

"So, what happened to the five thousand dollars that the client was due?" asked Louie.

"I don't know. It never made it on to the account statement, which is very strange," admitted the Branch Manager.

"This business about the corn futures is suspicious. Did the client actually purchase corn futures?" asked Louie.

"I can't be sure. The document you faxed to me indicates that he did, but our Back Office file says he did not. If he had purchased corn futures, his cost basis would be shown on the account statement and it is not there. Also, as you know, the transaction would be reported on the client's 1099 statement. I have the 1099 statement that was issued and it does not appear on the 1099 statement that we filed with the IRS. This is very strange, Agent Lipschitz," said Haynes.

"According to the document that I was given, the five thousand dollar corn futures contract was worthless after twenty one days," said Louie.

"Yes, that's correct."

"I assume that it is your firm's policy to have clients sign certain documents before they are allowed to buy and sell instruments such as options, puts and calls, as well as commodity futures?" asked Louie.

"That's correct. All clients must sign documents before they can enter into these types of transactions because of the significant element of risk," replied Ira.

"I'd like you to check the Back Office file and see if Alex Talbot signed the requisite forms to purchase commodity futures," said Louie.

After examining the Back Office file documents that he had on his desk, Ira Haynes said, "I don't see it here."

"Could he have purchased commodity futures without signing the requisite consent forms?" asked Louie.

"I suppose it's somehow possible, but it's a violation that would be caught by our Compliance Officers and the infraction would be part of the employee's performance record. The violation is not in any of the files," said Haynes. "I really don't know what to make of this, Agent Lipschitz."

"Mr. Haynes, you've been very helpful and I appreciate the time you've given me. I have one request of you before I let you go."

"What's that?"

"I would like you to provide me with an Affidavit that spells out everything of relevance that you've told me. If you like, you can fax me a rough draft first and I'll look it over," said Louie.

"Our office procedures require that the firm's Legal Department first review and approve the Affidavit before I can send it to you. I'll send it to you as soon as it's been approved," Haynes said.

Louie was now making real progress.

***

The next day, Louie received a phone call from an official at Bank of America. The bank was in the process of formally responding to his request regarding official bank documents that indicated the transfer was reported in error on Alex Talbot's account statement.

"Agent Lipschitz, this is Mary Sue Sloan. I'm a VP in the Customer Relations Department and I'll be coordinating your request for clarification regarding the transfer you have asked about. At this time, we haven't been able to reconcile the document you showed us with official bank records," said Mary Sue.

"Ms. Sloan, can you tell me if five thousand dollars was re-deposited into Alex Talbot's bank account once the alleged bank error was discovered?"

"That's a tough question. You see, I can't find it anywhere in the bank's records," admitted Mary Sue.

"Would I be correct if I said that the document that I showed you was created after the fact?" said Louie.

"Agent Lipschitz, I would agree with you. It appears that someone at the bank created a false document," said Mary Sue.

"Ms. Sloan, I'll need you to provide me with an Affidavit that addresses what we just discussed. How soon can you have this for me?" asked Louie.

"I'll get started on it right now. However, it will have to be reviewed by an attorney in the bank's Legal Department before I can send it to you," said Mary Sue.

"Please see about getting it to me as soon as possible."

***

Today is the first day Ben Newman has returned to the Federal Building since his dismissal. Ben is soon going to discover how times have changed.

When Ben entered the Federal Building, he was instructed by the screeners to prepare for a full body scan, followed by a strip search. Apparently, the only thing the screeners failed to do was have Ben turn his head and cough twice. After getting dressed, Ben was given the results of his diagnostic test and advised to go to the front desk where he can pick up his nutritional report to improve his diet.

As Ben proceeded to the bay of elevators, he wondered if the security guards remembered him from his having worked in the building for so many years. When no one struck up a conversation with him, Ben assumed that the IRS used some form of mind control on the guards so they would not say anything to Ben, such as hello or nice to see you.

Ben has a meeting with Alice Fisher and wisely decided not to mention that he used to work for the IRS. Letting someone know that you were forced to resign a government job because of employee misconduct is something that should not be disclosed because it is unlikely to impress anyone.

"Ms. Fisher, I've brought some of the documentation that you've asked to see."

"Why only some and not all?" asked the office auditor.

"My client was unable to provide me with all of the documents," Ben replied.

"What's the problem?" asked Alice.

"My client has difficulty keeping track of her records. She is challenged in this respect," Ben said.

"What did you bring with you?" asked Alice.

"I have copies of school report cards," Ben said.

"That's it? Copies of school report cards?" Alice questioned Ben.

"Yes."

"Look Mr. Newman. Here's my concern. Your client is a twenty five year old single parent who earns almost eighteen thousand dollars a year as a nurse's assistant. Ms. Jackson has claimed a total of ten dependents between the ages of nine and one. There are several sets of twins in this group. Ms. Jackson lives in a two bedroom apartment where she claims to raise ten children."

Apparently, it hasn't registered with Ben that it doesn't sound feasible for a single parent earning less than eighteen thousand dollars in a year to be able to support ten children in a two bedroom apartment. Furthermore, to claim that a child the age of one year old is attending the first grade of school is so outrageous that it undermines the client's credibility and does not reflect well on Ben.

"The report cards indicate that the children live with her," Ben said.

"That's another problem I have. I wasn't aware that five of her children under the age of four attended grade school," said Alice.

"I don't follow."

"Five of the children that she claims are hers are under the age of four. Your client has produced copies of report cards that show these children attended grade school. The one year old child attended the first grade and received A's and B's.

"Your client has represented that her two year old child was also in the first grade and earned straight A's. She also claimed that the three year old child was in the second grade while the four year old attended the third grade. Next, we have the four year old twins in the fifth grade. Need I say anything else?" Alice asked Ben.

"I guess not."

"I'm also questioning the authenticity of other claims. The social security numbers that have been provided do not match the Social Security Administration's official records for eight of the ten children. In addition, of the two children who do exist, they were claimed as dependents by another taxpayer who has established having provided more than fifty percent of the child's total support," said Alice.

"Can you share that information with me so that I can disclose this to my client?" asked Ben.

"No. I cannot disclose confidential taxpayer information," replied Alice.

"So, my client is not entitled to any dependents?"

"That's correct. We know that eight of the children do not exist. The two children who do exist live elsewhere. Your client's sister shares the apartment because we know that she used the same address as her residential address on her tax return. Clearly, your client didn't come close to earning nearly enough money to provide for the support of ten young children. You couldn't see that?" asked Alice, who was openly questioning Ben's competency.

"I've been so swamped with other work that I only picked up this case minutes before I met with you. I had no idea that it was this type of situation," Ben answered in a tone of voice that pleaded for mercy.

"For future reference, you should be better prepared before you meet with IRS officials," Alice said as she let Ben know that he would have to elevate his game if he expected to represent clients in future audits.

CHAPTER 26

Louie, Roger and Tom have been invited to see the Chief of Exam to brief him as to the status of the Alex Talbot audit.

"Let's get down to business. What's new with the Alex Talbot case?"

"Talbot's lawyers passed along questionable documents. I don't believe his lawyers did this intentionally. I think they were bamboozled," said Louie.

"I've spoken with officials at Morgan Stanley and Bank of America. I'm convinced that Talbot had more than one person create false documents to cover up the transfers. I'm waiting for Affidavits that will confirm what I've learned," said Louie.

"Who are the officials that conspired with Talbot?" asked the Chief.

"I suspect that it would be the late Ralph Adler who formerly worked at Morgan Stanley, as well as the late Gary Mandel who formerly worked at Bank of America," said Louie.

"They're dead?" asked the Chief.

"Ralph Adler was killed in a car accident near his house. He is believed to have created false brokerage account records to show the transfer was an error by the brokerage firm and created a false statement that reportedly shows Talbot invested five thousand dollars in a commodities contract which went belly up. However,

Talbot never executed the requisite documents to invest in commodities," explained Louie.

"Could this simply be an administrative mix up?" asked the Chief.

"No. There's no official record of Talbot having a cost basis of five thousand dollars in his commodities futures. It's not in the firm's Back Office files which are its official records and there is nothing in the 1099 statements," said Louie.

"Okay, what about the bank?" asked the Chief.

"Gary Mandel spoke with Alex Talbot a few days before he was terminated on a sexual assault charge. The next day he allegedly committed suicide by swallowing an entire bottle of sleeping pills. This makes no sense since his wife told the police that her husband never took sleeping pills. Mandel had a clean employment record and there was nothing in his past that suggested he would behave in such a manner or commit suicide," said Louie.

"How do you know that they spoke?" asked the Chief.

"According to Mandel's wife, he told her he had spoken with Talbot and was concerned about doing something that was improper. He told his wife he turned Talbot down on his request, but didn't go into specifics. The wife said he seemed distressed about the conversation. This is what she told the police," Louie remarked.

"I don't want to know how you discovered all this. What does the bank say about Talbot's claim?" asked the Chief.

"That there's no official record of five thousand dollars having been re-deposited into his account. All we have are statements from Talbot that don't match the bank's records," said Louie.

"Jesus Christ. I never trusted that slimy SOB when he got into politics," said the Chief.

Turning to Roger and Tom, the Chief asked, "You fellas have anything you want to add?"

Both managers shook their heads sideways.

"Louie?"

"I need to know about International Business Solutions. My guess is that Talbot's a nominee owner and that any revenue he's generating from his other business activities is being dumped into this company's Swiss bank account," said Louie.

"Okay, when I talk with the commissioner, I'll let him know that the audit is progressing. We've discovered contradictory information that we need to clarify. Further investigation is necessary," said the Chief.

**

Monte Monroe has been following the news regarding Stanley Scherr's legal difficulties. Monte, who has been practicing law for only two years, saw an opportunity to enrich himself at Stanley's expense.

Monte contacted those clients who were represented by Stanley Scherr in Tax Court. In an introductory letter to each client, Monte informed them that Stanley has been suspended from practice before the IRS for a period of twelve months because it was determined that his conduct did not meet the minimum standards. In other words, Stanley was found to be incompetent.

Monte then informed each person that it appeared that Stanley did not understand basic principles of taxation and cited the article in the Baltimore Sun that quoted the government's trial attorney that Stanley was reckless. Monte concluded his letter by stating that he intends to file suit against Stanley to recover legal fees that Stanley collected for which subpar legal work was performed.

Monte crafted a reasonably clever argument for each client. The thrust of his argument was that each client paid legal fees with the expectation that work was being done by a lawyer who was qualified to represent taxpayers before the IRS. In Stanley's case, he was ill prepared to practice tax law.

Monte's motivation for taking this action was not to serve as a crusader, but rather, to generate legal fees and publicity for his small law practice.

Upon graduation of law school and passing the Bar Exam, Monte applied for an associate's position at virtually every law firm in Baltimore. Of the hundreds of firms where he applied, Monte received only several acknowledgments but no interviews. Having sensed that he was not going to land a position at a law firm, Monte decided to start his own law firm.

Monte was able to obtain a bank loan and used the funds to rent a small office in a downtown office building that should have been condemned by the Housing Department years ago. Monte purchased some furniture at a consignment store for next to nothing. He then recruited his friends and family as clients, which is what most lawyers do when starting a law practice. Slowly, Monte was able to build a small practice out of nothing.

Monte was no legal scholar. In fact, Monte was probably the second worst lawyer in Baltimore. However, Monte's reputation was clearly better than Stanley's reputation. This allowed Monte to make a legitimate claim that Stanley, in essence, stole money from his clients.

After one week, Monte was able to obtain commitments from eleven of the twelve clients who were duped by Stanley Scherr. Monte has now initiated the filing of a lawsuit against Stanley to recover legal fees.

In Stanley's mind, this was the ultimate slap in the face. To be sued by a young upstart lawyer smacked of greed. When Stanley was served with the lawsuit, he exclaimed aloud, "How could another lawyer do this to me?"

CHAPTER 27

Louie has traveled to Washington, D.C. to meet with a few of his contacts at Treasury and the FBI. For Louie to make substantial progress in the Alex Talbot audit, he had to learn more about International Business Solutions. Louie believed that once he could pierce its corporate ownership and show that this Swiss company did business with Alex Talbot, he could build a tax evasion case against the former president.

Today is Timmy's day to appear in court for his plea bargain. Although Louie was not involved in Timmy's case, he was invited to attend the hearing by Debbie Macht and Gary Zimmer. Prior to the hearing, Louie made it a point to stop by Jennifer Lee's office to briefly chat with her.

It was Jennifer Lee who was the lead prosecutor in the refund litigation case that involved jury tampering on the part of Stanley Scherr's client. When Louie witnessed the jury foreman purchasing a luxury car for cash at a car dealership under audit the day after the verdict was announced in court, he knew that Stanley Scherr's client had bribed the jury foreman. Once the DOJ prosecutors were told of this, it didn't take long to obtain bank records and trace the money. After the verdict was quickly set aside, Jennifer let Louie know that she owed him a favor for saving the day.

"Louie, what brings you to Washington today?" asked Jennifer.

"I wanted to stop by and see my favorite prosecutor," said Louie.

"That's sweet. But I sense you have more important things to do," replied the DOJ prosecutor.

"I'm meeting with some of my contacts at Treasury and the FBI to see if they have alternative means of discovering what a certain Swiss company does and who the owners might be," replied Louie. "But first, I'm on my way over to District Court for the Timothy Bell plea hearing. Do you remember that case?"

"Sure. The Criminal Division assigned the case to Debbie Macht and Gary Zimmer."

"They've invited me to attend the plea hearing."

"Just make sure you behave yourself in court," said Jennifer who was aware of the munchkin's reputation.

***

Louie was seated in one of the last rows in the back of the courtroom next to several federal prosecutors who wanted to observe the judicial proceeding.

Sitting several rows in front of Louie were Timmy's parents. Both are sobbing softly. Prior to the hearing, Debbie and Gary had spoken to them and offered their sympathies for their son's misfortune and wished them well under the circumstances.

Before the judge can approve the Plea Agreement, he must ask Timmy a few questions.

"Mr. Bell, do you understand the ramifications to having entered a guilty plea?" asked the judge.

"Yes, Your Honor," said Timmy.

"And your plea is made voluntarily?" asked the judge.

"Yes, Your Honor."

"Were threats or promises made that forced you to enter a guilty plea?" asked the judge.

"No, Your Honor."

"Have you been under the influence of drugs or alcohol that would impair your ability to make an informed decision?" asked the judge.

"No, Your Honor."

"Do you fully understand the charges that have been alleged against you?" asked the judge.

"Yes, Your Honor."

"And you understand that your sentence will be one hundred and forty four months in prison, with time off for good behavior and credit given for time served at the federal correctional facility. In addition, you are personally liable for paying a court imposed fine of two hundred and fifty thousand dollars," said the judge.

"Yes, Your Honor."

"You also understand that one of the terms and conditions of the Plea Agreement specifically provides that you must cooperate with the IRS and you will be required to satisfy all civil tax liabilities the IRS determines you owe with respect to these tax years," said the judge.

"Yes, Your Honor."

"Mr. Bell, please recite the factual basis of your plea for the court," ordered the judge.

For the next hour, Timothy Bell explained how he created foreign corporations such as nominee entities in tax haven countries in order to evade the payment of tax. Timmy's account of how he structured foreign transactions was so riveting that even the judge was mesmerized by Timmy's brilliance.

Timmy had been told by Debbie and Gary that he needed to be specific as to certain factual events. In order to comply with the prosecutors' requests for specificity, Timmy said, "One such immensely profitable foreign entity that I created was the Universal Technology Company, which was incorporated in the Cayman Islands.

"Universal Technology was operated as one of many subsidiaries of Global Technology. This company was engaged in the business of designing computer technology for use in military applications. The military applications might include military defense or even the creation of military weapons. Because of its sensitivity, I couldn't sell it outright to foreign governments. Therefore, Universal Technology needed a middleman to assist in the transactions," explained Timmy.

"International Traffic in Arms Regulations imposes restrictions on the import and export of information and material pertaining to defense and military related technologies." Looking up at the judge, Timmy said, "As you probably know, these items may only be shared with US persons unless a special exemption is authorized by the State Department. All US manufacturers, exporters and brokers of defense articles, defense services or related technical data are required to register with the Department of State," added the defendant.

"It was my understanding that registration is primarily a means to provide the federal government with the necessary information as to who is involved in certain manufacturing and exporting activities. Under these regulations, a US person who wants to export defense and military related items to a foreign person must obtain authorization from the State Department before the export can take place. At no time did I or my corporate entities obtain State Department approval," admitted the defendant.

"Because of the political problems in many of these third world nations, Universal Technology had to utilize the services of a broker who had connections with other world leaders that could act as a middleman," Timmy stated.

As Timmy ever so calmly provided this account, Louie's ears perked up.

"Universal Technology generated over a quarter of a billion dollars in revenue each year. In order to generate this revenue, my former business partner and I agreed to sell the technology to the broker who, in turn, would sell it to the foreign governments. In essence, my partner and I were willing to pay fifty million dollars a year to the broker to assume the risk for brokering illegal sales of computer software technology. My partner and I assumed that a portion of the fifty million dollars was used to bribe foreign leaders," Timmy added.

"When my former business partner and I entered into this arrangement with International Business Solutions in Switzerland, we knew what we were doing was wrong, but we went ahead with the transactions because of the amount of the money involved," acknowledged Timmy.

"Holy shit," yelled Louie as he jumped up from where he was sitting in the back of the courtroom.

"Order in the court," yelled the judge, as he banged the gavel on the bench.

"I need to talk to him right now," yelled Louie as he approached the podium where Timmy was standing.

"No, you don't," said the judge. "The defendant is in the middle of his allocution and he is not to be interrupted. Now return to your seat or I'll have you removed from my courtroom."

"You don't understand. I must talk with Mr. Bell," Louie said.

"Who are you?" asked the judge.

"Louis Lipschitz. I work for the IRS and I have to talk to Mr. Bell before he is sentenced. It's an urgent matter that has implications of critical importance."

"Mr. Lipschitz, you have just disrupted this hearing and for that, I'm citing you for contempt. Kindly take your seat in the back and refrain from speaking in my courtroom during this proceeding," said the judge.

Louie must have tuned out the judge because he told the DOJ prosecutors that he has to speak in private with Timmy. The judge, upset at being ignored by the little guy, signaled to his bailiff and a Sheriff's deputy to escort Louie from the courtroom.

As Louie was led away, he yelled out to Debbie that he must speak with her immediately. Sensing the urgency in Louie's voice, she requested a brief recess, which the judge reluctantly granted.

Louie's outburst in court will cost him two hundred and fifty dollars. This is an expenditure that will not be reimbursed by the federal government.

Debbie came to Louie's aid and vouched for his questionable state of mind. The Sheriff's deputy agreed to leave the little guy in Debbie's custody and returned to the courtroom.

"What in the hell was all that about? Have you lost your mind?" said Debbie to the little guy left in her custody.

"Debbie. Listen up. I'm auditing Alex Talbot's tax returns. I have...."

"The former president?" Debbie interrupted Louie before he could finish his sentence.

"Yep. I'm investigating a connection to transfers to a foreign bank account that he has not disclosed. He provided me with false documents to cover up his interest in a Swiss company identified as International Business Solutions, which owns the Swiss bank account in question.

"Holy shit," exclaimed Debbie.

Louie proceeded to bring Debbie up to speed on his case. At least ten minutes lapsed before Louie had finally finished recounting the relevant facts.

"So, you think Alex Talbot had his stockbroker murdered and made it look like an accident and set up his banker to be fired and then killed? That won't be easy to prove," said Debbie.

"What I think I'll be able to show is that Talbot created International Business Solutions for the purpose of soliciting bribes in order to pay off foreign governments on behalf of Universal Technology. That was my initial suspicion. Now it all makes sense," said Louie.

"Jesus," muttered Debbie.

"What I believe is that Alex Talbot was operating as an unregistered broker of classified information relating to military and defense articles and services. Talbot played a material role in exporting technical data to foreign governments without first obtaining State Department approval. That is a federal crime that can involve criminal penalties. At the minimum, he can be subject to monetary fines if he provided foreign persons with access to this kind of technical data without State Department authorization," added Louie.

"Bell obviously had the technical data and Talbot had the foreign influence. Bell needed Talbot's connections to foreign leaders to make the sales because he knew that the State Department would never approve the exporting of this kind of technical data to unstable and possibly unfriendly third world countries. Without Talbot's assistance, it would have been extremely difficult for Bell to be able to approach and meet with the leaders of these countries and he couldn't risk the possibility of criminal prosecution by the federal government if he exported this type of technology without approval," concluded Louie based on Bell's admissions.

"Talbot did not report any consulting or advisory fees on his tax returns. And, he failed to disclose his interest in International Business Solutions. He concealed his ownership of a foreign bank account. He had several people murdered to prevent them from disclosing what he did. I'd be willing to bet that he probably pocketed most of the money that was paid to him by Bell and got the contracts for Universal Technology on the cheap," added the little guy.

"Jesus Christ," reiterated Debbie.

"I have to meet with Bell to find out how much was paid to Talbot. I'll need this information to write up my report and refer the case criminally," said Louie.

"Louie, do you know how long I've been sitting here with you?" said Debbie as she glanced at her watch. "I've got to get back in the courtroom," as she quickly got up to leave.

Before going back into the courtroom, Debbie turned to Louie and said, "Do not move from this spot. I will come get you when the hearing is over."

When Debbie returned to the courtroom, she heard the judge formally accept Timmy's Plea Agreement.

"What happened while I was gone," Debbie whispered to Gary.

"The judge waited five minutes. When you didn't come back, he started without you. Timothy was told to continue with his stipulation of the facts. When he was finished, the judge accepted the Plea Agreement and returned Timothy to his cell. You didn't really miss much," said Gary.

"Well, you certainly did," replied Debbie.

CHAPTER 28

While Debbie and Gary returned to their office to inform their boss that they will need Timothy Bell's assistance to build a criminal case against Alex Talbot, Louie called his boss with the latest news before he joined the DOJ prosecutors in their office.

Passing Jennifer Lee in the hallway, she stopped him and said, "Louie, didn't I tell you earlier today not to be disruptive in court?"

"Oh yeah, that's right. You did."

"And you didn't behave yourself. How much did that set you back?" asked Jennifer, who already knew the amount of the fine and everything that transpired in court from talking to her fellow prosecutors.

"Two fifty, but I'm thinking about filing an appeal with the judge to get him to rescind the fine."

"Don't worry, we'll take up a collection for you. It's the very least we can do," offered Jennifer.

***

Ben Newman is putting in fourteen hour days at his office. He has hired several young tax accountants to prepare tax returns for clients and is in the process of adding several lawyers to his staff. This morning, his appointment calendar is full.

"Mr. and Mrs. Corey, how can I help you?" Ben asked as he greeted his 10 am appointment and led them into a small meeting room in his virtual office which he was in the process of expanding into a real office with office space for a staff of at least six employees.

"Mr. Newman, we saw your advertisement on television and thought you might be able to help us with our problem," said Mr. Corey, a rather rotund man who resembled Porky the Pig and who looked to be in his early seventies.

As John Corey made his way into the conference room, Ben couldn't help but notice that his overweight client's pants were being worn well below his waist. The client had a gut the size of a gigantic watermelon which forced him to wear his slacks well below his midriff. To say this looked ridiculous would be an understatement.

"What's the problem?" Ben asked, wondering if the Coreys should be in an emergency room to have the watermelon surgically removed from Mr. Corey's stomach.

"Recently we were notified by the IRS that the settlement that we agreed to with the Baltimore Appeals Office is not being honored. We find this very disturbing because we are being forced to go to court to argue our case. Can you intervene on our behalf and persuade the IRS to honor our settlement agreement?" asked the obese client.

"Who in the IRS agreed to the settlement?" inquired Ben.

"The people in the Appeals Office," replied Mrs. Corey, who was also rather beefy looking and had a very fair complexion like her chubby husband. Clearly, these two people didn't miss any meals during the day. Judging by the pink color of their skin, they probably spent most of their spare time standing around the kitchen waiting for the next meal to be served.

Looking at the plump Mrs. Corey, Ben asked, "Who is it we are talking about?"

"We met with an appeals officer named Adam Coleman, who agreed to waive a negligence penalty if we agreed to the full deficiency in our case. He had us sign legal documents which he intended to send to the Tax Court. We spoke with him about a month after we signed the legal documents and he informed us that his boss had approved the settlement," the chunky Mrs. Corey said.

"Can you tell me the name of Mr. Coleman's boss?" asked Ben.

"Sam Fishman. He's an Associate Chief," replied Mrs. Corey, who appeared to be in a hurry to go to lunch.

"Let me give him a call and I will get back to you as soon as I know something," replied Ben.

"I'll tell you something, this isn't right. We agreed to the deal, the IRS agreed to the deal, everyone signed off on the deal, and now the IRS doesn't want to honor the deal. Does that make sense to you?" asked the fat man.

"No, it doesn't make sense. But there is a lot of stuff that goes on in the IRS that doesn't make any sense. I'll sort it out for you. That's my job," announced Ben, who had no idea what really went on and how he was going to sort this out to the satisfaction of his client.

As soon as Mr. and Mrs. Corey lumbered out of his office, Ben faxed a copy of his Power of Attorney to Sam Fishman so that he could discuss the case on behalf of his client.

***

Louie was told when he reached Debbie's office that he should go to the office of the Assistant Deputy Attorney General for the Criminal Tax Division. When he arrived there, he was introduced to David Harbaugh and asked to take a seat at the front of the conference room table because he would be the featured speaker. Debbie then asked Louie to discuss his findings in detail. After almost one hour, Louie had covered all the major points in his case. Debbie's boss had listened intently and saved his questions for when Louie had finished.

"I take it you'll want access to Timothy Bell at the earliest opportunity?" asked Harbaugh.

"The sooner, the better," was Louie's reply.

"While the FBI was conducting an investigation into Timothy Bell's overseas activities, a former business partner of his, received a 'target letter' from the US Attorney," said Harbaugh.

The purpose of a target letter is to advise the subject of the inquiry that he or she has been under investigation for possible criminal violations and is entitled to appear before a federal grand jury.

"The subject of the target letter cooperated during the investigation and was expected to be a government witness at trial. However, this person recently turned up dead. According to the police reports, his death, while suspicious, was ruled a suicide. Thus, we won't be able to obtain any information from Bell's former business partner about International Business Solutions and Universal Technology," explained Harbaugh.

"This means we must have Timothy Bell's cooperation," said Gary.

"And given the fact that we just sent him back to his cell so he can spend the next one hundred and forty four months in a federal prison may be awkward," added Debbie.

"Wait a minute. Don't we have a clause in the Plea Agreement that specifically provides that Bell must cooperate with the IRS?" asked Larry Baumgardner, a senior executive at the Treasury Department who was invited to attend this meeting.

"The stipulation that you're referring to is with respect to Bell's civil tax liabilities. He's expected to resolve any dispute as to his personal income tax liabilities which are to be determined by the IRS upon the conclusion of the criminal case. There is nothing in the Plea Agreement that requires his cooperation in another matter involving an unrelated party," answered Debbie.

"I see," said Larry, who was actually not familiar with the specific terms and conditions of Timothy Bell's Plea Agreement.

"So, here's where it stands. We have to cut a deal with a criminal mastermind who facilitated the largest tax evasion conspiracy case in history and allowed sensitive defense related technology to be sold to third world nations without first obtaining State Department approval, which I understand is also a federal crime. Has this person committed any other criminal offenses that I should know about?" said Harbaugh, to which no one had anything to say.

"Okay, here's what I want you to do. Gary, get in touch with Bell's PD and let him know that we would like to talk with Bell," stated Harbaugh.

"Debbie, I want you to put together a recommendation to reduce his sentence. The commutation will be based on the helpfulness of the information he gives us. Once we've worked out the commutation of his sentence, Agent Lipschitz will meet with him and collect as much information as needed for his civil case," added Harbaugh.

"But what if we agree to commute his sentence and Louie determines that there's insufficient evidence to pursue a criminal referral?" asked the Treasury Executive.

"The sentence reduction is contingent on a criminal referral," answered Debbie.

"You're making one condition contingent on the other?" asked the Treasury Executive, who was starting to get on everyone's nerves.

"We have no other choice. In Debbie's example, if we commute the sentence and we're unable to prosecute Talbot given what Bell has told us, we would look like idiots. Can you imagine what the press would say about our decision?" replied Harbaugh.

"Look, the whole point to this is we're trying to determine if another crime has been committed. If we do have another crime and it involves a former president, we have a responsibility to conduct a criminal prosecution. At the minimum, we need Bell's cooperation. We may even need his assistance if it requires finding documents and sorting out the evidence. To secure his help, we have to offer him something substantial. If the criminal case doesn't pan out, all bets are off," proclaimed Harbaugh.

"Agent Lipschitz, let me ask you this. Assuming that your turns into a criminal referral, how long do you think it will take to get it to us?" asked Harbaugh.

"I really can't say at this time because this isn't a typical criminal case. In view of the fact that it's a former president, I would think the investigation will take longer than other cases," said the little guy.

"And don't forget Alex Talbot's involvement in possibly two deaths," said Larry Baumgardner, who just couldn't keep his mouth shut.

"That's a matter for the FBI or state police to sort out," said Harbaugh. "We have enough to do just with the tax issues."

CHAPTER 29

The following day, Louie was told by Roger that the Chief of Exam wished to see him immediately, if not sooner. When Louie arrived, he was escorted to the Exam Chief's conference room and told the Chief will be with him momentarily. After a few moments the Exam Chief greeted Louie and said, "I heard you made a spectacle of yourself in court yesterday."

"I'm two hundred and fifty dollars poorer. Can I get reimbursed for the fine?" asked Louie.

"We can talk about that later." What this means is that the little guy is out two hundred and fifty dollars.

Your DOJ friends briefed me on yesterday's developments. It looks like you were in the right place at the right time. I want you to prepare a memorandum that summarizes everything to date," said the Exam Chief.

"It's done. I prepared the memo last night and e-mailed it to the DOJ lawyers, Roger, Tom and you. I guess you didn't check your e-mail this morning," remarked Louie.

"I'll get to it in a moment," said the Exam Chief as he stood up.

As Louie stood to leave, the Chief said, "DOJ is anxious to prosecute Talbot for what they believe are serious crimes that you think he committed. I hope you can support the conclusions you reached yesterday,"

"Me too."

***

"I'm sorry, Gary. I'm not sure I heard you correctly. Did you just say you wanted to arrange a meeting with my former client to discuss a commutation of his sentence? Were you not in court when he entered his plea and it was accepted by the judge?" remarked Derick Mason.

"Derick, I was there. Some recent developments have come to our attention and it merits reconsideration of the sentence. We need to meet. There's a lot to discuss," replied Gary.

"Are there factors in Timmy's case that impact his sentence?" asked Derick.

"No. There are no factors in your former client's case that are relevant to this matter," answered Gary.

"Then I'm confused. There's another case?" asked Derick.

"Yes."

"That explains the IRS person's outburst in court. That caught completely me by surprise," said Derick, who wasn't the only person who was taken by surprise by Louie's performance in court.

"That was Agent Lipschitz. He's the revenue agent who is performing an audit on an unrelated taxpayer. However, Mr. Bell is believed to have information that can have an impact on Agent Lipschitz's audit. If the information is deemed to be of significant relevance to the IRS agent's audit, Mr. Bell may be asked to testify in court," said Gary, who was trying not to disclose too much information to the Public Defender.

"I see and are you prepared to adjust his sentence accordingly?" asked Derick.

"Yes, we are. However, the sentence reduction is contingent on Mr. Bell providing information that results in a criminal case," replied Gary.

"Okay, first I need to talk to my boss and then we'll let Mr. Bell know what's in store for him. Bear in mind, that technically, I no longer represent Mr. Bell. It's up to him as to whether he wants the PD's office to handle his representation. After all, his case is considered closed," said Derick, who was wondering how the DOJ prosecutors could be motivated to administratively effectuate a reduction in sentence so quickly.

* * *

Ben placed a call to Sam Fishman to find out why the settlement agreement in the Corey case has not been finalized. During his ten years at the IRS, Ben has never met Sam. However, Sam is well aware of Ben's reputation.

"I have your Power of Attorney on my desk. What have Mr. and Mrs. Corey told you?" asked Sam.

"Mr. and Mrs. Corey told me that you approved the settlement agreement that they signed but that the deal was not being honored. Like my client, I find this to be extremely disturbing. I hope I don't have to take this over your head," Ben said as a threat.

"Before you get yourself worked up over this, you should know all the facts. This case is docketed before the Tax Court, and as such, the Appeals Division does not have ultimate settlement authority. Final authority rests with Counsel, because it is the trial attorney or the Associate Chief Counsel who must sign the Stipulation Agreement before it is entered with the Tax Court," explained Sam who sensed that Ben was not familiar with this rule.

"Are you familiar with this particular procedural rule?" Sam asked Ben.

"Umm………, no."

"Do you know anything about this case, such as what comprises the underlying tax adjustment?" asked Sam.

"No," admitted Ben.

"Your client invested in an abusive tax shelter. The write-offs generated a twelve to one ratio. That ratio reflects an extremely aggressive write-off percentage. When the admin file was sent to Appeals, we were advised that the entire loss deduction is not deductible and that all investors would have to concede the entire deficiency amount. However, someone had mistakenly left out the negligence penalty in the complete examination report. Because the appeals officer did not see it in his copy of the report, he agreed to waive the negligence penalty. When I reviewed the case for approval, I did not see the negligence penalty in the report and concurred with my employee that the penalty could be waived," explained Sam.

"Okay," said Ben.

"However, after the case had been sent to Counsel for approval of our settlement proposal, we learned that Counsel had designated this partnership as a litigating vehicle and that the negligence penalty is applicable. We were later given a copy of the entire examination report that contained the negligence penalty," Sam added.

"Okay," said Ben, not knowing what else to say.

"While I'm sorry about the confusion, as a procedural matter there is nothing that Appeals can do for you to eliminate the negligence penalty. Again, the case has been designated by Chief Counsel as a litigating vehicle so Counsel is not about to concede any part of the penalty. Because your client's case is in Counsel's jurisdiction, my office does not have the authority to overturn Counsel's edict," Sam explained further.

"But the case was in Appeals jurisdiction when the parties agreed to the settlement. Therefore, the settlement is binding on the IRS," said Ben, who thought he had turned the tables on the Associate Chief.

"That is not correct. Apparently, you're not familiar with IRS procedures," Sam replied.

"Once a petition is filed with the Tax Court, the case is in Counsel's jurisdiction. Appeals cannot conclude the matter by settlement because the only closing document that is permissible is a Stipulation Agreement that is entered with the Tax Court. And, the only ones who can do this are the trial attorney or the Associate Chief Counsel. Now do you understand?" asked Sam.

"My client will not be happy," was Ben's only comment.

"Your client can take it up with the judge when the case is called for trial," replied Sam who was anxious to get back to work as he hung up on Ben Newman, celebrity tax representative.

***

Debbie Macht has been called into a meeting with her boss to discuss Timothy Bell's Plea Agreement.

"Rule 34(a) of the Federal Rules of Criminal Procedure provides that the court may correct a sentence within fourteen days after sentencing," said Debbie.

"That won't work for us because we'll need more than fourteen days," replied her boss. "What else?"

"We can file a Rule 35 Motion," said Debbie.

In unusual instances where a Plea Agreement has been entered with the court and the Justice Department later determines that the defendant who agreed to the Plea Agreement has information which prosecutors need in another criminal case, the defendant's sentence may be commuted. The authority for doing so is Rule 35 in the Criminal Procedure Rules. The Motion is filed by a prosecutor under the authority granted by Rule 35(b). The Motion asks the court to reduce the sentence based on substantial assistance provided by a defendant after sentencing.

"I take it Bell is going to have to provide us with substantial information to go forward in our criminal case against Talbot," said Harbaugh.

"Providing information that leads to an arrest, indictment or conviction is considered substantial assistance. Testifying against another person is also considered substantial," replied Debbie.

"What kind of sentence reduction are we talking about?" asked her boss.

Debbie threw up her hands as if to say she doesn't know. "Under a Rule 35 Motion, I would ask for a reduced sentence. But the court is free to impose whatever sentence it believes is appropriate. I have no idea what the court would do," acknowledged Debbie.

"Theoretically we have the authority to commute the sentence to probation under a substantial assistance departure motion," replied Harbaugh.

"If the Public Defender figures out where we're going on this, Bell will insist on probation," theorized Debbie.

"And I'll be vilified by the press as the prosecutor who permitted Timothy Bell to avoid serving a prison sentence. This is a no-win predicament," complained Debbie's boss.

"From Bell's standpoint, there is a downside to all this. The most serious risk in cooperating is the defendant's safety and the safety of his family. If Talbot learns of Bell's cooperation, he could threaten to harm Bell or his family. Remember, we have at least two dead bodies," said Debbie.

"Right, the broker and the banker. But we don't know for certain that Talbot was behind their deaths," said Harbaugh.

"Also, Bell could be prosecuted for additional crimes that he discloses as part of his cooperation. We would have to give him a Proffer Agreement that protects him from this," said Debbie.

"You'd better line up your ducks and make sure this doesn't blow up in our faces before we grant probation to Bell," Harbaugh cautioned his prosecutor.

BRUCE BRONSTEIN

CHAPTER 30

Derick Mason has been advised by his boss that he should meet with Timothy Bell to let him know that the DOJ is interested in reducing his sentence, contingent on his assistance in another matter that is considered to be substantial.

"How badly do they want to cut a deal with me?" asked Timmy.

"They are quite serious about this. An IRS agent is anxious to talk to you about Universal Technology's business dealings with International Business Solutions," replied Derick.

"I saw Agent Lipschitz in court. What do you know about his audit?" wondered Timmy.

"Absolutely nothing. The prosecutors have not told me anything. And I have not spoken to Agent Lipschitz," said Derick.

"Is it possible they will commute my sentence if I have information that's helpful to the audit?"

"It's theoretically possible you could even be granted probation, provided your cooperation is so substantial that it results in an arrest or conviction. But it is more likely that they would merely reduce your sentence. Keep in mind, your case is the largest tax evasion case in history. They can't let you walk away without doing time in prison," said Derick. Pausing for a few moments, the Public Defender asked, "Do you have information the government can use?"

"I believe I do," Timmy said with a smile. "I think I can be very helpful to the investigation of International Business Solutions."

"Also, keep in mind that if you agree to cooperate, the investigation conducted by Agent Lipschitz may take a long time and getting the IRS to initiate a criminal case could take years. In the meantime, where would the government keep you? If they keep you in prison, there may not be sufficient motivation to cooperate. If you're placed in a federal witness protection program while you cooperate, that will seem like confinement at times, but considerably nicer than prison," offered Derick.

"Also keep in mind that if you cooperate and are required to testify, you could be at risk because threats may be made against you or family members. This is a serious matter and it should not be taken lightly," added Derick.

"I know."

***

Edward Smith and Larry Donnelly are meeting with Alex Talbot to discuss the IRS audit. The lawyers were asked to meet with their client at his District of Columbia apartment.

Both lawyers were apprehensive about representing someone who seemed to be unwilling to fully disclose his business affairs. While respecting the former president's preference for privacy, the lawyers had the feeling that their client was holding back on them.

The lawyers were met at the front door by an aide to the former president. The aide accompanied them to a large family room and told them that the president will be with them in a few minutes.

Alex greeted his lawyers as if he was still president and has an assistant bring coffee and a tray of refreshments into the room. Once the refreshments have been served, the assistant quickly left so that the three men can talk in private.

"Where do we stand with the IRS?" asked Talbot.

"The IRS agent has obtained the summoned information and informed us that he intends to follow up with officials at Morgan Stanley and Bank of America," replied one of the lawyers.

"What's his problem?" asked Talbot.

"He seems to be inquisitive. I'm of the opinion that he is not convinced that there were mistakes made by your brokerage firm and bank," said Donnelly.

"What's not to believe?"

"He has access to the official records of your brokerage firm and bank. He can interview officials at these companies and verify whether mistakes were made. He doesn't strike me as the sort of person who accepts things at face value," said Smith.

"But this bank account is owned by a foreign corporation. How can he attribute its ownership to me?" asked Talbot.

"The agent has not confirmed who owns International Business Solutions. Until the agent has confirmed that you do not have an ownership interest in this entity, he is not going to acquiesce on this issue," reasoned Smith.

Talbot mumbled something to himself that the lawyers could not comprehend. He then asked, "What about the other issues?"

"Agent Lipschitz has raised a question as to whether you were actively involved in different business activities when little or no income was reported. At the same time, there are substantial deductions claimed as business expenses," said Donnelly.

Talbot waved his hand as if to dismiss what he was just told as being of no consequence. "I'm involved in a variety of projects. I consult with foreign leaders. I advise companies both domestically and internationally on business deals. I'm active in charitable causes. I'm a busy person. In fact, I'm working harder now than when I was in the White House. And this little runt is questioning what I do?" Talbot said in frustration.

"It may be a problem of presentation." "What do you mean?"

asked Talbot.

"By that I mean, your tax returns do not provide an explanation as to what you do. It merely shows a form in which deductions were claimed. Perhaps if you set aside time to personally meet with the agent, you could explain each of your various business activities and offer an in-depth insight into why little or no income was reported," suggested Donnelly.

"Okay, I suppose that makes sense. Set it up when you talk with him."

After spending almost an hour with the former president in which the lawyers discussed other tax matters, they left to return to their law office. On the way out, Smith said to his partner, "Where did you come up with that nonsense about a problem with presentation?"

"Sorry. I couldn't think of anything else to say that would appease him. It looked like he was about to go on a tirade."

***

"Is that an offer?"

"Yes. It's an offer," replied Debbie.

"You're recommending a reduction of two years?" said Derick. "That's not an offer. It's an insult to my intelligence."

"Your client is the mastermind of the largest tax evasion case in history. What does he expect? A presidential pardon and a red carpet parade in his honor?" asked Debbie.

"Probation seems reasonable considering how badly your boss needs Timmy's assistance," said Derick.

"Granted, the Department does need your client's assistance in another case that is under the jurisdiction of the IRS. We need information, documentary evidence and perhaps his testimony. Admittedly, it's a lot. But we have to balance that with his crimes, in which he's admitted his guilt," answered Debbie.

"My client will accept a sentence of three years in prison, less credits for time served and good behavior."

"Are you kidding me? What kind of sentence is that? A three year term with credits means he'll never spend one day in prison," said Debbie.

"Consider how long an audit investigation may take. It could take the IRS years to send the case to your office for criminal prosecution. And you would have my client rot in prison during this time? If that's the case, there is no incentive for his cooperation," argued Derick.

At this point, Derick knew that he had made significant progress on a reduction in Timmy's sentence. The cost of his cooperation would have to be a substantial reduction in his prison sentence if Timmy were to provide assistance to the same prosecutors who sent him to prison.

"I'll have to get back to you," said Debbie, as she hung up and went in search of her boss who would have to sign off on the sentence reduction.

When Debbie caught up with her boss and advised him of the Assistant Public Defender's insistence that Timothy Bell not serve prison time, he erupted.

"Why don't we call a news conference and extend a public apology to him," said Harbaugh who was clearly annoyed that Timothy Bell was in a position to demand probation.

"If you want his help, it's going to cost. He's looking for an incentive to cooperate. Otherwise, he'll go to prison, do his time and he'll be out in eight years, when you factor in credits for good behavior and time already served. In the meantime, we don't have the evidence we need to make a criminal case against Talbot. It's your call," said Debbie.

"Tell him we'll recommend a reduction to eight years in prison. When we factor in credits for time served and good behavior, he'll end up doing two years, if that. This is contingent on his cooperation resulting in a criminal case for prosecution. If he agrees to cooperate, he'll be placed in a safe house. That time will count as creditable against prison time," said Debbie's boss.

"I think that will work," surmised Debbie.

***

It's after 9 pm and Ben Newman has finally made it home. Ben has put in another fifteen hour day and he is physically and mentally exhausted. There is no way that he can continue at this frenetic pace.

With all of the work that continues to come in, Ben will have to hire more help and open a second office. While pleased that he is finally making strides in his professional career, Ben sensed that he is simply doing what he had previously found so contemptible. In essence, Ben is preparing tax returns without independently verifying the questionable information that he has been given. It wasn't all that long ago that Ben was so critical of others for having done the same thing.

"Honey, you look as if you're about to collapse," Nancy said with a concerned look on her face as Ben walked in the house.

"Just another thirteen hour day, babe." Ben seemed to either have difficulty with his math or lost track of two hours.

"Sweetheart, you had a phone call today from an official at the Maryland Comptroller's Office," said Nancy.

"That's odd. I don't recall having any cases with the State of Maryland," Ben replied.

"No. They want to hire you for a sales tax examiner position. An opening came up and they were given your name by people at the IRS who recommended you for the job. This man wants you to apply for the job. He said that when someone is told to apply, that's an indication they are in line for the job. I think this may be a wonderful opportunity," Nancy said to her husband.

"Opportunity for what?"

"To live a reasonably normal life. To be able to have dinner with your family. To work a nine to five job and get paid every two weeks and not have to worry about running a business. To have time on weekends to play with your sons and watch them grow up," Nancy said.

"And if I get this job, how much money will I earn?" asked Ben, who could barely keep his eyes open.

"The man who called said it pays around seventy thousand dollars a year, with various benefits."

"Honey, I'm already earning seventy thousand dollars a month right now. By this time next year, I'll be earning seventy thousand dollars a week once I get this tax practice up and running. Babe, the secret is lining up clients. In order to attract more clients, I need to do more infomercials," said a weary Ben.

"So, you don't want to work for the State of Maryland?" Nancy asked her husband.

"Not when I already have the best job in the world," Ben replied as he threw his coat on the sofa and trudged off to the bedroom to grab a nap before getting up at 3 am the next day to go off to work.

CHAPTER 31

A tentative agreement has been reached between the Justice Department and Timothy Bell. Timmy's sentence will be reduced from one hundred and forty four months to ninety six months, subject to court approval. The prosecutors will file a Rule 35(b) Motion for a sentence reduction after Timmy has provided Louie with information that that meets the criteria for a criminal investigation of Alex Talbot.

Arrangements have been made for Timmy to be transported to the J. Edgar Hoover Building in Washington, D.C. where he will be interviewed by Louie. As Timmy has been granted immunity from prosecution in the event that he may have committed other crimes, Derick Mason will not attend the interview. In view of the fact that the interview to be conducted by Louie relates to a case that is a civil tax case, no one from the Justice Department will attend. This is a meeting between Louie and Timmy, and it is the first time they have formally met.

Louie waited in a conference room for Timmy, who was brought in by several FBI agents who then left the room.

"Good morning, Mr. Bell. I'm Louie Lipschitz, the IRS agent who will be interviewing you. Please have a seat," Louie said as he showed Timmy his IRS credentials.

"Agent Lipschitz, I remember you from the other day in court. You made quite an impression at my plea hearing," said Timmy.

"It was something you said that caught my attention. You connected Universal Technology to International Business

Solutions. I need to know everything that connects the two companies."

"Where do you want me to start?" said Timmy.

"At the very beginning. And don't leave anything out."

"I created a number of foreign companies that engaged in separate, but related, businesses. These entities operated throughout Europe and the Far East. One of these entities was Universal Technology. This company was incorporated in the Cayman Islands and was a subsidiary of Global Technology Systems, which was also incorporated in the Cayman Islands," said Timmy.

"Global Technology designed computer software programs for multiple applications. Global Technology wanted to do business in third world countries and created Universal Technology for this purpose," Timmy added.

"Universal Technology designed software programs for military use such as in developing military defense systems and designing weaponry. The profit potential was absolutely tremendous. Can you imagine what certain foreign governments would pay to acquire military technology superior to what their neighboring countries have?" wondered Timmy as if Louie had a clue.

Louie just sat there and took careful notes even though he was recording the entire interview. Louie notified Derick Mason in advance that the meeting would be recorded and Derick conveyed this to Timmy.

"However, I couldn't sell the technology to foreign nations because of US laws that prohibited the sale of computer technology to foreign governments. To circumvent this legal restriction, I entered into an agreement with a broker to act as a middleman," said Timmy.

"That would be International Business Solutions?" said the little guy.

"That's right. I sold the licensing technology to International Business Solutions, which then sold the military software to certain foreign governments. Even though I needed a third party to effectuate the sale, Universal Technology generated more than seven hundred and fifty million dollars in revenue over a span of three years. I don't know what International Business Solutions actually received for brokering the deal, but I would guess there was a mark-up of at least twenty percent. Can you imagine earning somewhere in the neighborhood of fifty million dollars a year for making a couple of phone calls?" said Timmy.

"The thing is, I needed a third party to serve as a middleman. So, the approximate fifty million dollars that International Business Solutions earned each year for brokering the deals was essentially my cost of doing business. Call it a consulting fee or an advisory fee or even a bribe, whatever. Look, I was willing to pay it if someone else was agreeable to assume the risk. In this case, International Business Solutions agreed to facilitate the transaction for me," explained Timmy.

"How did you get involved with International Business Solutions?" asked Louie.

"My former business partner had dealings with some venture capitalists who were approached by an associate of Alexander Talbot. Talbot was interested in brokering deals overseas and had valuable connections. Of course, when you're the President of the United States, you would be expected to have relationships with foreign leaders that extend beyond your term of office," said Timmy.

"Apparently word had leaked out to Talbot that we needed a middleman to sell our licensing technology. Talbot's people approached us and guaranteed that they could arrange sales to foreign governments.   I didn't want to have Universal Technology sell the licensing technology to foreign governments for fear of criminal prosecution," said Timmy.

"I assumed that bribes were paid to government officials to conceal the fact that illegal sales of software technology were being made to foreign governments," added Timmy.

"We're talking about federal government officials?" asked Louie.

"I would think so."

"Any idea who?" asked Louie who was anxious to hear their names.

"No."

"Who owns International Business Solutions?" asked Louie.

"I'm pretty sure it's Alex Talbot," answered Timmy.

"Do you know Hans Schumann and Klaus Bergmeister?" asked Louie.

"They're Swiss lawyers who have a small law practice that caters to wealthy clients. They're often listed as corporate officers on the corporate by-laws of many Swiss companies," said Timmy.

"Where are your documents to substantiate all this?" asked Louie.

"I think I can get you the contract that was signed with International Business Solutions several years ago. That contract is supposed to be in a file cabinet in an office that I maintained in the Cayman Islands. Every time a sale was made to International Business Solutions, we handled the paperwork electronically. The payments we received were electronically deposited in Universal Technology's bank account in the Cayman Islands. I would have to retrieve those records from the bank statements, and of course, from our computers," explained Timmy.

"I don't think you're going to be making any trips to the Cayman Islands anytime soon. You'll have to be specific as to where I can find the documentation that I'll need," said Louie.

"Do you think you can prove Alex Talbot has committed tax fraud?" asked Timmy.

"I don't have to prove it. I just have to provide the Justice Department with a case that they can prove," replied Louie.

***

Ben has returned to the Federal Building, or as he last remembered it, the scene of the crime. Not anxious to go through the indignity of having hundreds of strangers witness his strip search, Ben asked the supervisory screener if he remembered him from about a week ago.

"Oh yeah, I remember. Hey Charley, just frisk him for weapons and if he's clean, let him pass. We got too many exams to do today," Boris yelled out to one of his subordinates.

Ben quickly made his way to an elevator before Boris has a change of heart. When Ben arrived at the thirteenth floor, he went to the Baltimore Appeals Office for his meeting with Janice Eastman.

Janice greeted Ben and said, "You look familiar. Have we met before?"

Concerned that his reputation has preceded him, Ben answered by saying, "I don't believe so."

After a few minutes of small talk, Janice said, "Let's get started."

"In my Protest, you'll note that my client, the Computers R Us Company, utilized the services of Premier Pay, a commercial payroll tax service that was responsible for the preparation and filing of its payroll tax returns. All payroll taxes were paid through an authorized direct withdrawal from my client's checking account. Premier Pay was then expected to remit all funds to the IRS on behalf of my client," Ben said.

Janice nodded in agreement, so Ben continued.

"According to IRS records, several payments totaling twelve thousand dollars were not remitted on behalf of my client. Because the payroll service was authorized to remit trust fund taxes on behalf of my client, all delinquency notices were sent to the payroll service. My client didn't learn of the non-remittance until the IRS eventually sent a notice before enforced collection action was threatened," Ben asserted without bothering to determine whether this was true.

"When my client learned of the problem, the company attempted to contact Premier Pay but discovered that it was no longer in business. In fact, I was able to learn that its corporate charter had been revoked and that it failed to remit its own payroll taxes over a period of four years," Ben added.

"My client subsequently discovered that Premier Pay was the subject of a criminal investigation by the FBI and IRS for embezzlement of payroll taxes. This action was disclosed at the time Premier Pay had been placed into Chapter 7 liquidation proceedings. A trustee appointed by the US Bankruptcy Court was forced to hire a forensic accountant to ascertain to what extent funds were embezzled and from whom," Ben explained.

"In addition, my client has learned that the sole shareholder of Premier Pay owes the IRS more than seven hundred and fifty thousand dollars in unpaid personal income taxes. Last month, this individual was found dead in the Virgin Islands," Ben decided to throw in for emphasis.

"My client has provided the IRS with copies of its bank statements as evidence that its payroll taxes were timely remitted to Premier Pay for remittance to the IRS," Ben noted.

"Because my client had overpayment credits in its account, these overpayments were applied against the unpaid payroll tax liabilities. As a result of these overpayment credits, the balance due has been satisfied in full," Ben continued.

So far, Ben was doing quite well. He presented the relevant facts clearly and concisely. Indeed, Ben was starting to feel confident that he might actually win this case for his client.

"My client does not understand why the IRS has denied its claim for refund and retained my firm to review this matter. After an extensive analysis of the facts in this case, I am of the opinion that the IRS should issue a twelve thousand dollar refund to my client," Ben exclaimed, feeling quite proud that he did an excellent job in arguing his client's case. However, within the next moment, the wind was about to be taken out of his sail.

"According to a letter that was issued to your client, the IRS denied the refund claim because your client had a legal obligation to ensure the proper remittance of trust fund taxes to the IRS. The recovery of any funds remitted to a commercial payroll service is a civil matter between the parties involved. As a federal agency, the IRS is not a party to civil disputes," explained Janice.

"I understand. But my client should not be held legally liable for the non-remittance of trust fund taxes by its payroll service when the payroll service had a fiduciary obligation to remit such payments to the IRS in a timely manner. It is an undeniable fact that my client was unaware Premier Pay embezzled such funds, and to hold my client responsible for repayment constitutes double taxation," Ben argued.

"No. That is not a correct statement. Your client was notified by the IRS that the payroll taxes had not been paid and it was your client who told the IRS that its payroll service had remitted payment, which was not true," countered the appeals officer.

"Okay, but we're back to double taxation," exclaimed Ben, who was starting to grasp at straws.

"Do you have statutory authority to support your position?" asked Janice.

"I'm invoking section 3504 to assert third party liability against Premier Pay for failing to comply with its fiduciary obligation to remit my client's payroll taxes to the IRS," Ben asserted with confidence.

However, Section 3504 of the Internal Revenue Code only grants the IRS the authority to assert third party liability where there is non-remittance of trust fund taxes. Had Ben been aware of this requirement, he would not have raised this argument.

"Mr. Newman, your reliance on this code provision is misguided. The statute emphatically provides that the employer cannot be absolved of liability even when third parties are held liable as fiduciary agents," Janice remarked.

"What about section 6672?" Ben asked.

"What about section 6672?" Janice replied.

"I'm invoking section 6672 because my client lacked the element of willfulness in failing to ensure that its trust fund taxes were remitted to the IRS," asserted Ben.

Section 6672 of the Internal Revenue Code provides certain mechanical criteria for determining whether a taxpayer can be considered a responsible party, and as such, be held liable for the non-remittance of withheld payroll taxes. Apparently, Ben's strategy is to characterize the commercial payroll tax service that failed to remit the trust fund taxes as a taxpayer that falls within the definition of a responsible party.

"Mr. Newman, section 6672 is also not applicable because even if Premier Pay were held to be a responsible party and held liable for the trust fund penalty, your client is still liable for the underlying trust fund taxes. As a matter of law, a taxpayer is responsible for its trust fund tax liability and cannot shift the legal obligation to another party. Neither the Internal Revenue Code, its accompanying regulations, nor the courts provide authority for absolving an employer of its legal liability," Janice explained.

At this point in the conference, Ben has just had both of his nuts crushed. In essence, he has invoked two code sections that are not applicable. He needed to try a different strategy and quickly because Janice was about to put a bow around this puppy and wrap it up.

Janice Eastman has already sensed the trepidation in Ben's voice and the glazed look in Ben's eyes have betrayed him.

Several years ago, the Baltimore Appeals Office hired Professor Dimitri Zachoslavsky to teach the art of interpreting body language to its appeals officers. Professor Zach, as he was called by his students, was paid twenty thousand dollars to conduct a series of workshops on the subject of studying a taxpayer's body language. Included in the course was a class on Face and Mind Reading. At least the IRS didn't hire Maxine Kaminski for the mind reading part.

When it comes to spending money, the IRS can spend it like drunken sailors in a topless bar. Years ago, the Baltimore Appeals Office had leftover funds from its budget. Rather than not spend the money and have less funding in the next year's budget, the Chief decided to go on a spending spree and purchased the ugliest desk lamps in the history of the world.

These desk lamps looked as if it they were made by blind inmates in a federal correctional facility. These lamps were so hideous that they were stashed in cardboard boxes in a section of the library that no one used.

"Okay, but once funds are transferred to a fiduciary agent, the IRS is precluded from holding the employer liable," Ben said to Janice.

"I disagree, Mr. Newman. Your contention that the IRS has no cause of action because Premier Pay embezzled funds, thereby defrauding the federal government is also misguided. I'm afraid that there is no statutory, regulatory or judicial authority that allows an employer to escape liability from paying its trust fund taxes as a result of embezzlement by a fiduciary agent," Janice explained.

"No exceptions?" asked Ben, hoping his case might still qualify for relief.

"In unusual instances involving certain charitable organizations, exceptions to this rule may be made for public policy reasons. Other than that, there are no exceptions," Janice stated.

However, Ben wasn't about to give up without pulling out all the stops. "I think it's grossly inequitable to hold my client liable because the IRS did not provide adequate notification that the payments were not made until more than two years after the funds were made available to Premier Pay. Because Premier Pay is no longer an ongoing entity, it further compounds an otherwise harsh result if my client can't file suit to recover these funds," Ben asserted.

"Mr. Newman, this argument is also frivolous because the IRS notified Premier Pay as the fiduciary agent that payments were not remitted in a timely manner. As a point of fact, the IRS followed its rules and procedures in notifying an authorized party that was acting on behalf of another in a fiduciary capacity. Although it is unfortunate that your client was a victim of embezzlement, the tax laws do not allow relief from payment by shifting the burden to another party," Janice said.

It goes without saying that when taxpayers are left with an argument of inequity, this is an indication that there is no merit to their position. Experienced appeals officers such as Janice Eastman know this.

"Anything else you wanted to say?" Janice asked.

Defeated, Ben just shook his head no and got up to leave. This is obviously not what Ben had thought would happen today.

In light of his inability to obtain favorable results for his clients, Ben decided that he would refrain from doing tax representation work and instead, focus on administrative matters such as client development.

CHAPTER 32

"How soon do you want me to leave for the Cayman Islands?" asked Louie.

"You're not going to the Cayman Islands," replied Roger.

"Why not, Rog?"

"I'm not authorizing that trip because I know what you'll do. You'll make this a vacation at government expense. It'll take you five days to retrieve documents that should take five minutes. Do you plan to take your wife?" asked Roger.

"No. I'm looking forward to having a good time."

"Well, you can forget about going to the Cayman Islands. I'm not running a travel agency here. Let the FBI send an agent."

"We can't get the FBI involved. It's not a criminal case just yet," said Louie.

"He's right," Tom remarked as he walked into Roger's office. Taking a seat across from both men, Tom said, "The case is still in our jurisdiction. In view of the fact that we haven't made a referral to another agency, Exam will have to send someone to the Cayman Islands to get the documentation. It's Louie's case. Why not let him go?" suggested Tom.

"Tom, you've finally made a good decision. I see potential for your career," exclaimed the little guy.

"Louie, call the people who handle our travel and get on the next available flight. However, I want you back in the office ASAP. Do not pack beach wear, golf clubs, and anything else that suggests a vacation. You're going there on a work assignment. Do you understand?" said Tom.

"Tom, can you cut me some slack?   Once I have the documentation, let me relax for a few days," Louie said hoping that Tom would reward him.

"Louie, I know you and I know what you do on government time. I know you'll milk this little trip for all it's worth. So, here's the deal. I'll give you the day you arrive to get your documents and you'll have the remainder of that day to relax. You'll get a flight out the next day. I want you back in the office the following day with all documentation," said Tom.

"Now you're talking, boss."

"I'm not finished. The government will reimburse you for your travel expenses. However, you are not flying first class. Next, you'll be reimbursed for your hotel room for one night at the prevailing government per diem rate. Next, you'll receive per diem for meals and incidentals for up to two days. Everything else is on your dime. Understood?" said Tom.

"This doesn't look as if it's going to be much of a trip," sighed Louie.

***

When men often use the expression, "How's the little woman," they could be referring to Louie's wife. Lucy Lipschitz is indeed a little woman. Lucy stands about several inches shy of five feet in height and weighs no more than eighty five pounds. If Louie is a munchkin, Lucy is a smaller version. Sort of like, munchkin-lite.

Lucy learned of Louie's trip to the Cayman Islands almost by accident when he casually brought up the subject of an out-of-town trip while they were having dinner.

"Wait a second. Back up. What did you just say?" asked Lucy.

"I'm sorry?"

"What did you just blurt out in an almost hushed tone of voice that you didn't want me to hear?" asked Lucy.

"Could it have been my flying to the Cayman Islands tomorrow?" asked Louie.

"That must have been it. You're going off to the Cayman Islands? Is this some kind of a top-secret trip?"

"I just learned that I would be flying out tomorrow. The office didn't give me any advance notice," pleaded Louie.

"You couldn't have given me a head's up so I could fly down to the island with you?" said Lucy.

"I swear, I just found out only a few hours ago."

"And how long do you expect to be there?" asked Lucy.

"Tom told me to wrap up my business by the first day and take the next flight out the following day," said Louie.

"In that case, I'll help you with your packing. I guess you won't need your swim suit."

***

Louie's flight arrived in the Cayman Islands only thirty minutes late. After Louie checked into his hotel, he took a taxi to the address that Timmy gave him.

The first stop was to meet with the realtor who leased the office building to Timmy. Presenting the realtor with his credentials and a letter from Timmy authorizing him access to his office, Louie had the realtor escort him to the office building.

The realtor is an attractive female in her mid-thirties who is a sun worshipper when she's not working. Louie was tempted to ask her how long it would take him to get a tan like hers but thought otherwise when she said something about looking forward to spending the afternoon sunbathing at the beach rather than waste her time showing him an empty office building.

The realtor let Louie into the empty office. When Louie inquired as to where the file cabinets are, the realtor replied, "What file cabinets?"

Louie immediately headed over to the bank where Timmy maintained the bank account for Universal Technology. Louie identified himself by presenting his IRS credentials to the bank manager along with official government documents in the form of a summons and a notarized letter from Timmy requesting that the bank allow Louie access to Universal Technology's bank statements.

Louie was given copies of the bank statements. The cost of copying the statements was paid by Louie who will be reimbursed for this expense since it is a cost to the federal government and not an employee expense.

Louie returned to his hotel and planned to take an early evening swim using the swim suit that he smuggled into his suitcase when Lucy wasn't looking. The little guy can be very devious. Before Louie left for the hotel pool, he placed a call to the local police to inquire into whether he can stop by the police station first thing in the morning to see the chief of police.

After a quiet dinner with no one to look at and talk to, Louie returned to his hotel room to think. While he has the bank statements, he doesn't have Universal Technology's contract with International Business Solutions. Louie needs this contract to establish that there was a direct relationship between the two entities and that services were performed for an express purpose, albeit illegal.

The following morning, Louie met with the police chief to find out if he knows who removed the file cabinets, office equipment and furniture from the Universal Technology office building.

"Do I look like I'm in charge of policing office furnishings?" asked the police chief.

Louie ignored the sarcasm and said, "Mr. Bell didn't authorize the removal of any furnishings. Nor does the realtor know of anyone entering the office to remove anything. Someone had access because it doesn't appear that the office building was entered by force. So, I'm asking you if you know of anyone who could have done this sort of thing," said Louie.

"No,"

However, Louie sensed that the police official knew who engineered the heist of Universal Technology's file cabinets. This suggests that the chief a bribe to look the other way. It appears that Alex Talbot knows the police chief in the Cayman Islands.

CHAPTER 33

Louie returned to Baltimore without a suntan and without the documents that established Universal Technology entered into a contractual relationship with International Business Solutions to sell its computer software technology. IRS management is not happy because the overriding purpose of the trip was to come back with the contract.

"I'm certain Talbot had someone remove everything in the office and he did it with the blessing of the police chief," declared Louie.

"I'm sure you're right, but we can't prove it just yet. You'll have to work your case with what you have. Call the DOJ lawyers and let them know you've come to a fork in the road. Maybe they'll have some suggestions for you," said Tom.

"Maybe I should go back to the Cayman Islands and poke around for the documents," thought Louie.

"I have a better idea. Go back to office and do some real work. If I need someone to snoop around, I'll get a detective," replied Tom.

***

"Someone get Heather out here. Ben needs some touch up work on his face before we shoot," Lars yelled.

After Ben received some additional make-up from Heather, who was the most popular person on the film set, the crew was ready to shoot the next infomercial. "Lights, camera, action," yelled Lars as he gave Ben the sign to start.

"Hi folks. Are you concerned that you pay too much in taxes every year? Are you worried that the IRS will come after you because you haven't paid your correct taxes? Are you in need of tax planning? Are you being audited and need a qualified person experienced in tax matters to represent you? If you answered yes to any of these questions, you need to call me," Ben said.

Looking to the camera on the other side of the room just as Lars told him to do, Ben said, "Trying to handle tax problems yourselves can be stressful and difficult for those not qualified to do so. If your house collapsed in an earthquake, would you re-build it yourself? Of course not. Then why not use a team of highly trained professionals to help you re-build your financial foundation. Call me and I'll have my diligent team of tax experts solve your problems so you can sleep soundly at night, worry-free," Ben said.

"Beautiful. That's a wrap. Ben, you were great. You should be nominated for an Academy Award for your performance," Lars said as he shook Ben's hand and then gave him a pat on the back in appreciation for his solid performance.

Ben wondered if he was doomed to be a pitchman for late night television. He had the sales pitch and could bring in business. However, he wasn't capable of actually doing the work that involved tax controversy and client representation. As long as he could employ qualified people, his tax practice would be fine. The problem is qualified people do not work for knuckleheads for long. When Ben returned to the office, he called a brief staff meeting to announce the opening of a third office and his intention to add several more accountants and lawyers to his staff.

"By the end of the week, I anticipate another three hundred clients. We're going to be inundated with compliance work. That means everyone is going to have to put in longer days until we have more staff to help out," Ben said.

"Longer hours? Are you kidding me. I'm already working fifteen hours a day. I can't put in any more time. If I do, my wife will divorce me," said Julio Gonzales, whose parents immigrated to the United States when he was four years old so he would have an opportunity to get a better education and enjoy a better life in the states.

"Ben, I haven't been home in two days. My husband thinks I'm in the federal witness protection program. If I'm not home in time for dinner, my husband plans to call the police," said Sandy Benson.

"Ben, this office is run like a slave ship. I'd rather collect unemployment benefits than continue to put in seventy five hours a week, with no end in sight," said Kwan Lee.

"The problem is you've taken on too much work too quickly and your employees just can't keep up with everything they need to do."

"Who said that?" Ben asked his employees.

"I did," said Maria, the cleaning lady who was collecting garbage from one of the trash bins in the room.

***

After several telephone conversations with Timmy to clarify certain facts, Louie was prepared to write up his report. This report will serve as the basis for a referral to CID for its criminal investigation of Alex Talbot. If the special agents are convinced of criminality on the part of the former president, they will forward the case up the chain of command for referral to the Justice Department for acceptance.

If DOJ accepts the case, the prosecutors will file the Rule 35 Motion with the District Court and recommend that Timmy's sentence be reduced pursuant to their agreement.

Louie's report detailed the improprieties by Universal Technology and International Business Solutions. In his report, Louie discussed the motivation for seeking a broker in the computer software technology sales. Louie then explained that the transactions were improper and that all parties to the transactions knew this.

Louie then addressed the issue of ownership of the Swiss bank account and attributed its ownership and control to Alex Talbot. Louie referred to the former president's official brokerage and bank account records as evidence and noted the discrepancies in other documents submitted to the IRS by the former president.

Finally, Louie concluded that International Business Solutions is owned by Alex Talbot. Louie attacked the validity of this entity as a foreign corporation when its sole purpose was to collect a fee for brokering improper business deals with foreign governments, which constitutes an illegal act.

In addition, Louie noted that Alex Talbot failed to report any income with respect to his ownership of International Business Solutions throughout each of the three tax years that he examined. As part of the fraud case, the unreported income is being re-attributed to Alex Talbot and the corporate entity is disregarded.

However, Louie has expressed reservations as to Timmy's claims that International Business Solutions generated one hundred and fifty million dollars in profits over a three year period. Based on Louie's analysis, some of the records that he was given are in conflict with other documents that he examined.

In view of the fact that Louie has questioned the authenticity of certain documents that Timmy provided, he believes that Alex Talbot's income should be re-examined. This suggestion will not go over well with the Chief of the Examination Division who is anxious to have Louie send the case to CID.

There is also the matter of Alex Talbot's failure to disclose his ownership of a foreign bank account, as required by law. In addition, information returns must be filed with the IRS by any citizen who controls a foreign corporation. The penalties for these infractions are quite substantial. This is a matter that Louie will address separately from the fraud case and these penalties will automatically be assessed by the IRS.

Before the little guy can submit his case to Roger, he must obtain a legal opinion from Counsel with respect to his decision to treat Alex Talbot as a nominee owner of International Business Solutions. , which is an entity that was created without economic substance. Under his theory that this company was created without economic substance, the individual who has beneficial ownership is the true owner. This is commonly referred to as "piercing the corporate veil."

It is Louie's contention that if a corporation is not formed for valid business reasons, its corporate form cannot be recognized. Louie has asserted that the corporate formalities of International Business Solutions are merely empty gestures and not indicative that it was carrying on a business. In addition, Louie has raised a question as to whether an entity that is engaged in an illegal activity could even be engaged in a valid business for tax purposes. By definition, it cannot because an illegal activity cannot be considered a trade or business.

Once Louie has completed his request for a legal opinion as to whether he can disregard the formation of International Business Solutions and attribute ownership to Alex Talbot, he hand-delivered the case files to Lindsay Cooke who is the Acting Associate Counsel while Warren Simonsen recuperates from eye surgery.

"For me? Louie, you shouldn't have," said Lindsay.

"How soon can I get approval?" asked Louie.

"You mean a legal opinion," corrected Lindsay.

"No. I know the answer to my request. I mean approval," corrected Louie.

"Well, were you thinking about writing the legal opinion yourself?" asked Lindsay.

"Sorry. I'm just a worker bee who serves at the pleasure of management."

"I hear you. Tom Collins called me earlier to give me a heads up that this was coming my way. Warren is expected back tomorrow and I think he'll want to handle this himself," said Lindsay.

The following day, Warren Simonsen was back at work and the first thing he saw on his desk is Louie's case. Warren has devoted the entire morning to reviewing the admin files and reading Louie's lengthy memorandum in support of disregarding the creation of International Business Solutions and attributing approximately one hundred and fifty million dollars in income to Alex Talbot. Louie's request for a legal opinion has addressed virtually every relevant judicial decision on the subject.

Warren went to work drafting a memo and by the end of the day, the files were returned to the munchkin with Counsel's concurrence.

With Counsel's approval, Louie was now prepared to submit the case to Roger for his review before it is reviewed by Tom and his boss before it is referred to CID. Two days later, the files were sent to CID and assigned to Margo Alifano and Mark Brown in the Criminal Investigation Division's Washington, D.C. field office.

Due to its sensitivity, the Examination Division had one of its field agents in Baltimore drive to Washington, D.C. in order to hand deliver the files to Margo and Mark who were anxiously expecting the files that morning. The special agents were already briefed during a conference call with the Examination Division officials once the decision was made to proceed with the criminal investigation. Upon receipt of the case, Margo sent a letter to Alex Talbot and his lawyers letting them know that she had been assigned the criminal investigation and would be meeting with them in two weeks.

The lawyers took the news in stride that Alex Talbot was now the subject of a criminal tax investigation. Alex Talbot did not take the news nearly as well.

CHAPTER 34

"Those bastards. I should have abolished the IRS when I was president." Alex Talbot was close to blowing his top and the person on the other end of the line was not about to encourage him. So, Scott McCall said nothing.

Scott McCall has served by Alex Talbot's side for over ten years. Before Scott accepted a job as a Secret Service Agent, he worked as an undercover cop. Scott left the police force when he was caught having an affair with his supervisor's wife. Scott's connections in the military enabled him to be selected for a position in the Secret Service and he eventually became a favorite of Alex Talbot.

How Scott McCall became a favorite of Alex Talbot is another story. Scott had been stationed on a security detail in the White House. During his tenure at the White House, Scott became romantically involved with an attractive lobbyist who often attended White House social events. Apparently, Scott had forgotten he was supposed to be ensuring Alex Talbot's personal safety when he brought his lover into a reading room for an afternoon lovemaking session that went on a few minutes longer than it should have.

Alex Talbot had unexpectedly entered the room while the two naked lovers were all over each other. Talbot stood there for a moment while Scott was practically pile-driving his lobbyist girlfriend. When the two lovers looked over at the president, Scott said, "Sir, can I help you with something?" Without missing a beat, Talbot replied, "No thanks. Just continue with what you were doing and keep up the good work."

Later that day, Alex Talbot made it a point to call Scott McCall into the Oval Office for a chat. Talbot essentially told Scott that he would not be reprimanded for his indiscretion while on duty, but that he expected unqualified loyalty from Scott in the future. Scott willingly agreed to this.

When Talbot lost his bid to be re-elected, Scott resigned his position with the Secret Service and went to work for his old boss as an administrative assistant. What this really involved was doing odd jobs that posed difficult problems for the former president. In other words, if a sensitive problem needed to be addressed, it was Scott who was told to deal with the problem.

Indeed, Scott was very good at dealing with sensitive problems. A third degree black belt in Kenpo Karate, Scott trained almost every day for several hours at a nearby dojo. In addition to his martial arts training, Scott was an expert marksman and spent several days a week practicing his skills at a Virginia police academy shooting range that he was allowed to use.

Scott usually kept himself busy but always made it a point to be available whenever Alex Talbot called him. Today, he got the call to be available.

"Jesus! That little runt has put me in a real bind," said Talbot.

"Bell?" asked Scott.

"I thought that when you got rid of his business partner, that would put an end to the criminal case. But I was wrong. Now, you'll have to take care of a few more people," said Talbot.

"You want me to whack federal agents?" asked Scott, who couldn't believe what he was hearing.

"Not yet. But Bell needs to be taken care of before he can testify against me," replied Alex.

"I can't get to him. He's in federal custody." "What about his

family?" Alex asked.

"What about it?" Scott asked.

"Stop answering my questions with a question. If you get rid of his parents, that might discourage his cooperation with the feds," said Alex.

"Whacking people who are corrupt is one thing, but killing innocent people is another. I really don't think I should have to kill someone's mother and father just to make a statement," said Scott.

"I didn't put this up for a vote. Think of our relationship this way. You'll be the star quarterback and I'll be the football coach. I'll tell you which play to call and you'll execute the play. Got it?" said Alex.

"Okay, but this job is going to cost more than the others. I want an extra million," said Scott.

"Okay, but I want that nerd Bell to know that his parents were whacked because he's a cooperating witness. At the same time, make it look like an accident so I don't have to deal with a homicide investigation in addition to a criminal tax investigation."

"When do you want it done?" asked Scott.

"I have a meeting with the IRS investigators in several weeks. Don't do anything just yet. After I know what kind of a case they have against me, I'll let you know what I want done," said Talbot.

***

Once Margo and Mark had finished reading the Alex Talbot audit files, they called Louie to ask him some questions. Satisfied that they had everything in the audit files that Louie was able to learn from his investigation, they called Debbie Macht to make arrangements to interview Timmy.

When Debbie was not available to take their call, the agents called Gary Zimmer, who picked up on the second ring. Both agents had worked with Debbie and Gary on prior criminal prosecutions, where it is normal for special agents to continue to assist DOJ prosecutors after they have completed their criminal investigation.

"Margo, it's good to hear from you. I take it you're calling about Timothy Bell," Gary said.

"That's right. We're going to need information about the Swiss banking records," said Margo.

"That shouldn't be a problem," replied Gary.

Since 2009, the federal government has been successful in working with the Swiss Government to release account holder information and more recently, other nations such as France, North Korea and India have convinced the Swiss Government to further relax its bank secrecy rules.

"As long as you can provide the Swiss with the name of the account holder, the account number and the name of the bank and brokerage firm, you'll be allowed access to transaction details," Gary assured Margo.

"Gary, we also need to interview Timothy Bell. I see where you and Debbie are the DOJ contacts to call to make arrangements," Margo said.

"I can set it up for you. When do you want to meet with him?" asked Gary.

"Mark and I would like to meet with him ASAP. How about 1 pm today?" Margo asked.

"Let me make a phone call to set it up. I'll call you back shortly," replied Gary.

Ten minutes later, Margo heard back from Gary who had set up the meeting with Timothy Bell.

"Hey Mark," Margo said as she walked over to where her partner was standing. In a low tone of voice, Margo said, "I've got the address where the FBI is keeping Timothy Bell. I want you to memorize it and then swallow the paper," as she handed him the note with the address.

"Eight hundred Sixteenth Street, Northwest. Isn't that?" asked Mark.

"The Hay-Adams Hotel," Margo answered.

"They have him in the hotel?" Mark asked.

"They have him in a suite. Let's grab a bite to eat before we head over to see him," suggested Margo.

***

Margo and Mark parked their car in the parking garage at The Hay-Adams Hotel. The cost for parking their car is going to test their supervisor's volatile state of mind.

"What do you think a suite in this place is going to cost taxpayers?" asked Mark.

"Maybe DOJ got the room at the government rate," Margo said.

"I would seriously hope so. Would you like to order room service when we get to the room?" Mark asked.

"Are you kidding? Our esteemed boss would have the room charge taken out of our pay," exclaimed Margo.

"Just a thought."

"Mark, do me a favor and don't think," joked Margo.

When the agents arrived at the hotel suite where Timothy Bell was staying, they presented their credentials to the FBI bodyguards on duty and signed in for the record. The agents introduced themselves to Timmy, who in turn, told them to call him Timmy.

Mark took out his tape recorder and placed it in front of where Timmy sat while Margo took out yellow legal pads for note taking. In addition, Margo removed sheets of paper that contained questions she and Mark wanted to ask Timmy.

Before Mark turned the tape recorder on, the agents engaged Timmy in casual conversation for a few moments so that he would be at ease before they got started.

After several hours of listening to Timmy explain how Universal Technology did business with International Business Solutions, the agents were satisfied that they had evidence of criminality. The only issue that remained open was to what extent Alex Talbot was involved in the crimes.

"Did you deal directly with Alex Talbot?" asked Mark.

"No. My former business partner handled the business side of things. He was involved in negotiations, securing contracts, that kind of stuff. I handled the technology side. So, I never did business with Alex Talbot," answered Timmy.

Mark looked at Margo as if to ask if they should tell him. Timmy picked up on the look Mark gave his partner and asked, "What?"

"Your former business partner recently passed away," replied Margo.

"Oh no. What happened?" asked Timmy.

"The coroner ruled his death a suicide," answered Mark, who said it in such a way that it left the nature of his death in doubt.

"But you think he was murdered?" asked Timmy.

"We don't know because we don't have all of the details as to his death. According to the police reports, the circumstances surrounding his death are somewhat suspicious. In light of what has transpired, the Justice Department is not taking any chances with you. You'll be protected around the clock with FBI agents as long as you are not incarcerated. And we've been advised by the DOJ that your parents will be getting protection as well," explained Gary.

"Getting back to Alex Talbot, what evidence do you have that shows a connection to International Business Solutions," asked Margo.

"International Business Solutions had connections to foreign governments.   We had the technology that these nations desperately wanted but we couldn't risk dealing with them. International Business Solutions could deal with these countries because of its connections. They knew who to call upon, who to negotiate with, and who to bribe. These deals were done quickly. To be able to do that, you needed someone of importance who had connections. And Alex Talbot was their man," stated Timmy.

"But you weren't in the room when these deals were done. So, you can't implicate him in your testimony," Margo said.

"That's right. But Franz Gruber can," replied Timmy.

CHAPTER 35

"Who is Franz Gruber?" asked the agents in unison.

"He's the one who can tell you what went on at that meeting," said Timmy.

This is the first time Franz Gruber's name has been mentioned by Timmy. Although Timmy had an opportunity to disclose Franz Gruber to Louie, he chose not to do so because he did not want to implicate his former business partner in this matter and expose him to potential criminal tax problems.

"But who is he?" asked Margo.

"He owns and operates a private security company in Switzerland. It's very high tech and among the best in Europe. Franz's people installed surveillance equipment at my late partner's request. He recorded everything that went on in our Swiss office. It's all on tape," Timmy explained.

"Wait a minute. You have everything on tape?" Margo asked Timmy.

"No, I don't. But Franz should have the tapes you want to see," Timmy replied with confidence.

Turning to Margo, Mark said, "We have to get these tapes without delay."

"Does anyone else know about these tapes?" Margo asked Timmy.

Timmy shook his head as he said, "No. Just Franz and his staff. And most of the people who work for Franz are family members."

"Okay, before we contact Franz Gruber, tell us what happened," Margo asked Timmy.

"My late business partner was concerned about his personal safety given the fact that he was doing business deals that were illegal. I remember him telling me that he hired Franz Gruber's company to install surveillance equipment that provided both video and audio recordings in our Swiss office. I recall that the equipment was placed into service two days before he met with officials of International Business Solutions," said Timmy.

"How do you know this to be true?" asked Mark.

"Because he told me that he was meeting with the two Swiss lawyers who were listed as the corporate officers, but that the real owner of International Business Solutions was going to attend the meeting because there was a glitch with regard to the purchase price involving one of the contracts that had been negotiated. I remember him saying that the owner was vacationing in the Swiss Alps and intended to leave for the Greek Islands after the meeting," Timmy said.

"That sounds like Talbot," added Margo.

"Now tell us about the recordings," said Mark.

"The recordings start and end with the push of a button. It was suggested that we only record when we felt it was necessary. The recordings are tracked by date and time, to the second. Franz's system is computerized so anytime you want to see a tape, all you have to do is provide him with a date and he can identify the recording session," added Timmy.

"Do you remember specific dates?" Margo asked Timmy.

"Vaguely. But I can guess close enough so that you don't have to ask for several hundred tapes," replied Timmy.

"How far back does Franz keep tapes?" Mark inquired of Timmy.

"As far back as you need," answered Timmy.

"Who owns the tapes?" Margo asked Timmy.

"Technically, the client owns the tapes. It's included in the cost of the service. However, Franz keeps the tapes in storage for quite some time and when it becomes necessary to recycle the tapes, he'll notify us that the tapes will no longer be retained, at which time the client can ask for a specific tape," explained Timmy.

"We need to get Franz on the phone," said Margo. Turning to Timmy, she asked him, "Do you still have a phone number for him?"

"I can't recall the number," Timmy said as he shook his head.

"That's okay. We'll get it," said Mark.

"Mark, why don't you track down the number for Franz Gruber and I'll check in with our glorious leader. If Franz still has the recordings, he'll have to send it to us since I don't think a trip to Switzerland is in our budget," said Margo.

"Timmy, you may as well relax. Mark and I will make a few phone calls and then we'll let you talk to Franz," said Margo.

***

The first person Margo called was an Associate Chief Counsel in the Criminal Tax Division to discuss the admissibility of the tapes. Looking forward to a vacation in several days, the last thing Ellen Decker wanted to hear at this moment was that CID was conducting a criminal investigation of a former president when Margo mentioned Alex Talbot's name.

"Margo, please tell me that you're not requesting legal advice."

"Relax Ellen, it's an informal request for guidance that's off the record. I think I know the answer but I still need to run it by you just to be on the safe side. We have a case where tapes were secretly recorded by a third party. There may be incriminating evidence on the tapes. We don't have actual possession of the tapes at this time. The subject of our criminal investigation is allegedly in the room and we believe that his voice is on the tapes. The tapes were made in Switzerland. I assume the tapes are inadmissible in court. However, can we still use the information on the tapes for purposes of investigation, but not criminal prosecution?" asked Margo.

"I'm glad you brought up the Swiss. The Swiss are very strict when it comes to the unsanctioned invasion of privacy. A person is guilty of violation of privacy if that person installs or uses in a private place without the consent of the person entitled to privacy in that place, any device for observing, photographing or recording sounds or events in that place. Under Swiss law, information must be legally and fairly collected, and limits are placed on its disclosure to third parties including other nations. If the subject of your investigation was not put on notice that he was being photographed or recorded, the tapes are inadmissible in court," answered Ellen.

"However, there is nothing that would preclude you from using the information in your investigation. Just make sure you don't build your criminal case on the tapes itself," advised Ellen.

As soon as Margo finished with this call, she called her boss to give her the news. "I have good news and I have bad news," relayed Margo.

"I'm sixty five years old and not getting any younger. What is it that you want to tell me?" replied Becky Harmon.

"A third party secretly made tapes that may incriminate Talbot. We are in the process of trying to get the tapes. However, the tapes are inadmissible in court. I just got off the phone with Ellen Decker and she said that the tapes can be used in our investigation, short of going into the file as evidence," explained Margo.

"Okay, get the tapes and we'll go from there."

***

Margo had already concluded her phone conversation with Becky while Mark had several phone numbers and a website address for Franz Gruber. Timmy was told to use Margo's cell phone to call Franz Gruber and if they could not personally talk to him, they were prepared to send him an e-mail requesting that he contact them.

By the time Timmy made the phone call to Franz Gruber, it was almost 9 pm in Switzerland. Fortunately, the agents were given Franz Gruber's home phone number so Timmy was able to reach him at his home.

Timmy was told not to discuss his personal situation with Franz. Instead, the agents instructed him to say that it was of critical importance that Franz send him certain tapes that were made in Timmy's Swiss office from several years ago. Because the recordings were the property of the client, Franz quickly agreed to ship a duplicate copy of each recording to him.

In view of the fact that Timmy was in federal custody, the agents instructed him to have Franz send the tapes to them and gave him a Post Office Box address. Margo was concerned about the possibility of the tapes being accidentally destroyed if the package were sent to the IRS and electronically scanned. Therefore, by sending the package to a Post Office Box, it should not be subject to electronic scanning and potential damage.

***

It didn't take long for the Swiss banking authorities to provide the IRS with the account information it had sought. The agents now had access to the activity in the bank account of International Business Solutions. Both Margo and Mark did a double-take when they saw the amount of the deposits from the illegal sales.

"Based on the bank deposits, Talbot had to be pocketing in excess of fifty million dollars a year from these sales," exclaimed Mark.

"I would say that's motivation for his denials. That would come to additional tax deficiencies of about fifty million dollars over the three year period, without taking into account interest and the civil fraud penalty. And we still have a criminal tax case. I don't expect him to play nice once he realizes how bad his case is and how much worse it's going to get," added Margo.

"And we still have the video tape recordings to look forward to seeing," said her partner.

***

Franz Gruber was able to locate the tapes without any trouble. As promised, he had the tapes copied and mailed the duplicate copy to the address given to him. Within the next ten days, the agents should have the recordings that will incriminate Alex Talbot to a series of crimes for which he will be prosecuted.

It took eight days for the package to arrive at the Post Office Box that belonged to Margo. Once the agents reviewed the tapes, they knew they had a very promising criminal case against Alex Talbot, except for the fact that the tapes were inadmissible in a court of law.

CHAPTER 36

Today is the day that Margo Alifano and Mark Brown are meeting with Alex Talbot and his lawyers. The meeting will be held at their upscale law office.

On the drive to the meeting, Margo and Mark went over last minute details.

"As much as I hate to listen to politicians, I think we should let Talbot ramble on when we ask him questions. That way when we come back at him the next time, he'll probably contradict what he's already said," suggested Mark.

In a criminal investigation, special agents will ask numerous questions during the interview process. Some of the questions are simply re-worded. It is not unusual for special agents to conduct another interview with the same person at a later date and go over the same material as before. While the questions may be re-phrased, the subject matter remains the same. The special agents intentionally do this to see whether the answers are suddenly different. If the responses are different than before, the special agents may have to investigate further and more interviews may be necessary.

"I don't know. My sense is if we allow him too much latitude, he'll just waste our time with a bunch of nonsense. You know how politicians can bullshit. I think we should keep him on a tight leash and not give him a lot of wiggle room," replied Margo.

"Do you want to arm wrestle for it?" asked Mark.

Turning to her much larger and heavily muscled partner who was behind the wheel, Margo said, "I don't want to embarrass you. Let's give Becky a call and get her input."

"Forget calling the Beckster. We'll do it your way," Mark said in mock surrender.

"And if Talbot rambles on too much, you can slap him around if you want," Margo joked.

"Great. You want me to beat the snot out of a former president in front of his lawyers?" Mark asked. "Can you imagine what Becky would have to say about that?"

"You could always kill the lawyers so they won't be able to incriminate you and it will be Talbot's word against ours," Margo said in jest.

"Don't tempt me."

***

When the special agents arrived at the law office, Alex Talbot and his lawyers were waiting for them in a conference room located behind the reception area. When the receptionist greeted the agents, Larry Donnelly was the first to come out to say hello to them. After shaking hands with the agents, he led them into the conference room to meet his partner and the former president.

Margo and Mark were respectful and cordial to Alex Talbot and his lawyers. In fact, the agents even made it a point to engage them in small talk for several minutes before getting down to business.

"We're going to set up our recording device now. Do you need time to set up your recorder?" she asked the lawyers.

"We're ready to go," Smith replied.

After Margo stated for the record the date and time, the identities of those in attendance and where the meeting was being held, she covered some housekeeping items as required by investigation procedures. Before she started the interview, she asked the former president if he had any questions.

Alex Talbot went postal when he received a letter from Louie advising him that the IRS had assessed first and second tier penalties for failing to file IRS Form 5471 by the required due dates with respect to his ownership of International Business Solutions. As the former president has continued to assert that because he did not own the outstanding stock of this foreign company, he was not required to file this form.

When Alex raised this issue with the agents, he didn't expect to hear, "That's a matter that we cannot discuss because it's outside the scope of the criminal case. I suggest that you address any objections to these penalties with the Examination Division. Do you have any other questions before we get started?" said Margo.

"Do you plan to indict me today?" asked Alex Talbot, partially in jest. As he said this, his lawyers looked at each other, rolled their eyes and questioned their client's sanity. Challenging the investigating agents at the outset of a criminal investigation is not a wise tactic.

As the tape recorder was on, neither Margo nor Mark could respond with a flip answer. "Mr. Talbot, the purpose of this meeting is to conduct an investigation to determine if the tax laws of this country may have been violated. This is a fact finding investigation on our part. If it has been determined that criminal prosecution is warranted, it will be the responsibility of the Justice Department to issue an Indictment," Margo explained.

"Sorry. I didn't mean to be flippant with you. I guess I'm just on edge at having to undergo a criminal investigation dealing with my taxes. Please proceed," Talbot said to the agents.

"Mr. Talbot, did you own, control or have an interest in a foreign bank account at Banque SCS Alliance in Geneva, Switzerland within the past four years?" asked Margo.

"I believe that my lawyers already answered that question on my behalf when Agent Lipschitz met with them at the outset of the audit several months ago. This is ancient history. Let's move on," suggested the former president.

"For purposes of this interview, we require from you, a yes or no response, sir" stated Mark.

Pausing for a moment as if he wanted his lawyers to interject, Alex Talbot replied, "I don't believe that I did."

"You sound less than certain. Are you sure you did not have a foreign bank account?" asked Mark.

"While I understand that you want a yes or no response to your questions, I think it best if I could elaborate on my answer. I happen to be even more active now than when I served in the Senate and spent four years in the White House. I am constantly in discussions with foreign leaders, joint venture capitalists operating overseas and a number of international corporations. I frequently travel overseas and there are times when I do open foreign bank accounts as a matter of necessity. However, when my business is finished, I usually make it a point to close the foreign bank account. To the best of my knowledge, I have no recollection of any such Swiss bank account," stated Talbot before he decided to further clarify his response.

"However, there is a remote possibility and I stress the word remote, that I could have opened a bank account in Switzerland for my convenience. Because it is not something that I remember, my answer would be no," answered Talbot who was attempting to create some wiggle room so that he could later say that he had forgotten about this account if shown documentary evidence that the account belonged to him.

"Mr. Talbot, you provided Agent Lipschitz with documentation that indicated you purchased corn futures at a cost of five thousand dollars. This transaction does not appear on any of the official Morgan Stanley records," Margo said.

"I can't explain that," said Talbot.

"I haven't asked my question yet. Instead, your brokerage account statement shows a five thousand dollar transfer to the Swiss bank account in the name of International Business Solutions. Are you familiar with this company?" asked Margo.

"Yes. I've heard of IBS," replied Talbot.

"Can you explain the transfer of funds?" Mark asked the former president.

"No. Didn't Morgan Stanley acknowledge that this was a mistake?" asked Talbot, who was hoping that the agents would conclude that it was the firm's error.

"No. According to officials of Morgan Stanley, it was not a mistake on the part of the firm. The official brokerage firm records confirm that it was a transfer," added Margo.

"I don't know what to say," responded Talbot.

"We realize that you have a job to do and we can appreciate the thoroughness in which you conduct prospective criminal investigations, but this appears to be overkill. Our client has said he can't explain the discrepancy with respect to his account statement. Can we move on?" asked Donnelly.

"Let's talk about your investment portfolio. Did you purchase any other futures contracts?" Mark asked the former president, who was now starting to squirm in his seat.

"No."

"Who recommended that you purchase a contract for corn futures?" asked Mark.

"My broker."

"But according to Morgan Stanley's Back Office records, you did not sign any of the required in-house documents authorizing your broker to permit you to trade commodities. Surely your broker knew this," said Mark.

"Is there a question for our client?" asked Edward Smith.

"How is it possible that you could have purchased a contract for corn futures when you were not eligible to do so?" asked Mark.

"I don't know."

"Perhaps this is a matter that you should take up with Morgan Stanley," Donnelly said to the agents.

"Actually, we have. That's one of the reasons why we're here," Margo responded.

"We have the same problem with the five thousand dollar transfer out of your Bank of America checking account. The bank's official records contradict your explanation that it was a mistake on the part of the bank," added Mark. "Can you help us with that?"

"I can't explain that either. But I can say this. Neither banks nor brokerage firms are perfect. They do make mistakes," said Talbot, who was now starting to show some agitation in his voice.

After about thirty minutes of pleading ignorant to the two transfers, Alex asked the agents, "And how does all this prove that I filed fraudulent tax returns?"

Ignoring the former president's question, Margo asked him, "Please tell us about your involvement with the business dealings of International Business Solutions."

Margo intentionally phrased the question this way to make it seem that she already knew of Alex Talbot's involvement.

"IBS? Who said I was involved in IBS?" replied Alex.

"Are you saying that you had nothing to do with this company?" asked Margo.

"That's right. I know of IBS. IBS has an international reputation in the business community. But I had no involvement with its business," replied Alex.

"Agents, if you have evidence that our client was somehow involved in this foreign company, we'd like to see it now. Otherwise, please move on with your questions," said Smith.

Neither Margo nor Mark were willing to disclose the video and audio recordings that showed Alex Talbot negotiating on behalf of International Business Solutions to sell unauthorized military and defense license technology to certain third world countries. In addition, from listening to the audio, it was clear that Alex Talbot was the principal owner of International Business Solutions. To disclose this now might undermine their chances of catching Alex Talbot do something really stupid.

"If you had nothing to do with this company, how is it that a total of ten thousand dollars was transferred to it from your brokerage and bank accounts?" asked Margo, coming back to the same question she posed only moments before.

"My client has already said he doesn't know," a perturbed Edward Smith responded. "Can we move on to something else?" he asked as the tension in the room was starting to build.

"Do you recall your meeting with Jeremy DeMille on September 28, 2008 in Geneva, Switzerland?" Mark asked the former president.

"Who is Jeremy DeMille?" asked Donnelly, before Alex could respond.

"Jeremy DeMille was a former business partner of Timothy Bell. At one time, he maintained an office in Geneva and was actively involved in marketing computer technology on behalf of Universal Technology," answered Mark.

Donnelly nodded to his client that he could answer the question. "No," Alex replied to the question and shook his head sideways for effect.

"You don't recall the meeting or you didn't meet with Mr. DeMille?" asked Margo.

"The answer is no to both."

"Perhaps I could jog your memory by saying that you told Mr. DeMille that you were the principal owner of International Business Solutions. In fact, at this very meeting you even boasted that these deals could only be consummated because of your political connections. I believe this was said to justify the money you were going to make for brokering these deals," Margo said.

"I don't know where you're getting all this, but it never happened. I don't know anything about this DeMille character or any meeting with him," Alex Talbot emphatically declared.

A line has now been drawn in the sand. Alex Talbot intends to play hardball and deny any association with International Business Solutions. Without seeing documentary evidence that contradicts his denial, Talbot's lawyers will support him for the time being. The agents, well aware that the former president had an ownership interest in this company, have provided ample opportunities for him to acknowledge ownership. As Talbot failed to do so, the agents will stress in their reports that the former president repeatedly lied to them.

"If your client is unable to answer questions concerning International Business Solutions, we will conclude the interview at this time," said Margo as Mark unplugged the recording equipment and Margo gathered their files. On their way out, the agents promised Alex that they would schedule a follow-up conference at a later date.

After the agents left the office, Alex Talbot said to his lawyers, "They have something that indicates I own IBS. I want you to find out what it is so when they come back, we'll be better prepared."

"Alex, I think if they had something, they would have put it on the table for us to see," replied Donnelly.

"I agree with Larry. If there is evidence of your involvement with this company, we'll eventually see it, so why not disclose it now?" added Smith.

"Unless the evidence is so damning that they've already concluded this is a criminal case and they intend to send it to the Justice Department for prosecution," replied Donnelly.

"If that's the case, they have no intention of showing their hand. And they did seem confident that there was some connection between you and IBS," added Smith.

"Jesus. That's all the more reason to find out what kind of evidence they have," Alex Talbot exclaimed.

***

Once the agents got to their car, they high fived each other.

"Did you notice how Talbot waffled when he admitted that he could have owned a Swiss bank account?" Margo said.

"He did quite a job dancing around the question of ownership. Remember that baseball player a few years ago who was asked if he ever took performance enhancing drugs?" Mark asked.

"You mean the one who, at first, emphatically denied ever taking drugs?" Margo asked.

"Right, but then he qualified it by saying, it's possible that he could have, but he didn't recall ever doing drugs," said Mark.

"But then he added a caveat by saying, upon reflection, maybe he could have taken drugs without knowing it, but he didn't think he did. He then said he could have inadvertently taken drugs if his teammates provided him with pills that he thought were multi-vitamins," added Margo.

"Convenient, don't you think?" asked Mark.

"Yep."

"Well, we've given him something to think about. If he takes the bait, the trap is set," said Margo. "I think Talbot knows we have something and he'll put two and two together and …."

"Assume Timothy Bell is providing us with information," Mark finished Margo's thought.

"That's right," Margo replied.

CHAPTER 37

"That problem we talked about a few weeks ago? I want you to take care of it for me."

"What is it that you want me to do?" asked Scott McCall, who had a pretty good idea, but wanted his employer to make it crystal clear for him.

"This IRS investigation is getting out of control. These IRS investigators know something and the information has to be coming from Bell. I could go to prison if I'm found guilty of tax evasion," said an irate Alex Talbot. "And I don't plan on going to prison."

"I'll ask you again. What do you want me to do?"

"These agents have evidence. They're getting information from a confidential source, which they won't disclose. Find it," ordered the former president.

"Could you be a little more specific?" asked the former president's Secret Service bodyguard.

"You're supposed to be the hot shot Secret Service agent who knows how to find out things. Start investigating," exclaimed Talbot.

"How about a clue as to where to start?"

"There's only one person still alive who could possibly know anything about my using IBS to broker illegal business deals and that's Timothy Bell," stated Talbot.

"I thought Bell's in prison on tax evasion charges. Do you think he cut a deal with the DOJ?" asked Scott.

"Go find out."

"Right. I'll call the Justice Department and ask if anyone knows anything about a secret plea bargain with Timothy Bell. That should work," replied Scott.

"I don't need your sarcasm. I pay you to deal with problems. I have a problem and I want you to make it go away," said Talbot as he hung up the phone.

***

Several days later, Scott phoned his boss and told him what he had learned. "It seems that Timothy Bell worked a deal with the DOJ prosecutors. In exchange for his cooperation in your IRS case, the prosecutors have agreed to reduce his prison sentence," Scott said to the former president.

"How did you learn about this?" asked Alex.

"I have a female friend at Justice who saw the documents that were filed with the court. It wasn't all that difficult to get her to talk," said Scott.

"Can you get to Bell?" inquired Alex.

"Are you nuts? He's in a federal prison," said Scott.

"Then I want you to take care of his family. That ought to scare the shit out of him. With his parents dead, he'll have second thoughts about cooperating with the feds and testifying against me," replied Talbot.

"Jesus Christ! You're really serious about me whacking his parents. I want five hundred thousand in advance and another five hundred thousand upon completion of the job," Scott said.

***

Scott McCall had his orders to kill two innocent people. He really didn't like it, but the psychopath that he worked for paid well and he was the only employer Scott McCall had.

As a person who is called upon to terminate others, Scott has the option of choosing the means to die. Scott considered starting an electrical fire in the home of Aaron and Ella Bell to make it look like an accident. However, he concluded that they might survive which would complicate a second attempt on their lives. Also, he was told by his employer that their deaths should appear to Timothy as a contract hit so that he understood that if he continues to cooperate with the feds, he will soon be joining his parents sooner than he thinks.

Scott eventually decided to shoot them in their bed in the middle of the night. For this assignment, Scott selected a Beretta 92FS. Because the house is in a residential neighborhood, Scott will attach a sound suppressor to his gun to reduce the amount of noise and flash generated by firing the gun.

At approximately 2 am, Scott entered the back of the house by inserting a lock-pick in the rear door. After only a minute, Scott was able to pick the lock and enter the house. Removing his shoes so that he will not make any noise, Scott went up the stairs one step at a time. Once he saw the master bedroom, Scott screwed the suppressor to the Beretta and fired two shots in each body and turned to leave.

At that moment, Scott heard someone say, "FBI, drop your weapon and put your hands up over your head! Do it now!"

Scott surmised that the person who just said this was addressing his comments to him.

It seemed as if a hundred FBI agents were in the room and surrounded Scott McCall with high powered weapons aimed at his face. In reality, it was only four FBI agents, but to Scott, it seemed like a hundred.

Placed in handcuffs and read his rights, Scott was led away to a detention facility. Tomorrow morning, he will be charged with the attempted murder of Aaron and Ella Bell, who are at this very moment, sound asleep in the presidential suite at The Hay-Adams Hotel, courtesy of the federal government.

While the Bells will be pleased to know that it was a good idea that they were not asleep in their bedroom that night, they will not be happy that their favorite pillows were ruined by gunshots. However, replacing pillows is a small price to pay in lieu of not being assassinated.

It is almost 4 am and the FBI agents are still euphoric over the capture of the person they believe killed Ralph Adler and Gary Mandel.

At 5 am, Debbie Macht received a wake-up call from the FBI's Special Agent in Charge. "We got him," was the agent's message.

Debbie relayed the news to Gary a few minutes later. Gary's wife, who awoke from a peaceful night's sleep, handed the phone to her husband with the message, "This had better be good."

That morning, officials at the Justice Department got together to hold an important meeting. Because this involves a potential high-profile criminal tax case as well as a high-profile criminal non-tax case, there are a lot of senior executives in attendance. In view of the fact that the IRS has not concluded its criminal tax investigation, the criminal case that will be litigated first will be for the attempted murder of Aaron and Ella Bell.

At the same time, the IRS is holding several meetings. It looks like there are a lot of meetings being held in Washington, D.C. this morning involving a lot of executives.

Becky Harmon is running the meeting in CID. Becky is pleased that her plan has worked and she graciously commended everyone for not screwing up her brilliant plan. Acknowledging that her plan was coordinated with the Justice Department and FBI, Becky has to thank those agencies, which she is often loath to do.

"From the young lady at Justice who so skillfully leaked the information to our suspect, to the FBI agents who protected the Bells around the clock, and to Margo Alifano and Mark Brown who played their roles so convincingly that Talbot took the bait we set for him, I congratulate you all," Becky proudly announced. "I'm very pleased that our efforts were coordinated so smoothly."

What Becky really meant to say is that her ingenious plan worked because everyone did what she told them to do.

***

Scott McCall was taken to a jail cell where he will await his booking on the attempted murder charge. For some reason, the FBI thought it might be prudent to put Scott in its filthiest and most deplorable holding cell. Scott is not happy with his living quarters and will have plenty of time to consider his fate.

Alex Talbot has been anxiously awaiting word from Scott that the job has been satisfactorily completed. However, the one telephone call that Scott made was to a criminal defense attorney.

It wasn't until the following day that an enterprising crime reporter learned of Scott's arrest and the murder charge. Philip Townsend, who covers the crime scene for The Washington Examiner, reported that Scott McCall, a former Secret Service Agent once assigned to a White House detail, has been arrested by federal agents and charged with the attempted murder of the parents of Timothy Bell, who recently pleaded guilty to the largest federal individual income tax evasion case in history.

In his article, Townsend posed the question as the motivation for having someone allegedly attempt to assassinate the parents of someone in prison. The writer then speculated that Timothy Bell may be cooperating with federal authorities in another case. Insofar as the IRS cannot disclose the subjects of its tax audits, Alex Talbot's identity is protected under the confidentiality rules until it is disclosed in court. Once the Justice Department makes its criminal charges public through either the issuance of an Indictment or Information filing, the press will learn the identity of the suspect.

Once Alex Talbot read the article in The Washington Examiner, he called his lawyers to let them know that he will no longer be requiring their services as they do not practice criminal defense work.

Alex then called the Managing Partner at Baker & Collier in order to obtain legal representation by their criminal defense attorneys.

After finally retaining new legal counsel, Alex Talbot left for his Virginia countryside estate to be alone with his thoughts and a bottle of whiskey. As the former president sat in his expensive executive leather chair with his feet propped up on his oversized custom-made executive desk, he gulped down another shot of whiskey, perhaps thinking that the booze will solve his legal problems. If it could, why would he need to hire expensive criminal defense attorneys?

Alex is alone in his Virginia estate. His wife Karen is in New York, consulting with a client on some interior design work. Karen's absence has left Alex alone with his thoughts.

After about an hour of staring off into space, Alex removed a small handgun from one of his desk drawers and began to run his hands over the hard metal. The booze has clouded Alex's thinking as he lifted the gun to his temple. With tears running down his face and his hand trembling, Alex exclaimed, "I can't go to prison."

However, just as Alex was about to blow his brains out, the unlisted telephone on his desk rang. When Alex answered the phone, he was given the bad news by an aide.

"Mr. President, I am so sorry to have to tell you this, but the networks are reporting that earlier this morning Mr. McCall was apparently found dead in the cell where he had been detained by the FBI."

"That's terrible news. Do you know what happened?" asked Talbot who was thrilled upon hearing that Scott McCall is dead.

"According to CNN, it is believed that Mr. McCall may have killed himself late last night. I'm so sorry to have to tell you this," said the aide.

"It's okay that you called. I appreciate you telling me this," replied Talbot, who thought that this is wonderful news.

Believing that with Scott dead, the government has only circumstantial evidence that he conspired to have the Bells murdered. While the press may speculate that Alex Talbot conspired to have the Bells killed, Alex's criminal defense lawyers will vigorously argue otherwise.

"I guess one man's misfortune is another man's fortune," chuckled Alex, who had apparently forgotten about the five hundred thousand dollar wire transfer to Scott McCall's overseas bank account just twenty four hours ago that could present a problem for him.

"It's fourth and one and I just scored on a quarterback sneak on the last play of the game to win the championship. And what the hell was I thinking about when I wanted to blow my brains out? I'm back in the game," Alex said, without bothering to get the full details as to what exactly happened in Scott McCall's cell late last night.

If only Alexander Talbot, former President of the United States of America really knew what happened in Scott McCall's cell last night and what his former business partner has planned for him. As a former football player, Alex should know better than to underestimate an opponent, particularly one who is brilliant and has carried a grudge that goes back eight years.